FATAL

SNOW

ROBERT WALTON

SUNBURY
PRESS

Mechanicsburg, Pennsylvania   USA

Published by Sunbury Press, Inc.
50 West Main Street, Suite A
Mechanicsburg, Pennsylvania 17055

www.sunburypress.com

ISBN: 978-1-62006-379-8 (Trade Paperback)
ISBN: 978-1-62006-380-4 (Mobipocket)
ISBN: 978-1-62006-381-1 (ePub)

FIRST SUNBURY PRESS EDITION: February 2014

Product of the United States of America
0 1 1 2 3 5 8 13 21 34 55

Set in Bookman Old Style
Designed by Lawrence Knorr
Cover by Lawrence Knorr
Edited by Amanda Shrawder

Upper front cover photo "DS1122-Teton Winter Panoramic" by Doug Steakley

Continue the Enlightenment!

Dedication

To my wife and daughter.

Acknowledgments

I could not mention this book without calling to mind Carmen and Don without whom I would not be published. I am extremely grateful for the staff at Sunbury Press for their faith in me, and not least to Amanda for being such a great editor.

"She spake in language whose strange melody might not belong to Earth."

--Percy Shelley,
The Revolt of Islam,
Canto 1 stave XIX

Buffalo

1978

Winter comes early in the high west. The winds blow hard across the open spaces, making it feel colder than it actually is.

Harry and Conner drove through patches of rain alternating with blue sky, as though the earth were shaded with a gigantic venetian blind. The temperature had turned for the better that day, and the clouds finally subsided.

It was Harry's turn to drive Conner's '73 Volkswagen Beetle—his pride and joy. He drove slowly, looking left and right, up ahead. Usually he drove the car as if it was some indestructible behemoth, some four-wheel off-roader, but now he drove with care because they were looking for a place to camp. Night would fall soon.

By the time he was thirty, the Vietnam War was four years over and Harry Thursday had already been married twice. He had been about to open that door once again, but the third time would lead him from the innocence of youth into the dark reality that accompanies one until death.

Conner pointed to a road up ahead.

Harry stopped the car in the intersection and looked down a dirt road with deep ruts and grassy knolls.

"It's too much for the car," Conner said.

Harry grinned. "Nah. Piece of cake," he said, his blue eyes brightened. He turned the wheel suddenly to the right and stepped on the gas, spinning the rear wheels and flinging stones and dust into the air. It bounced and shimmied and then hit a deep hole, sending the both of them to the roof of the car. They could hear the metal pop under the pressure of their heads. Harry was thrilled, and Conner visibly upset.

He slowed the car after catching a glimpse of Conner's sour face, and took care to avoid the unusually large potholes.

Small tufts of grass grew on the middle hump of the road, and at some parts the road disappeared where the underbrush grew freely. A downed tree loomed ahead, and Harry stopped the car. They got out to have a look around. The road ended abruptly just twenty feet ahead, so they parked the Bug and went to find a place to camp for the night.

Harry stepped to the side of the road and relieved himself, while Conner headed off into the brush.

"This looks as good as it gets, hey Conner?"

He started to unpack sleeping bags.

Conner yelled over to take the cooking gear and the machete along. When he reappeared, the sun had moved closer to the horizon.

"You ready now? It'll be dark soon."

Conner hoisted his bag over his shoulder, took the cooking gear, and started on what looked like a path. He was smaller than Harry, but arguably the better looking of the two. He had brown eyes and light brown hair marked by a dark oval spot, likening itself to the spot on Jupiter, just above his left temple. Two tours in Vietnam and years of skiing in the Canadian Rockies had kept Conner fit. Yet he spoke with an unpretentious voice. "I don't think this road has been used in years."

Conner was a semi successful playwright working hard in New York to make a living at what he did best. He produced his last play, *Wormhole: Mumbo Jumbo will Hoodoo You,* at an off Broadway playhouse.

After being released from the service at the end of the War, he had begun his career writing for a skiing magazine. He had logged hundreds of hours perfecting his skills as a skier and a writer. Four years later he had already produced two plays and preferred the warm walls of the city.

They walked for several minutes and suddenly the patch of woods opened into a large clearing. The tall grass blew lazily in the soft autumn breeze. The hill rose steadily until it dropped off, leaving behind it a view of the distant mountains that sat high above the setting sun. The snow-covered peaks looked jagged, and the sun reflected brightly off the tallest of these. Trees sat on the horizon and behind them the sunlit mountaintops.

The few trees turned out to be the focal point of a large mire that slowly spread into the distance. The hill crested and turned into open grasslands that meandered over toward a large creek about one hundred yards away. The mountains that looked so close from down below were actually miles away.

They made camp.

It was late, but they both had enough energy to build a small fire with some of the loose branches Harry had collected. With the last rays of dying sunlight, Conner sat down with his notebook and pencil to write while Harry prepared dinner.

Harry was an archeologist and used to all sorts of climate; although, he would remind Conner often, the summer months were when he did most of his work outdoors.

After failing to enlist his friend's aid in hunting for food, Harry headed down the hill to where he had seen rocks and a few varieties of vegetation. He felt certain he would find onions at least and—if there was enough decay—mushrooms.

He found a tussock of onions growing in the open glade along with Queen Anne's lace and dandelions, but no mushrooms. Using a knife, he dug the vegetables and carried them back to camp in a bag long used for such gatherings.

Conner had tended the fire and made sure the meal didn't boil away. They made quick work of the food Harry found by rinsing it off in the nearby stream, adding it to the pot, and cooking it quickly.

"I could use a beer right now," said Conner after they had eaten.

"I thought you'd be working on the new play," Harry said as he stood and looked up at the sky. The ambient light had dimmed, and everything was turning to shadows. The setting sun lit the mountain peaks from behind, and looked as though they stood apart from the world.

He was restless and furtive, trying to remember why he had come on this trip. He sat down on his sleeping bag, rustled through his backpack, pulled out a bottle of vodka and held it in the air like he had just pulled a lobster out of a barrel.

"Tada," he said, smiled, and then took a long drink. He passed the bottle to Conner, who had already put away his writing.

They sat quietly for a while with the fire throwing flickering light on their faces. The stars filled the sky, covering them like a warm radiant blanket.

Conner broke the silence. "How's your Mother doing?" he asked.

Harry looked over at his companion. "Died two years ago. Didn't I tell you?"

"You pretty much dropped off the face of the Earth after you went to Peru."

"Chile."

"South America." Conner spoke frankly.

"You ass. After I got back from Chile, I took a vacation in Europe. I only came back to sell the business and bury Mother." He dug at the fire with a stick and watched the sparks float into the air. "That's how stars are made," he said, "according to the Yeshret."

"I always thought they were made by a big gigantic explosion four and a half billion years ago."

"Some poet you are," Harry said. "When I was younger, my father took me to South America to look for new natural replacements to the plastics in the aircraft we made. He heard about this tribe called the Yeshret, who made rubber from some wild plant. He wanted the secret and we headed off into the Amazon to get it. That's when I met my first wife. They believed

4

that giants made stars by throwing sparks into the night sky from their giant fires."

Conner, who knew Harry traveled a lot, raised his brows. "Wife? At fourteen?"

"Well, she was a gift from the chief Yamniut as an offering of 'Great Friendship,'" Harry explained. "I had just gotten over a severe and inauspicious case of dysentery, and Father just came down with an unfortunate case of malaria. Father was a sick puppy lying in sweat and fever, and in comes Yamniut dressed in full regalia wearing everything he had ever gotten from the outside world. He had a wheel cover from a Ford Fairlane around his neck; a gift from the gods, he claimed. We suspected he found it on some abandoned truck somewhere. Anyway, he had his oldest unmarried daughter with him and gave her to me. We figured we should oblige him rather than suffer ostracism, or worse."

"Worse?"

"They were cannibals and ate their enemies."

"What did you do?"

"I married her and spent the rest of the time naked bonding with the young warriors who taught me to hunt, make poison arrows, and eat nasty things." He leaned back down and said, "The girls were magnanimous."

Later that night the bushes provided some comfort from the breeze. It was not cold by Wyoming standards, as fall weather goes, but they knew that at any given night they could possibly wake up under a foot of snow.

Harry thought he would clean up in the morning, but the pragmatic playwright convinced him that the food would only draw unwanted critters. As it did that time in Oklahoma, when they had to fight off a pack of ring-tailed weasels after leaving the cereal out of the pack.

Early in the morning hours, they woke up simultaneously to the sound of chewing. As it did not sound like snow, Harry was under no obligation to open his eyes. The less he knew about what was making those noises the better off he felt he would be.

Conner hissed at him until he answered.

Harry opened one eye and saw a silver moon swimming in a pool of stars as thick as sand on the beach. A bison stood three feet from his head. There were hundreds of them—dark, shadowy figures lumbering nearby aware of their presence, but unconcerned. One such creature stopped long enough to consider a wide-eyed Harry staring back, and then returned to his midnight meal.

The moon threw no light, but the stars that filled the sky burned an eerie silhouette of these great beasts that haunted their sleep. In the morning, they woke alone, their ghostly visitors gone.

The Diner

Conner drove, not wanting to do any more damage to the Bug, and insisted Harry had taken years off the life of his precious car.

"That's at the end of its life," Harry said. "It's been a good car all these miles."

"It's my baby." Conner took quick glances at Harry.

They drove slowly for hours stopping once at a small diner for something to eat. It sat alone at the foot of a slow rising hill covered in thinly spaced pines and juniper. Rocky outcroppings surrounded by laurel and aspen spotted the terrain. The whitewashed building was now faded, and under the fading paint they could still see the old sign painted in red from when the building was a tack shop.

A new sign claiming the best flapjacks in the west twenty-four hours a day, beckoned visitors to enter. Out in front of the building were two small gas pump islands, clues to the building's ancient history.

The pumps were old and still had the glass tubes, "O'Toole's Gas," could still be seen in faded and patchy color; the hoses and nozzles had been removed. It reminded Harry of a friend back home whose garage housed at least a dozen antique cars and even more gas station paraphernalia. He called it the Limbo Lounge because everything was in a state of continuous repair.

They pulled up and parked at what looked like old hitching posts. There were seven cars parked in front.

"Are you sure this is a restaurant?" said Conner.

"This looks good enough. Don't you think?" Harry said.

"For a perfectionist, you sure lower your standards when it comes to food."

"Who are you kidding Conner? You'll eat anything anywhere. You only fancy yourself a gourmet when ladies are involved."

Harry thought back to the jungles of the Amazon, to the unmentionable things they ate there. Harry and his father were obliged as a courtesy to eat their food. They found themselves eating large thumb sized grubs, which the natives ate raw, but, for the sake of the White Ones, they toasted in a fire. He thought at the time it tasted a lot like chicken, or maybe beef marrow.

"Hey, seven cars can't be all that wrong."

Conner put the car in park, pulled up the brake, and turned off the engine. He looked dubiously at his friend, got out, and headed for the building.

A crudely made vestibule adorned the front of the building. It had a wooden floor, and thinly framed walls. Air and light seeped through the aluminum framed louvered windows that covered the front and sides. The cranks were missing, the screws rusted, and the windowpanes either damaged or gone. Thick remnants of ancient spider webs clustered at the ceiling near the windows and door.

Just as they were about to enter, the windowless door opened and a very large man with a red knit cap came out laughing, filling almost the entire vestibule with his bulk. He walked past them, pushing both aside with his huge frame, and let the door swing closed behind him as he walked out to his car.

Inside, two people sat at the counter talking to an old man in a plaid shirt and apron. Shelves full of glasses and liquor flanked an opening behind the service bar. Beyond that was the kitchen where the sound and smell of cooking came rolling out. The counter looked more like a bar. It had stools bolted into the floor that swiveled and a brass foot rail that ran along its length. The bar itself was made of linoleum, pieces of which had been broken off over the years. In the middle were two beer taps. In the one corner next to the kitchen sat a lone door marked "Private," written in crayon.

The bartender walked up and down the length of the bar on a wooden riser. With each step, the glasses on the edge of the counter would clang together, and it sounded to Harry like he wore spurs that jingled when he walked.

To the right of the bar was a small dining room that led to a hallway and the bathrooms. To the left were some tables and windows. A jukebox sat unplugged at the entrance. Rings left from glasses and cigarette burns adorned the glass cover. Harry went to look for a bathroom and Conner found a table. The old man behind the bar glanced at them without stopping his conversation.

Harry walked into a small room lined with booths. It was empty except for three men sitting in the corner table playing cards. One man casually looked up as he passed by.

"Two," the man said, and laid two cards down. When Harry came out of the bathroom, only one man sat at the table.

"Where'd you go?" Conner asked.

"Bathroom," Harry said. "No soap."

"Doesn't surprise me," said Conner.

The old man at the bar twisted his head toward the window and called out, "Sara."

A woman in her twenties came out of the kitchen, grabbed a tablet off the counter, and walked over to their table. She wore a low cut blouse and tight blue jeans. She had tied her blonde and sweaty hair in a ponytail; a loose strand hung down over her one eye, which she kept brushing out of her way. She said nothing, but stood pen in hand ready to write down their order.

"Hi," said Conner.

She smiled back. As she moved, Harry could smell a hint of perfume. Her hands were smooth and well groomed, and she seemed at ease with herself and the world.

Her eyes were bright and clear and she looked through them into some other place.

"What's good?" Conner asked.

She looked from Harry to Conner and back again, and then rolled her eyes. "Number one special," she said, and wrote that down.

She looked over at Harry, who asked, "What's number two?"

"You don't want that, trust me," she said, and waited for him to order, but he hesitated.

"Two number ones," she nodded, raised her eyebrows, and turned back into the kitchen to prepare two number ones.

The old man came over with coffee and poured two cups.

"I'd rather have a beer," said Harry.

"Comes with coffee," he said. "Beer is fitty cents extra."

"Well, that'll be fine."

He went back behind the bar, set two Coors on the counter, and opened them. Then he reached down and put two tiny glasses on top of the bottles.

As they watched, Harry turned and said, "F-i-t-t-y? This place would make good fodder for one of your plays. Look at these people. No one seems to be enjoying themselves. That guy has his face buried in his coffee, the bartender has about three teeth and looks like a character out of a science fiction movie, and the waitress seems like she hates this place. You could call it *Zombie Diner*."

"Damned Diner," Conner said. They waited while sounds of someone cooking came out through the open window behind the bar.

Conner fussed with the silverware and looked out the window; then looked over at Harry, who stared at the kitchen.

"Nice tits," said Conner, craning his neck toward Harry so no one else might hear. He raised his eyebrows and winked.

Harry feigned ignorance. "Oh. I hadn't noticed."

"You're full of shit. I don't think she's up to flirting with you."

Sara came over with the beer and set the two bottles on the table, bending over as she did so. They both stared down her open shirt, she had no bra, and their eyes were riveted on her breasts.

"What's your name?" asked Harry. He already knew, but he wanted to hear her say it.

She didn't respond, but looked at him as if to say, "Please no."

When she walked away, her hips swung pendulously like Marylyn Monroe's. She walked behind the counter and stepped in front of the old man, grabbed the coffee pot and refilled an empty cup for the customer there.

"They don't learn to walk like that, Harry. It's nature made."

"I thought we weren't supposed to think of women on this trip."

"That's easier said than done."

"Well, it took me two years to get this trip together and I'd like to stick to the plan. You're a hard man to pin down, Conner. Your plays are getting a lot of attention. Before you know it you'll be so famous you won't even recognize me."

"At least I don't gallivant all over the globe in search of gold and 'jooles'."

The cook was banging pots and pans in the kitchen. They looked over and the kitchen door swung open and Sara came towards them with two plates in hand.

"The name's Sara," she said. "You want anything else?" She brushed the hair out of her face again.

"Sara," said Harry. "You working late tonight?"

"Oh, like I ain't never herd that one before," she said and smirked.

Her breasts were all Harry could see by now, but he took an occasional look at her face.

"Just asking," he said.

"Don't bother." She went back to the kitchen. Once there, the pots and pans started banging again.

"Now who's thinking about girls?" Conner said wryly.

They both looked at their food for the first time.

"What the hell is this shit?"

It was pale and unappealing, and looked like hot turkey with gravy. "I thought Number one was supposed to be meatloaf," Conner said.

Harry was starving and ate his food regardless of what he thought of its appearance. Conner played with his at first and nibbled, drank his beer, and sipped the coffee. Harry finished his meal and pulled Conner's uneaten food over and ate that as well.

Conner watched him as he ate. "Shovel that in."

"I learned to do that in college," he said and wiped his mouth with a napkin. "The food wasn't great and it was best to get it over with."

Harry finished and joined Conner, who had already gotten up to pay at the counter. Only one customer remained and he sat alone in the corner of the diner. His poker pals had gone and he had not moved at all, looking as though he had grown out of the furniture. His eyes never lifted off the coffee cup, which he held firmly between two hands.

"Two-fitty," said the old man in plaid. He was talking to Harry who couldn't take his eyes off the lonely man. "Two-fitty," he repeated.

Conner fumbled in his pocket for his share of the bill.

Harry was non-responsive and too focused on the man in the corner. He'd seen him before, or men like him, in the lonely cantinas of small villages in Chile and Bolivia. On the table next to the man was a weather-stained fedora with frayed edges. He reminded Harry of the Russian they had met in Chile. He tried to remember that day, but something disrupted his train of thought.

Harry suddenly realized everyone was staring at him.

"Let's go," said Conner. Clearly, he had noticed Harry's distraction and had paid for Harry's share, too.

Harry looked at the man behind the counter and raised his eyebrows. The old man looked at Sara and held up the twenty-dollar bill, and said, "Fer two-fitty."

With the change, Conner put a tip on the table.

Once outside, Harry looked around and counted the cars in the parking lot.

"There are three people in the diner and seven cars in the lot," Harry said.

"So?"

"That doesn't seem odd to you?"

"It belongs to the cook," Conner said dismissively.

"Yeah, I guess." He could not shake some vague trepidation. It almost felt to him like that whole experience was significant in some way, which he could not put his finger on. He kept thinking about Sara and how out of place she looked.

"She looks better than that place," he said suddenly.

"How's that?" Conner asked.

Harry slowly looked over at Conner who was driving now, "Just thinking."

Her destiny, Harry thought, was elsewhere.

Dagon, Nancy and Don

1976

In 1974 Harry got a job as a professor for a small college called Ogden Sumner University. He had been leading an expedition in the Tolfa Mountains in northern Italy for a year and returned to gather more supplies and students. Carl, the chancellor of the school, took on a new professor, and invited Harry to dinner to meet him along with the rest of the staff.

The campus was small and no more than a fifteen-minute walk from end to end. It lay deep within the Rocky Mountains, on a high plateau that offered a bucolic atmosphere, low sloping hills, and a view of the distant mountains. Bear Creek River ran straight through the center of campus and was prized not only for its beauty, but also for its sport. OSU won conference in rowing three straight years, and sent four students to the '72 Olympics the year before.

Few people used their cars on campus and most walked to classes and even to town. When school was in session, the size of the local community would double even though most students and professors lived on campus.

The chancellor's house was a large stone mansion built in 1810 by a British architect. He sold it to Ogden Sumner for twice what it was worth just before the war of 1812. The college came along in 1822.

Dinner at the Chancellors house was always a formal affair. Harry dug his tuxedo out of storage and was surprised he still fit into it. He even shaved his beard for the occasion.

The dinner was a success, as usual, and Carl paired the new man, Dagon, and Harry with splendid results. Although the affair was to welcome the new

14

professor to the family, most of the females, either wives or teachers had eyes for Harry, the conquering hero.

Professor Jim Barnes, from the math department, came up to Harry after dinner and thanked him for keeping his wife company so he could maneuver closer to the new graduate assistant with the extraordinary assets. The male population assumed that Harry's advances were merely polite, but the women knew better, and took turns with the adventurer.

This worried Carl who hoped that some of the women would fuss over Dagon.

"Harry," he said, pulling him aside just after dessert. "I want you to share some of the affection you receive with the new guest. I want him to feel comfortable."

Harry scanned the crowd and locked his eyes on Dagon who was already three deep in women. "I don't think you have too much to worry about, Carl. I'm guessing he'll do just fine."

Dagon told stories of his adventures in the mountains of South America, being chased by bandits and thugs, "And they were just the government officials!" The women near him laughed solicitously. In his left arm, he held Mrs. Buxley, the librarian, in his right hand; a glass of wine, which he sipped from occasionally in between descriptions of the cold dark tombs he had exhumed.

"He's doing okay for an old man, Carl."

"Old, Harry." Carl looked surprisingly offended. "I'm a year younger than he, and I'm only 58."

"It must be the grey," Harry said with a wry smile. That seemed to quell Carl's insecurities, although he and Dagon both had greying sides.

Carl stood by the door talking quietly with Dagon for several minutes. Harry approached and they stopped.

"I'm heading back home, Carl," he said. Then he looked at Dagon and put his hand on his shoulder.

"Dagon, would you like to walk with me? I think we're heading in the same direction."

They walked back to campus together.

"Professor Benicia," Harry said, "how do you like the school so far?"

"Dago, everyone calls me Dago." However, before Harry could say his name, Dago read his expression and said, "I'm Italian. I grew up in Brooklyn and we all had politically incorrect monikers." He paused and stopped to pick a twig off the ground. "I've just dipped my feet into the pool, so to speak, and I'm going to teach a course this spring on the influence of mummification on the Indian culture in South America; a specialty of mine." He stopped to look at his watch.

Harry noticed they were standing in front of an old cottage with a freshly painted white picket fence.

"Ah well, anyway, I'm home." Dago swung open the little gate to the path leading up to the front door. "The others should be here by now. Why don't you come in for a drink? There's a lot to talk about."

The others turned out to be two graduate students: Nancy Tully and Don Cassopolis.

Dago offered them a vintage bottle of wine. "It's from Argentina. They have a young wine industry there. This bottle is from a French gentleman who brought over several thousand cuttings from a very old vineyard in France after the war."

Harry looked at Nancy, who sat quietly next to him on the couch. She was an attractive woman with light brown hair and a short turned-up nose. When she smiled, her eyes sparkled and she had dimples. She was a graduate student transferred from the History department to work specifically with Harry

"And what is your story," he asked her. "What brings you over from history?"

She explained that her ex-husband worked in that field and she had done her masters under his tutelage. "But he was a drunken slob with an insatiable appetite." She winked and raised an eyebrow.

"For the women," Harry ventured.

"I caught him in bed with a professor's wife. That's when I came here for my doctorate." She held a glass of wine in her hand swirling it, but never taking a sip. She held his gaze for a while and Harry smiled.

He turned to Don who looked as much like a wrestler as anyone he had ever seen. He was a handsome enough fellow, with a Slavic looking face: square, blonde hair, blue eyes, and even some freckles across the bridge of his nose.

"I'm a Nebraskan. We never sleep with any man's wife, Dr. Thursday," he said, his face stern.

"Well, you've never slept with any of mine," Harry replied. "I'm sure."

"Any?" Dago inserted.

"I've been married twice. Both were short term and I'm not sure if either was legal in the king's eye."

They talked into the night. Dago told them of his lifelong work, and of the Chilean mountains. "There are mummies there and so much work to do. My last post let me go after I failed to produce any substantial return on their investment, but I am very close." Then he went on about Europe and his time spent there during the war in Italy and France. "I was with the 101st airborne," he said. "We'd got around a bit."

He brought out a humidor filled with cigarettes and offered one to each. Don refused, but Nancy and Harry accepted. Harry rarely smoked; in fact, he quit the year before going to Italy. It was easier to smoke with alcohol.

Harry pressed the European thing, wondering how a corporal could be in so many places in so short a time.

"I stayed on after the fighting stopped. I spent thirteen years in Europe as a private citizen. Started my career there. You can't believe how much the Germans stole in their short stay in power."

They finished the evening when the sun came up unexpectedly. Don had already gone home, promising to be ready in two days to head south. Harry took the opportunity to walk Nancy home across campus. She was tall, reaching nearly to Harry's eyes. She wore a cotton dress that flared from the waist down. Rather than wearing high heels, she had a pair of flats, which revealed her true height. Harry found himself holding her hand by the time they reached her cottage. The cool morning air was calm and dry. Leaves rustled in the tops of the trees, and they could smell the roses in the garden. Somewhere, a student shouted for his girlfriend, calling her name.

Nancy looked over. "He must be lost."

"It doesn't get any more romantic than that," Harry said.

She invited him in for coffee.

This was no young coed, and Harry felt the temptation, but politely suggested that he was tired and had a lot to do to prepare for the trip south. He kissed her gently on the cheek instead, and stood watching as she entered her cottage.

The New Girl

1978

Skinny was a thinly built man in his late fifties. He had dark hair that was receding and greasy, but he still managed a small patch of it in the front of his head. It looked like an island in the midst of a barren sea. This he grew long, and instead of combing it over, he combed it straight back. He had muttonchops for sideburns that met in the middle of his face and formed a mustache, making him look as though he stepped right out of the 1890's. All he needed was an apron, bowtie and a bowler.

He stepped out of the private door next to the kitchen and watched as Sara leaned over to pick her tip up off the table.

"Fuh! Big spenders," she said, stuffing the money into her pocket.

A young girl, avidly chewing gum, stepped out of the room behind him. Her cheeks were blushing, and her brown eyes darted all around the restaurant. With her hand, she brushed back her ruffled hair. The buttons on her blouse were askew.

Others might think that the heat was the cause of the sweat on Skinny's shirt, but Skinny and the young girl knew better.

Skinny's handmade cowboy boots, with spurs and silver cleats, clicked as he crossed the wooden floor.

The girl followed him to the counter and waited timidly near the kitchen door.

Sara stood in his way.

He eyed her for a moment and then walked around her to get to the register.

"How's business?" he asked.

Sara looked at him with disdain. "Great. We were slammed."

He opened the register, took out the twenties, and counted them. There were only four, and he kept one of them and put the rest back. He turned slowly to the girl and looked down her blouse. Her large breasts begged attention, so he slid the bill into her cleavage.

She stared up at him and smiled.

He patted her on the rear, put his foot up on the counter, lit up a cigarette and said, "You'll do fine kid. Sara will show you the ropes. You can follow her to the hotel around eight tonight."

The girl beamed at Sara who granted a weak smile in return, "What's your name, kid?"

"Bonnie." She walked to the door, put on her coat and left.

"They're getting younger all the time, Skinny."

"She said she was twenty. That's all I know," Skinny said.

"That's all you want to know."

"Shut the hell up," he said, and made like he was going to swing a backhand at her.

Sara seemed unimpressed. "She looks like my friends little sister. She's sixteen. Tops. She in school?"

"Said she graduated in 74, and went to some college in Colorado."

"Yeah, she got an education alright," the old man said, and chuckled.

"No doubt." Skinny took a long drag on his cigarette and blew a steady stream of smoke toward the ceiling.

"Who were your friends there?" he asked.

"You mean those two easterners? My new boyfriends. Whata'ya think?"

"Ya wanna know what I think? I think you had better start acting nicer to our customers," he looked over at the bartender, who quickly looked down at the bar and cleaned it with a towel. "I heard ya out here." He patted her on the cheek and wrapped his arm around her waist and pulled her closer. "We're in this for the money."

Skinny looked over to the corner of the room and saw the dark figure sitting motionlessly, watching his cigarette burn. His eyes slowly rose as if he was following the smoke trail upwards. He stopped when his eyes met Skinny's and then tossed his head slightly.

Skinny looked at the other two at the counter and wondered if they knew he was being called.

"Check in with Mouse when you and what's-her-name get to the hotel later," Skinny told Sara.

He took a beer out of the cooler, popped the top off, and took a long steady draft, never taking his eyes off her. "It's fucking hot in here," he said all of a sudden, and ran the bottle across his forehead. "Open the back door," he shouted into the kitchen, and walked to the man in the corner and sat down.

The Arapaho

They drove away from the diner at leisure. At some point they would see signs for the Yellowstone National Park, or so they hoped. As the day went on, they looked for a place to stay the night. Kampground of America was always a safe place—clean and comfortable—and they looked for one. Up ahead they saw a sign that said, "Yellowstone National Park 70 miles north." A half hour later they came on a sign for Yellowstone one hundred miles in the opposite direction.

"We're doomed," Conner said.

Harry sloughed it off as an adventure, but Conner wasn't the type that enjoyed misdirection. He had to know what to expect and when and where it was coming from.

"What would you have done if Sara had responded favorably to you?" He asked Harry.

"Asked her if she had a friend."

"Oh, no thank you," he said holding up his hands like a traffic cop. "Remember that time in Wildwood when you had a date with that little redhead, and you got her cousin for me?" Conner laughed.

"You're laughing."

"Yeah, now I am, but I didn't used to. That is a prime example of our differences."

"What differences?"

"Harry, you were born with a silver spoon in your mouth. You always came out on top, and I had the worst of it, fighting for every bit I could get."

"We were kids then, Conner. Barely thirteen. You made out better after you had your teeth straightened, I remember. Besides, it was my date. That means you get the cousin."

"Did I ever tell you about my play, *Majestic Twins*?"

"No. Can't say I heard about that one."

"It was loosely based on those girls, two cousins who were in love with the same man, but one cousin was wealthy and the other was actually her sister adopted out as an infant. They met later in life by serendipity and both fell for the same man. Guess which one he chose?"

"The rich one."

"No. And do you know why? Because he was socialist and he scoffed at the wealthy in spite of his own family's wealth. It flopped on the circuit after a two month run in a Soho house slash hippie hangout."

"Too bad."

"So it goes."

They eventually came to a heavily wooded area where the road meandered through the trees, climbing as it narrowed to two lanes with no shoulder. The forest became thicker, the trees taller and the sky disappeared behind Ponderosa Pines that were thick as hundred-year-old oaks. Brown pine needles carpeted the forest floor, allowing for little else to grow. They almost passed a large driveway to their right, which was marked by two life-sized grizzly bears carved out of what used to be living trees.

Conner stopped the car and backed up to have a look. A black wrought-iron sign with the name Arapaho Hotel, written in white, bridged the space between the two bears.

Conner looked at Harry.

"Go for it," Harry said.

At the end of the gravel road sat the hotel, a grand log structure surrounded by a short lawn that wrapped itself around the entire building. A fine line separated the forest from the lawn as though some invisible barrier kept nature from encroaching upon its parasitic neighbor. The gardens along the sides of the hotel battled age-long neglect.

They parked the Bug in the lot and made their way to the front door. A sign by the steps welcomed visitors to the Arapaho, "The Friendliest Place West of the Mississippi River."

Leading up to the front door were steps made from thick quarter logs of the same sort that comprised the building. The door was framed first by two trees that branched out at exactly the same distance from each other; forming a large, gothic, cathedral-like frame, which was crowned at the pinnacle with a gigantic moose skull with its antlers flaring outwards. Beneath that was inscribed the date: 1857. Within this framework, an elaborate concentric molding led to progressively smaller frames down at last to the doorway.

The doors, rather than being heavy and cumbersome, were light and easy to push in. As a newcomer, one would believe they were entering a grand lobby with bellhops and ballroom, and perhaps an orchestra playing Teutonic waltzes. What they found instead was an eclectic nightmare.

"What the hell is this place?" said Harry, talking softly. It took a moment for their eyes to acclimate to the change of light.

Conner said, "I don't know, but I'm not sure I like it."

"It'll be fine," Harry said, trying to reassure his friend. "How bad could it be? I've seen worse." Black velvet paintings and Tiffany lamps dominated the décor, which drew their eyes to the bar.

Between the foyer and the barroom were two flanking velvet paintings of naked women. The painting on the left showed an Amazon wrapped in deadly battle with a giant two-headed snake that wound suggestively between her spreading legs. One serpent rose above her with its mouth agape. The other—headless—hung limply between her breasts.

Two much larger paintings framed the bar. One was of Elvis in his classic sequined body suit, and the other of him playing a guitar in front of the Pearly Gates, angels and all. Heavy natural colored log beams, beautifully mortised and elaborate, supported the high arching ceiling that rose thirty feet above the floor. At one time, this was no doubt a fine establishment, but now the bar acted as both the front desk and the focal point of the entire business. Behind the bar, a man stood with his foot propped upon the sink talking with a big man, who was standing on the other side of the large slate top.

He watched as the two approached.

Harry sat at the bar and smiled. Conner stood.

Although they had never seen one another before, the bartender stared long at them, sizing them up as a fighter might do before a match.

They ordered two beers.

Conner seemed uneasy and coughed to get Harry's attention.

Harry was in his element. As an archeologist, he would spend a bit of his free time, in the only place in 48 states where he could legally relieve his tensions: a bar. He had seen or heard it all by the time he was a graduate student, and he could forget half the things he had done and still remember too much. Perhaps in memory of his father, or because of his father, Harry liked living life as fully as he could.

Harry had seen this type of person before and preferred not to give the bartender any more attention than was necessary.

"How you boys doin?" he said. "My name is Steve. My friends call me Skinny. I run the hotel." A cigarette hung, burning, from his lower lip.

Conner extended his right hand, which Skinny did not accept, and said, "I'm Conner. We need a room Skinny."

Skinny looked blankly back.

Harry broke in. "Steve, we'd like a room please, and two beers."

Skinny's head turned suddenly and he lifted his foot back onto the bottle trough. He wore black leather cowboy boots with silver cleats on the toes and heals. He looked over at the huge man, who was now in the far corner talking to a young woman. The man looked briefly at Skinny, and then went back to the girl.

Skinny looked at the two guests, his lower lip protruding slightly. He popped the top of two beers with an opener attached to the cooler and placed them on the bar. As he did this, he opened his mouth a bit and Harry could see a glimmer of gold.

"You want it for the night?" Skinny asked.

"All night, sure," Conner said. "Why do you ask?"

"Ain't got no bags is all." He turned around, grabbed a large register, and plunked it down on the bar in front of them. It smelled musty, old bookish, like something you would find in the deep recesses of a library. It was beer stained.

"Y'all wanna sign the book?"

Conner took the book, turned it around, and registered their names.

Skinny dashed the cigarette out on the bar top, and lit another. "Thirty-five dollars for the night. Twenty if you want it by the hour."

Conner leaned over to Harry and whispered, "By the hour?"

Harry drank his beer. He looked around the room. It was dark. The shutters were drawn to keep out the sunlight, and oil lamps scattered around gave off enough light to see by. Over in one corner, a jukebox sat quietly waiting for a coin, and next to that was a pool table with four players. Covering the eastern wall was a walk-in fireplace made of local flagstone, and it rose up and through the roof. Two people sat on a couch in front of it watching an empty grate, but they did not seem to mind there was no fire.

Two couples were playing pool in the corner of the main room. Someone broke the cue and three balls fell in one after the other. One of the girls walked over to the jukebox and put a quarter in it. "Tuesday's Gone" came on.

On the opposite side of the bar was a hallway that turned a short way back. A stack of dusty boxes rose up beside it blocking a door from view. It slowly opened and squeaked sharply. It stopped at a crack. A face appeared from the dark, vaguely visible by the light of the main room. A second later, it swung open and a girl stepped out. The light flooded in behind her. She had long hair that hung just to her shoulders. He guessed her to be about twenty years old. She looked over in their direction, and smiled.

Conner meanwhile paid the thirty-five dollars but did not get a key in return.

"Check it out," Harry said.

He watched her walk across the floor. Harry finished his beer and asked for another. The girl had moved closer all the while talking to different people in the place, her eyes always returned to Harry. Soon she was standing right on top of him, smiling. They locked eyes and she crossed her arms so that her breasts came together, accentuating her cleavage.

"Hi there, I'm CJ." She was wearing white Capri pants that fit snugly, and a button down denim shirt with the top few buttons left open.

"I'll bet you are." He offered his hand and she took it. "Harry, and that's Conner."

CJ smiled and Harry found it hard to look away. Her skin was smooth and fair, and her green eyes stood out against her dark brown hair.

Conner was still talking with Skinny. "We're tired. We'd like to sleep now." Still no keys exchanged hands.

"When you're ready, my girl will show you the way. Room 17 C."

"I take it you work here?" Harry said.

"Stave's my brother. I help out." She had the same southern drawl as Skinny. If she were any closer to Harry, she would have been in his lap.

"Ready?" she said.

"That's all right," Conner, said forcing a smile. "We can find our way just fine, I'm sure."

"I ain't in no hurry," she said, and sat down next to Harry, twirling her hair with her right hand. She gathered her hair, somehow making tiny braids with only one hand, while supporting her head with the other. She winked. "You gonna buy me one?"

"Oh sure." She caught him a bit off guard, and before he could get Skinny's attention, he had already put a beer down in front of her.

"On the house fellas."

Harry looked at CJ as she lifted the bottle and said, "My lucky night." He had now turned his back to his friend and gave his full attention to CJ.

"Where you boys from?" CJ had a deeper voice than her frame looked as though it should carry.

"Back east," Conner put in.

"I thought you weren't listening," Harry said.

"I wasn't until just now," Conner said, looking uneasy. Then to CJ, he said, "We're just passing through."

"Most folks do round here 'cept the locals. Only thing happenin' round here are the tourists."

"And they ain't bitin tonight," said Skinny. He chuckled and CJ gave a knowing look. "Yellowstone?"

"Huh."

"You folks going to Yellowstone," said CJ. "You know, the park."

"Yeah, how'd you know that?"

"Lucky guess," she said.

Conner downed his beer, slammed it on the table, and said, "You ready?"

CJ walked around the end of the bar, grabbed a set of keys, and took one off for room 17. "Come on then."

Harry's heart began pumping faster. He was excited by what could happen next.

CJ led them through a side door down a dimly lit hallway and outside. She looked over her shoulder every couple of seconds and smiled as she sashayed in front of them. Harry was certain she was trying to seduce him. She walked slowly and he could smell the powdery perfume she wore. He noticed how her ass swung back and forth so naturally. It was just like Sara's back at the diner.

He glanced back at Conner who was looking at the same thing. "Déjà vu," he said. He wondered if a girl really could learn to walk that way. How old was she? "Old enough," he muttered to himself. *She is going to be trouble*, he thought, but somewhere inside his head came the reply—*maybe not*.

At the back of the hotel, she headed up a set of stairs and outside along a balcony that overlooked the lawn, and past several rooms until she came on a short hallway with more rooms. Theirs was at the far end. "Should have taken a cab," Harry said.

"These are our private rooms." She emphasized the word private. She opened the door without a key, flung it open, and stood with her back against the frame with her foot up on the jam. Harry had to squeeze by her and he could feel her breath against his throat. Her breasts pressed tightly against him.

"Here you are boys. Do you need anything?"

"No."

The room lacked certain savoir-faire. It did have black velvet paintings of two naked girls displayed on the wall.

"Are you sure this isn't the hourly room?" Conner said. He looked over at Harry and smiled.

She did not get it.

"This is one of our best rooms boys," CJ looked offended. "You sure you don't need anything at all?" She said this slowly and let the last word draw out a bit, making her l's sound like o's, like 'a-tow.' Conner seemed uneasy, and asked, "How old are you anyway miss...uh?"

"CJ," she said. "Old enough."

Harry began to heat up under the collar, and he blushed.

Conner by then had already dismissed the girl and was staring at the floor over by the bathroom. "Thanks Katy, I don't think we need anything else for now."

"That's CJ."

Sovth to Chile

1976

He had fallen in love with Nancy from the first moment he met her in Dago's house. He knew she was something different, certainly not like the other co-eds he had made love to. He remembered reading how Hemmingway said that making love to a woman was as essential to a man's needs as was eating, or breathing, and Harry lived that belief. But Nancy held for him something deeper, something everyone searches for and few really find. There was a truth in her that he needed.

By late October Harry, Dago, Nancy, and Don were in Lima Peru. Dago seemed to know a great deal about the area, and deftly took them through the city, and to the coast to a small fishing village about fifty miles south of the capital city. The village sat nurtured by a river that ran across the desert from the blue Andes. The village of Xico was once a major hub of the Spaniards in their own quest for gold. These tiny villages retain some of the original architecture they left behind in their search for the Capital city.

Within one mile of the protection of the coast and the river, is the harshest desert in South America, if not the world, Dago explained to the crew as they drove along old, rutted dirt roads from Lima to the village. Harry remembered his own experiences here years ago with his father, Alfred, in their search for caves rumored to have housed ancient civilizations before the Incas. They spent a month searching the mountains around Ayacucho, and came away with more of an understanding of the effects of heat on the human body than the lost civilization.

They traveled all night, arrived in Xico in the early morning hours, and headed for the fishing village along the coast where they had a boat waiting for them. There had to be nearly fifty boats of sizes varying from small rowboats to the larger schooners like the one they would be boarding.

They pulled up to one such boat painted white with blue trim. On the bow was a carved figurehead of a woman riding a dolphin—her paint had faded over the years. The name painted below her was "Ouro Maia"

"This will take us to Chanaral, Chile," Dago said. "Niko here will take good care of us. Next, we will take a train ride to Santiago, and there we will have to hire some means of transport to Vallicia where we will base the operation. We have reservations at a small hotel there."

They met Niko on deck, and he embraced Dago. They spoke Greek together like old friends, almost forgetting there were others with him. He finally introduced Harry and the others to Niko. When Harry shook hands with Niko his grip was vice-like, and Harry thought he could probably crush a sack full of stones into powder with it if he wished.

"Dago, ask him how long it is to Chanaral Chile," Harry asked.

Dago said something in Greek.

"Two days," Niko said in surprisingly good English, but it sounded more like, "Today's." He smiled brightly, showing his three gold teeth. Niko was in his sixties, at least Harry assumed, it was hard to tell with fisher folk who spend their entire lives in the harsh elements. His hair was black and grey and brushed straight back. It was coarse and thick, fed and watered by the salty air of the Pacific. His nose was long, and he had large ears that stood out. He stood stoutly at 5'6," and commanded great respect from not only the passengers, but also the crew.

They traveled lightly, carrying only what they would need for a month, relying on the local markets for subsequent supplies. The only equipment they had with them was a few metal detectors, a Proton

Magnetometer used to detect sub-surface structures, and crude but serviceable surveying tools.

Later that night, Harry woke up and felt the boat racing through the water. There was a great deal of commotion on deck.

Nancy and Don had burst into his room in alarm.

"Harry," she said. "I think I heard shooting."

"Okay," he said, trying to chase the sleep out of his head. He got up and sent them back to their rooms, but only Don would go alone. He had to escort Nancy back to her room, a small closet adapted for the use of female travelers. The head was directly across from her bunk.

Then he went upstairs on deck to look around. As he was about to open the door, Dago came running through. "Oh, Harry," he said placing his hand against his chest. He looked worried, and glanced behind him as if someone might be following. "Stay out of sight. I am supposed to be traveling alone, they've already seen me."

Harry looked skeptical, "Who saw you?"

"The Coast Guard," he said. "Or at least their version. More like pirates." Dago pleaded with him to listen. "Trust me, please. The worst is over besides. We have stopped, and they insist on boarding us, but Niko's resisting. He is in open international waters, but you know these people down here, they go by their own rules."

Niko's first mate came down and spoke in rapid Spanish to Dago, who gave a final plea to Harry, "Please, they don't know you are here or else they would come aboard." He turned, and ran topside.

Harry agreed to stay below. He went back to his room and found Nancy standing behind him. She looked up at him with large, frightened brown eyes. "He said they shot one of the crew, and needed him above to help explain to the police why we are here."

"Who said that?"

"The mate. To Dago."

"It'll be okay, Nancy," he said, and took hold of her shoulders. He had never touched her before—aside from holding her hand—and had not realized how soft, and petite she was. Beautiful. She looked alluring in a thin t-shirt and boxer shorts, barefoot, and cold. She wrapped her arms around him and held on tightly. "I'm scared," she whispered, and trembled slightly.

He gently put his arms around her. "I think we should be okay."

He looked down at her. Her long, shiny dark auburn hair was parted down the middle in a straight line. He could feel her breathing deeply, and her breasts pressed tightly against his chest felt reassuring.

Here was a young woman, by no means a schoolgirl, who was an outgoing and flirtatious person. Her effusive behavior often seemed sexual to the man with whom she was interacting. In addition, she flirted equally, with whomever she pleased. She was highly sexual and a true academic, and could hold her own in the tightest of oratories. The night they met at Dago's, she argued successfully with him about the role of science in government.

She took him by his hand, led him to her room, and opened the door. She turned, and at that moment, Harry felt it would be a difficult thing to live down should they make love that night. They had just begun working together and had many months ahead. It could become difficult later should something come between them. It happened all the time.

She tugged at his hand slightly, playing with his fingers, wrapping them between her own. But he stood his ground. Their fingers separated, and he quietly said goodnight.

The next morning, Harry stood on deck looking at the vast blue sea. He held a cup of coffee the cook had given him, and he sipped it thoughtfully.

"You sleep like a dead marlin, Harry," someone spoke suddenly.

Harry turned and saw that the voice belonged to Niko. He stood behind Harry, ready for a hard day's work.

"Will we be bothered again before we reach Chile?" Harry asked.

"No, I don't think we will."

"Your English has improved overnight, Captain."

"Oh yes, well." He shuffled his feet and pushed a piece of seaweed through the bilge holes on the deck sides. "I don't like to give out more than is necessary to strangers. Especially in my business."

He was not sure he should ask what business the captain was in without rousing suspicion. But what the hell, he figured he was well paid.

"What exactly is your business?"

"Fishing when the fishing's good. It is a small schooner, and mostly we carry passengers. And sometimes they fish too."

"Oh. How long have you known Dago?"

"Many, many years. I guess we met..."

Dago Benicia finished the sentence for him. "We met in the late forties, after the war ended. I saved Niko's life once. I was passenger on that freighter you had, remember Niko?"

"Oh sure Dago. ' El Paramo de Vuelo,' The Flying Moor, out of Spain. You called it my garbage scow. I do not know why. It was a beautiful ship. Just a little shot up after the U-boat had its way. That's when you hired me on board."

"I changed Niko's business from hauling cargo to hauling people. Many people were moving to South America after the war, Harry. You should know that. Europeans came over in sheets."

Take Your Pick

1978

Back at the bar, CJ approached Skinny. He was talking with the big man. Skinny stood in much the same position he did earlier, resting his right foot on the bottle trough of the bar. He had a beer in his hand and gently nursed it. *He's wearin that same goddamn outfit again,* she thought. He had a closet full of the same type of shirts, and she had washed them all for him over the years. She often thought of throwing them out and buying new ones for him, *but he'd kill me if I did.* He sipped the beer and looked at it closely, turning it around in his hand. *Look at him reading the label,* and she chuckled to herself.

She admired Skinny, used to think he was all there was to life, when he wasn't hitting her. She had begun to wish for something else in life, and secretly hoped for a new beginning at best, or a vacation with Skinny, at least. Without him would be best. She thought about that a lot. Then she began to formulate a plan.

The big man stood at the corner of the bar where he always did. His mouth opened slightly as CJ neared. *He's starin' at me again,* she thought, *big fat load.* He always leered at her. Sometimes she would see him licking his lips, and then he would move them, talking silently with himself – nodding his head and smirking. She chilled at the thought of him on top of her. *Not for any money.*

She looked at him and thought, *you make me sick.* She wanted to talk with Skinny alone. "Why don't you get lost for a while?"

He stared dumbly at her. He muttered something to himself. His mouth hung open.

"How's that," said Skinny.

The big man's mouth closed with a snap.

"Uh, nuttin' Boss. Just thinkin' to myself."

"Skinny told you about that thinking, Moose. Said you shouldn't aught' a do that sort of thing. Get ya in trouble."

"Mouse," he protested the misuse of his name.

"Moose," she sneered back. "You look more like a moose anyways."

Mouse looked to Skinny desperate for help. "Boss, she ain't fair."

"Shut up, both a ya." Skinny looked over his shoulder at Mouse and said, "Go and get more beer and stock the cooler will ya? Make yourself useful."

Then he turned back to CJ and grabbed her chin, turning her face from side to side. "Can't even see it no more."

"Don't be too proud of yourself, asshole."

Skinny raised his hand as if to backhand her again, and she flinched and pulled her head back.

"Skinny," she said, hoping to distract him. "How's about you an me get the hell outta here for a while, you know, a vacation. Huh?"

He finished the beer and slid the bottle down the bar to the end where it tripped on the padded edge and toppled over and landed in a trashcan.

"He scores," he said and lifted both arms in the air.

She knew what he was going to say before she asked. She knew him better than he did himself. He looked at his nails and reached into his pocket and pulled out a knife, switched it open and began digging at them.

"You gonna go for him?" Skinny asked.

"Huh?"

"You know the big one. Blue eyes."

"Him? Maybe I like a challenge once't in a while," she said.

"He wants you. Easy money sweet heart."

She knew she could have anyone she set her mind to. She was Skinny's pride and joy, his best girl in the place. However, she was tired of living like that. It was a living, sure and she was damned good at it. Made more money than she ever thought she could even after Skinny took out his cut.

She looked over at Skinny, who was at the bar counting his money with Mouse behind him. He was always counting his money and putting it down in that little book of his.

Here at least, I can call my own shots, she thought to herself. *He never really hits me that hard and he needs me anyway.* She sighed and drank her whiskey. "Let me try some of the good stuff," she said as she emptied her glass and slid it over to him. He kept counting. Annoyed at losing his count, he picked the pile up and started counting again.

"Jack's good enough for you. Shut the fuck up, will ya?" Then he looked at Mouse. "What are you smiling' at? Didn't I tell you to get more beer?"

CJ went behind the bar to help herself to the Jack Daniels.

"But I did Boss. I got the beer just like you said. I did." He looked down at his hands, and tapped them on the bar. Then he looked up with eyes wide and said, "Do you want I should go and get more, Boss? Huh, do ya?"

Skinny lost count again and threw the money down on the bar. "Why don't you do that? Why don't the both of you get the hell outta my sight and do something else?"

She thought about the two men from earlier. Something about them, especially the one named Harry, made her feel a bit different. They weren't like the usual slobs that came in here. The Arapaho's regulars were mostly drunks who came in after their wives kicked them out for coming home after a night of doing what, they would not guess.

She took the glass of whiskey and sat at the table by the fireplace and watched one of the girls make out with some new guy. She thought more about her secret. She didn't want Skinny to know what she was feeling, or what she had on her mind. She'd had enough.

Back at the Bar

Harry and Conner inspected the room. The bathroom was condemnable by most gas station standards. A double bed sat in the middle of the room, and they threw their bags on top. Next to the bed was a nightstand with a small lamp on it. Harry tried the lamp and it didn't work. A small couch stood alone in the far corner of the room. In another corner was a vinyl chair. By the door, a floor lamp stood like the Leaning Tower of Pisa; its shade, with a hole burnt through it, hung off the side. The walls were old plaster and probably painted with pre-war lead paint. The paint, yellowing and peeling in spots, actually gave the room a rustic look.

"Smoke," Harry said. "You smell it?"

Conner drew his finger across the wall by the bathroom leaving a streak. His fingertip was now dark yellow. "Yeah, I smell it." His eyes traced around the whole floor "Look at those dust balls."

Harry saw one of those dust balls run into a hole under the heating vent next to the lonely vinyl chair. He kept that to himself and continued looking for a light switch. He found one in the bathroom and turned it on. It put out a dim yellowish light that barely cast a shadow.

"Must be 15 watt."

Suddenly a bright light went on and nearly blinded them.

"Here it is," said Conner. "I found the switch."

Conner stood in the corner farthest from the door. The light came from a single bulb in the middle of the ceiling.

Harry took the shade from the floor lamp and hung it on the ceiling bulb.

"Ambience."

The room not being what they had expected, they decided to have a few more drinks before daring to sleep. They left the light on and walked out. The sun had set, and as they stepped out onto the balcony Harry could smell the powdery perfume left by CJ.

"You smell that?" said Harry. They had stopped to look out over the lawn of the hotel toward the woods beyond. There was certain stillness to the night, a dead silence as if snow lay on the ground. In the nearby woods, the trees swayed and creaked heavily in the thin air.

Leaning on the railing, Conner took a deep breath. When he exhaled, it formed a thick white cloud that quickly dissipated. "Smells like cold air."

"It's cold," Harry said, deciding not to bring up the girl. "Let's go have a beer," he said instead.

They re-entered the main room from the little door they had used earlier. It was warm despite the tall ceilings. Years of neglect had coated the polish with grimy dust.

Harry looked for the girl. "There's CJ over there." She intrigued him. "How old d'ya think she is, 20?" he asked Conner.

"You hope," Conner said. "Cool your jets. That's trouble there. She's not the kind of adventure we're looking for. You're supposed to get away from women, relax."

Harry took a deep breath and stretched his arms. "I'm going to talk to her just the same."

They ordered a drink and Conner walked over to the pool table where some people had been earlier. There was only a man and a woman there now. Another woman joined them. She was dressed much the same way as CJ. A group of college-aged kids came in just then. They were laughing and seemed to be having a good time. One of the girls with them walked behind the bar for a moment and grabbed a bottle of vodka. She gave CJ a wink and patted Skinny on the rear end.

"Some trouble," said Harry as Conner walked away. He decided to have a talk with CJ and see what kind of adventure she might be. The jukebox played, "Love me do," by the Beatles.

Harry watched as CJ came around the bar toward him. She smiled. He wanted to buy her a drink, but she saw to it herself.

She kept her eyes on him the whole time. It was an art that she had clearly mastered. She could make a man feel as if he was the only one in the place without overacting. No dramatization, no hips swaying. She simply kept her eyes on him, like a King Cobra holding the gaze of a frightened mouse.

She stood near Harry and reached over the bar with her whole body.

He watched as she stretched to grab a bottle of Jack Daniels. Her blouse pulled up revealing her abdomen. The low fitting jeans exposed her hipbones. The soft fuzziness of her body hairs glistened in the under-light of the bar. Then she looked over her shoulder and smiled as she sat back down on the stool next to him, bottle in hand, and picked up two glasses.

"You got twenty dollars?"

Harry tried to keep his mouth closed as he pulled out a twenty and put it on the bar.

"Not for the bar, for me." Now he knew what this adventure would be like. With cocktails in hand, she made her way for the door. Harry looked around, no Skinny. He picked up the bill and followed her out the door.

Mouse followed them carefully and slipped into a service room on the second floor adjacent to Harry's room. Once there, he took his favorite seat and opened the tiny tin plate that covered the hole only he knew about.

She locked the door and poured two drinks. She chugged one down and Harry did the same. Then she slowly undressed, stopping on occasion to help Harry with his clothes.

Once they were undressed, he poured two more drinks and raised his glass.

"Over the lips, Harry." She said, and downed it in one gulp and walked over to the switch. Harry put his drink down and she turned off the overhead light, leaving only the bathroom light on.

She stood silhouetted in the frame of the bathroom door, the dim light wrapped around her, highlighting her hips and breasts. Earlier, Harry had tried to imagine her measurements, but that seemed pointless now. Her breasts separated slightly. Her nipples stood out exposed by the light behind her.

Harry was in heaven. He reached for her, but she held him back.

She walked over to the bed and ripped the covers off. "I told you this was our best room."

When they had finished, she stayed on top. Her breasts seemed to grow and recede with each breath. Her tight body began to cool and tiny beads of sweat formed on her skin. Using her long damp hair, she tickled his chest and face. Never taking her eyes off his, she played with him, teasing, lightly trailing the ends across his flesh, all the while the softness of her curly mound stroked back and forth across his belly.

He was her slave and she played with him. Taking his hands in hers, she lowered herself slowly until his world diffused in a muffled paradise.

Spent and tired, they lay next to each other, breathing heavily. She turned on her side and got up on her elbow.

"Are your eyes, green or blue?" she asked.

He said nothing, and she pressed her body against his, and ran her hand along his thigh.

He felt as though she had eyes only for him, although he knew better. Her ability to please a man gave her some power of bewitchment. What man could fight this? Who would, but one who wished only to deny his own humanity? Was she why the Puritans, who fought relentlessly with human nature to cover the sins of the flesh, used the character of the witch to punish their sexuality? Why? If CJ would get up and fly around the hotel on a broom, he would hardly be surprised.

After they made love again, he sat on the edge of the bed and poured CJ another drink. A chill ran through his body, and he took his drink from the table next to the bed and drank it.

CJ swung her feet over next to his and sat beside her lover.

His feet touched the floor, while hers dangled from the side.

He thought about his plans to get away—it was supposed to be a vacation without the complications of women and he thought about his marriages, the two that failed. Nancy had died before that marriage could fail. Then he looked at CJ.

What am I doing? He lay back down pulling her along with him. How many hours had they been at this?

"Conner will be coming back soon."

"I wouldn't worry about that. The girls will keep him long enough. They have a good sense of timing."

"How long have you been at this?" He was curious, more than concerned.

CJ said nothing, but sat up and poured another drink. "That's not fair Harry," she said. "How long have you been at it? That's the question." She looked back at him.

"I was a virgin until tonight, believe it or not," he said.

"Bullshit. Bet you've spent the time real good."

"I was on a dig in Flagstaff," he said.

"A what?"

"A dig, an archaeological expedition. You know where they dig up bones?" He waited for it to register. "We had to examine this site before they could begin construction on a housing development. Pity. It was a beautiful area, but now it's covered with a huge residential community."

"So you lost it there?"

"No. That was just one of the most memorable."

Just then the door flew open and in came Conner looking no less the conquering hero than Harry.

"Oh, sorry. Didn't think you were still here," he said.

"Well, you've been busy yourself, haven't you?" CJ said. Then she hopped out of bed and started getting dressed. Conner followed her movement with his empty eyes. She walked over to the chair where her clothes were and bent over. He nearly lost his balance, but managed to make it to the bathroom bumping into the doorframe.

"He's a cheap date," Harry said. "Two drinks and he's done."

"I am shit-faced," he said and closed the door behind him. They heard a loud crash and a thump. CJ ran over and opened the door to the bathroom and peered in, laughed, and then swung the door open so Harry could see.

Conner leaned against the toilet, his arm in the bowl, and the shower curtain and hardware all on top of him.

"Katy," he said. "You are naked." He tried to get up, but slipped on the wet floor. "Sylvia looks nothing like you. In fact, I'm not even sure she made love to me. She just got me drunk. Bitch."

"Who is Sylvia?"

"One of the girls. I told them to take care of Conner. He seemed a little uptight."

She helped Harry get him into bed and take off his clothes as best they could, then she finished getting dressed. "Well, I gotta get back to work," she said as she headed for the door.

"You mean you're not finished?"

"A girl has to earn a living, Harry," she said. She was toying with him. She stuck out her bottom lip and pouted.

"I'm just helping my old man close up the bar, is all." She gave him a pat on the ass and opened the door. "I'm too beat to do that again."

The Expedition

1976

When Dago, Harry, Nancy and Don were in Lima, Peru, they hired a boat to take them to a small fishing village near Chanaral, Chile. From there, they went by train to Santiago; and by rented truck to Vallicia, a small coastal town far from civilization they would use as their base.

The town had been cut out of the forest years ago as the base camp of a logging unit, and grew into a small, but thriving village. It had since returned to a near ghost town, offering to the occasional wanderer guided tours of the two national parks in the nearby mountains.

The mountains loomed ahead like giant guardians. But to Dago, they were Sirens.

"There in those mountains, about a day's travel by mule, is our objective," he told his crew. They checked into the local hotel and prepared for a trip they hoped would be uninterrupted and profitable. "There's mummies in them thar hills," he quipped.

From the moment they arrived, it seemed to Harry that Dago's personality changed. He was in his element, perhaps. A famed Inca historian, he languished in any task other than this.

They soon had three pack mules and a mountain horse hired and ready to load. Harry had purchased some of the heavier tools they would need while Nancy and Don were responsible for the surveying equipment and the Magnetometer, which they brought along, as well as the food and medical supplies they would purchase locally.

Harry purchased a large .45 caliber Smith & Wesson and three boxes of ammunition. "I never travel anywhere in the wilderness without some sort of firearm," Harry explained.

"I totally agree, Harry," Dago said, and he held up a lacquered pine box, inlaid with a personal crest—a swastika and a diagram of the globe covered by a fisted hand. Inside was a Luger he claimed to have captured from a SS Captain at a rather fierce poker game in occupied France during the Battle of the Bulge.

The night was warm and the others slept soundly. The opened window offered little comfort and Harry was restless, thinking of Nancy and the trip south during which time they almost succumbed to the desires of the flesh. He noticed Dago getting dressed.

"Where are you going?" he asked. "Is it time to get up?" Harry looked out the window and saw the darkness. "It's still dark out. What time is it?"

"It's just after midnight. I can't sleep. I'm going to check on the animals."

"I can help if you'd like," he started to get out of bed.

"No," he said. "Go back to sleep, there's still lots of night left. I won't be too long. Be ready to eat at five O'clock. If I'm not back by breakfast, I'll meet you on the trail out of town." He opened the door to the hallway and the light shone in across the room and onto Harry. When the door closed, Harry—who was sitting on the edge of the bed—got up and looked out the window. He waited until he saw Dago cross the street and disappear into the darkness.

Harry didn't see him again until the end of breakfast when Dago walked into the hotel dining room and sat down. Don and Nancy were sitting at the adjacent table and stopped talking as he walked across the floor and sat down with Harry. The owner of the hotel brought him a plate without speaking.

Harry pushed aside his empty plate, eyed Dago and said, "You were up early."

Dago bent over the plate, shoving food into his mouth. He reached for the coffee, looked at Harry, and smiled. "Just some final touches," he said and swallowed. "I hired a couple of guides." He nodded and grunted. "Yes, two guides." He went back to his food, eating like a man who had not eaten in days.

Harry and the others stared at their companion. Nancy came over to the table where Harry and Dago sat. She had attached herself to Harry and he offered no resistance. Vallicia was a cold and lonely place, and her company was enjoyable.

Harry stole a quick glance at her and then asked Dago, "Do we need guides?"

"They sort of came with the animals. A package deal. And well worth it, Harry. These hills are treacherous, and travelers are cautioned about robbers." He stopped talking and looked up from his plate.

Nancy stared intently at him, and frowned.

Her concern made Dago laugh. "Don't worry, I'm told that this time of year, the danger of trouble is less likely. It's off season."

"I didn't know that banditos had a season," she said.

"Tourists are an easy mark, and the local government isn't too helpful when it comes to protection. They suggest hiring it. So I did."

Peeping Mouse

1978

The girls were off limits to Mouse. All he could do was watch. That was his favorite thing to do anyway, and he had watched it all from behind the bed. CJ was the best. He would always imagine it was himself with her instead of whomever. He had always hoped she would love him more than she did Skinny. At least he would not beat her. He would hold her so softly.

Still, Skinny sent him there to watch, and when he put CJ or any of the other girls in one of those rooms Mouse knew his job. Skinny always wanted to know all about it; what they did, how many times, what they said, and especially how much they paid her. Mouse did not see any more than the twenty go into her pocket and he would tell Skinny when he saw him later.

Still, CJ was his favorite. They moved here together and he formed a bond with her that he felt with no other woman in the place, especially the one called Sara. He watched CJ with Harry and found it hard at times to keep quiet on the other side of the wall. He watched her having sex like he watched a movie, he even stored candy in the one room he would spy from.

The more he watched, the angrier he got and the more he fell in love with her. Often he thought about not telling Skinny some of the things that went on in those rooms. He liked to keep that to himself. Still, he had strong feelings of rage and remorse, and they confused him. He liked the girls like a man should, but never had the courage to do anything about it. He would convince himself not to, saying Skinny would not like it. Even when he got a hard on he wouldn't do anything about it and just hold it all inside him.

Killing was his only relief, and he had the opportunity over the years to do some of that for his boss. Then he could stop thinking about the women. It hurt too much.

Pay Back

CJ waited for Mouse to head off to his second favorite hiding spot—the kitchen—and made sure he had his head in the refrigerator and then sneaked past the open door and headed down the hall and down the stairs in the back. It was dark and she kept the lights off for fear Shithead would wake up. She went down the hall to the end, through the dusty old tunnel, and into the safe room.

"I'll show you all right, bastard." She knew where the safe was and even remembered the combination from last year. Skinny never changed it; he did not know how. She opened the safe and searched through its contents; cash she had. There were guns, passports, deeds, and a bunch of papers that she couldn't identify. None of that mattered. She wanted more and knew that what was in there was worth a fortune. And he would miss it, and that was satisfying enough. She found the hefty leather bag that was tied with a string. She opened it up and made sure it was all still there. Then she closed the safe and quietly sneaked back up to her room and closed the door.

The Real Skinny

Harry had just managed to doze off when she came back and threw open the door. Conner snored loudly, splayed like a boned fish next to Harry. Cold air followed her into the room. She walked over to the bathroom and threw on the light. It was brighter than he had remembered, and it hurt.

CJ was leaning over the sink when Harry approached her; blood dripped from her swollen lip. Her eye was the same crimson color.

"What happened?" He knew; it was not hard to figure out.

He got a towel and helped her with the blood, examining her as he did. He tried to lift her torn blouse over her shoulder, but it fell again. Her brassier was missing. Harry began to wonder what kind of situation he had gotten himself into.

"He's a pig," she said.

Just then, the door banged open. Moonlight cast a lissome silhouette of a very angry Skinny.

"You bitch," he said. "You ever do that again and I'll slice your tits off."

Skinny stepped toward CJ, his cowboy boots clicking on the hardwood floor.

Harry stepped in between.

Before he could say anything, Skinny had both arms up, one holding a switchblade at his throat and the other warning him back.

There are all sorts of tough people in the world. Harry knew that those with knives were dangerous, and he stopped cold.

He was close enough to Skinny now to see the welt above his right eye. That too, was bleeding. His wet shirt smelled of whiskey. Around his neck, he wore a

Bolo necktie of turquoise in the shape of the Incan god of war—Tezcatlipoca.

"Well, won't you come in?" The tip of the knife was just under his chin. The looseness of his skin yielded slightly to the blade. They danced intimately toward the bathroom, toward CJ. Skinny looked oddly at Harry, and squinted a bit as if he recognized him from somewhere but couldn't place it.

"Nice tie," said Harry.

"Shut the hell up boy, she ain't free. Sit down."

Harry backed away and sat reluctantly.

Skinny folded the knife back and replaced it in his pocket in one quick motion, rubbed his mustache with his knuckle and made his way to CJ. She backed a bit into the bathroom and stopped when she touched the toilet. Harry watched as she pushed him away and they exchanged some colorful metaphors. Skinny reached behind him to close the door, but a towel blocked it. She continued to push him, looking up at him. He told her to stop. Finally he grabbed her by the collar and turned her around and pushed her out into the room where she fell into Harry who was now standing.

Harry pulled her to his side and put himself between the two of them and stood unafraid and unwilling to yield. Harry stood at least eight inches taller than Skinny, who stopped for a moment as if he was gauging how a fight would go between them. He pulled out his knife again. But this time CJ rushed between them.

"Put it away asshole, unless it makes you feel like a big man," she said.

Skinny held the stiletto in his hand balancing it. He hesitated.

"Yeah, that's right big man," CJ said scowling, almost crying, "go ahead cut him. Then what? Kill him too?" She waved her arm towards Conner who only now began to stir. "I swear if you hurt him I'll never do another thing for you." And she ripped open her blouse and offered her own chest to him, daring him, "Go on. Do me first."

Harry couldn't believe this was happening. He had seen some tough fights between men and women before, but they never involved him, directly. He had broken up a fight in Italy between two lovers where the man came at his girlfriend with a bottle of wine. That time all it took was a few punches to lay the man out cold on the floor. He had received a round of applause and an unwanted kiss from the girl. But this one, Skinny, was a bit crazy and CJ's defense astounded him.

Conner was now sitting on the edge of his bed shaking his head. "What the hell is going on Harry?"

"Shut the fuck up, puke," Skinny said. He was still plenty mad and had the knife in his hand.

Harry remained still, not wanting to encourage him to use it.

Conner ran into the bathroom and threw up.

Skinny held CJ off with his hand—this time a bit more gently—and kept looking at Harry, who tried to show as little fear as possible.

Harry took CJ by her shoulders and pulled her away from Skinny. He figured if Skinny tried anything he would position himself to get a few throws in.

While Conner puked in the bathroom, Harry closed the door and Skinny explained to the both of them about how the free market system worked in real terms. How the vendor, Skinny, supplies goods and services: CJ. And the consumer, Harry, pays for them. Then he explained how, "Twenty bucks just ain't gonna pay the shipping costs. Do you dig me?"

"Funny thing, I was just on my way over to pay you."

CJ clucked her tongue. "Leave'im alone asshole. He didn't do anything wrong." She walked up to him and shoved her chin in his face. "I'll charge what the hell I want to. This was on me."

"Oh yeah? I figure he's into me for at least a hundred bucks. After all the fun you two had. What d'ya think?" He turned to Harry. "Let's see, how many times d'ya do it, maybe three, more like four? Huh? Plus the booze. That sound about fair, huh, buddy boy?"

Skinny knuckled his mustache and held out his hand. "Shut up," he said.

"Yeah sure slim, I'll pay you in the morning."

"When?"

"You want it now?" Harry walked over to his pack and rummaged for the money. While he bent over looking in the dim light he suddenly felt a sharp pain and saw a flash of bright light.

Harry slowly opened his eyes. He had somehow ended up on the couch.

"You got a hard head Harry," CJ applied a wet cloth to his forehead.

He tried to get up, but she had her hand on his shoulder and held him there.

"What the fuck?"

"He's gone." She looked over her shoulder. "Are you okay?"

Harry sat up anyway and felt the back of his head. He looked at his hand and thought it felt wet. He rubbed his fingers together and examined them for blood. He looked over at Conner. "He's still asleep," he said incredulously.

CJ looked over. "Yeah, well he actually helped me get you on the couch."

"Did he see anything?"

"Well, not exactly. By the time he came out of the bathroom you were already on the floor and Skinny had taken his money and left."

Harry got up and went over to his pack and looked for his money. He counted it.

"He took too much and threw a twenty on the floor," she explained. "Said you should get the fuck out in the morning." She sat on the couch with her hands tucked under her legs, which she gently kicked back and forth and looked up at Harry. "I'm sorry honey, I should have warned you he can be a bit hot."

"Hot Christ. I'd hate to see him downright mad."

"That was his good mood," she said emphatically. "Usually someone would have gotten hurt."

Harry raised his eyebrows and opened his eyes wide.

"If he had his bodyguard here," she said, "it wouldn't a been pretty.

Usually? He sat next to her on the couch and examined her face. Blood dripped and had dried from her lip. She had blood smeared here and there and a bruise on her cheek. "You'll have a black eye soon."

He went to the bathroom and ran cold water on the back of his neck. "I don't think he has to worry about us leaving in the morning."

He took a towel and wet it with hot water, walked over to her, and started cleaning her face with it. His hands shook slightly as he dabbed at the blood.

"He shake you up, did he?" she said.

"A bit." The blood washed away revealing a small cut on her lip. "Any harder and you'd need stitches."

It bled a little and he held the towel to the cut and told her to press. "You look like a prize fighter."

"Yeah," she giggled. "An' you look like you got hit by one."

Conner moved on the bed. "You drink too much last night Harry?" He asked with a rough, dry throat.

"He came out of the bathroom and saw you lying on the floor." She said. "I told him you were drunk and couldn't get up and somehow we managed to get you here," she patted the cushion, "on the couch." She smiled.

"Go back to bed Conner," he said, and leaned on his knees holding his head down.

"Don't mind him, he's all talk," she said, patting his back.

Somehow, that did not seem the case to Harry.

"How did he know what we did?"

She explained about the peepholes. Harry looked around for a likely spot and figured the picture over the bed was a good place to start. He tried to lift the frame, but it would not move. So, he hung a towel over it. She thought that would be all. He sat back on the couch.

Like the dark shadows of ancient souls cast in stone, they sat motionless and cold. Moonlight leaked through the window softly lighting their faces. Then Harry leaned back and put his head back on the couch and closed his eyes. CJ sat looking on.

Harry shifted his position and looked at CJ, "Why are you here?"

"Never had no reason to go," she said. "No place to go."

"You could leave."

"Asshole wouldn't like that much. What do you care anyway? I do it because I'm good, and it ain't a bad way to make a buck."

"The hard way."

"I don't need no help from anybody. Just forget about it would ya?" She got up to leave, but Harry held on.

She said, "No one's holdin' a gun to my head Harry."

How was Harry supposed to make anything out of her? Why did she come back to his room, they had just met that night. What did he know of saving lives? His own life was always the focal point. Others came and went, and nothing he said or did would change that. It was going to take more than a beat up hooker to stimulate altruistic behavior in him. Yet he wanted her to confide in him, to tell him her innermost secrets, her needs, but she would not. How could he blame her for that?

The Sponge

1976

The base camp was located near a mountain stream and had a commanding view of the pine-barrens below. Things went slowly. Days went by and they found nothing, even with the magnetometer they had little success.

As the days turned to weeks, Dago withdrew. He told the others he was upset with the slow progress, or concerned for their safety, and things like that. His moods worsened and he would argue often with the guides, who felt they shouldn't do any work. He would often go back into town and once returned with a dirt bike. He said that it would cut travel time to almost nothing.

Still, they settled in and this became their new home. As seasoned veterans of the dig, they learned to live on very little comforts

On warm days, they would bathe in the stream. Nancy felt uncomfortable doing that with so many men around, and preferred to bathe in the main tent, which was roomier and private.

One day, Harry returned from canvassing and walked in on her. She was naked, covered with soap, and standing in the tub. He blushed and turned to leave

"Harry wait," she said as he stepped outside.

He stopped, and went back inside. He slowly raised his eyes to meet hers. She was beautiful: soft, not rugged, yet she could hold her own when it came to doing the heavy work. She faced him with her arms at her side.

He scanned her body, slowly savoring each inch. Her breasts were small, but neatly cupped and her hips were wide and smooth. Her freckled skin, scratched from the digging they had done, blushed under his scrutiny, but she stood still, luring him closer. He watched as bubbles slid down her stomach and came to a stop. Her hair was red. And she called to him, like a nymph calling a sailor to the shore of her tiny island.

He swallowed hard with a dry mouth. He smiled, and she smiled back. He walked over to her until he could feel her breath. "You, uh," he said slowly feeling the thumping of his heart, the blood rushing through his body, "you need something?"

"My back," she said, and she turned and waited.

He took the sponge out of her hand and gently washed her back, slowly up and down. "There," he whispered, and she turned back around and pressed her lips to his. The sponge fell to the ground.

The Runaway

1978

Harry brought something out in her, a courage and resolve she didn't know she had. She felt good about herself stopping Skinny from killing Harry. She knew he wouldn't have hesitated to stick that knife in him, and if she hadn't been there, things definitely would have ended up differently.

She remembered the first time she saw the big hotel. It seemed immense compared to the places she had lived in her short life. Trailers, mostly, and once an apartment overlooking the California coast – that was nice. That was just before her mother went to jail, and she ran away to Reno and met Skinny.

She thought about the first time he molested her— her old man. *The pig.* It was hot all the time. Seemed as if they lived in Hell. He always sweated all over her. It *was* hell.

The cockroaches were as big as the mice and there were scorpions, too.

Arlene, her big sister, had been getting it for some time and would confide in CJ. She told her about how their father would come into the room at night and take her out back to the truck behind the trailer. It was usually late and Momma and the neighbors were all asleep.

"He told me," she said to CJ, "that it was all right, that I would be a woman soon." She was only 12. When she turned 14, she ran away. CJ was just 11. Her father told her that Arlene would be proud of her and that she should not say anything to Momma or something bad would happen. He began by having her sit on his lap and touching her gently under her dress. She was scared. She remembered Arlene telling her how it hurt at first, but after a while it didn't, how his breath stunk like shit and alcohol.

He liked to have friends over to watch games on TV while Momma was out. The first time it happened, he showed his friends what a good little girl CJ could be, and had her prance about naked in front of them. They whistled and hooted. John, his one friend grabbed a hold of her with his big rough hairy hands and forced her to have oral sex with him. They all did it – over and over, until she could not stand it anymore and she ran out of the house.

The police brought her back a week later. She was outside of town looking for her sister, sleeping in bushes, starving. Her Momma was worried sick about her and locked her in her room. Momma was beginning to suspect something, and came home early one day only to see it all going on. She was mad, and the old man's friends left. He beat her badly that first time for interfering.

They found Arlene a month later in a dry riverbed, the next town over, with her throat cut from ear to ear. After that, Momma was too frightened to say anything. If she did, he would beat her until she passed out. She lost her job at Wal-Mart. After that, it became easier.

She would sit in the back room while he raped CJ, and ignore the protestations. They both began drinking heavily, and the old man even gave CJ some. She liked that even though she threw it all back up at first. It made things more bearable at home made the experiences tolerable.

After Momma lost her job for the last time they lived on disability from the old man and whatever they could make on selling CJ out. When she turned 16, she dropped out of school and ran away to Reno. She was working the streets for tricks, making only enough to eat and sometimes get a room. One of the older girls took her in and let her stay for a piece of the take. That is how she met Skinny.

He came along and took over a lot of the activity in town. He just muscled his way in. The streets were an open playing field then. Most of the casinos had their own business and never considered the streets. However, there was a lot of money on both sides, once Skinny figured out a system. He made a deal with the local mob by offering them a piece of it all.

Then, one day Skinny left Reno in a big hurry, taking CJ and some of the girls with him.

Whiskey

Harry was shocked. Maybe he really did think he was doing her a favor by talking to her. He wouldn't bother asking Conner—risky business to be sure—and asked her again to come with them, but she declined. She got up and left him there on the couch feeling sorry for it.

He tried to convince himself he did the right thing by asking her along. She brushed the idea off like dandruff, yet CJ looked so demure, hurt, and vulnerable, it forced a lump in his throat.

CJ was far from those things, not demure by any means. She had no more interest in changing her situation than Harry did in changing his. What could a twenty-dollar whore give him that he did not already have, besides VD?

Conner snored heavily. The smell of alcohol escaping with each breath he took.

Harry got out of bed and turned on the bathroom light. In his bag, he kept a journal he started in college. He got it out and sat in the chair to write in it.

He sat in the dark and looked out the window at the moonlit trees. A million things went through his brain. His life flashed through his mind like a film on fast forward. Like a projectionist, he hurried through all the old stuff and stopped at the Arapaho: Skinny, CJ, and the big fat guy at the bar.

He woke the next morning and saw the book had fallen to the floor out of his hands. He had not written a word.

Viscacha

1976

Nancy had a passion for things new to Harry, and sometimes their passions would keep the others awake. Don was without reservation and told them one morning that they kept him up the whole night. Dago didn't like their tryst; he thought it would interfere with the job.

But he wasn't there as much as Don who had taken on the job as cook, and liked to get up early to prepare the food for the whole day. His favorite meal was the Viscacha, a chinchilla like rodent that was tasty but stringy, and had to be braised a long time.

One morning a cold front had drifted in and laid frost on the ground.

Harry stood in the tent's dull lamplight. It was still dark and smelled like snow.

"Are you coming or going?" Nancy said.

"Oh," Harry said, startled. "I thought you were sleeping."

She smiled at him.

"I just had this odd discussion with Dago," he said. "I had to piss and went to the latrine." He sat down on the edge of his bed and looked at the little package he held in his hands.

"What's wrong, Harry? You look as if you saw a ghost."

He looked up at her and smiled. "Oh, do I?" He moved to the edge of her bunk. "I saw a light on in the main tent," he began, "and decided to have a look. Dago was in there packing his bag—the one he takes into town.

"So, I asked him, 'You going into town again Dago?'

"'Well, I'm going in again and this time I don't know when I'll be back.' He said it rather definitively,"

Harry said. "But I just stared at him, expecting more of an answer. He was circumspect, and changed the topic from himself to me again. He bought you up." He glanced at Nancy. "He said, 'Are you sure you're not fucking things up getting involved with her?'

"'Nancy,' I said. I got pissed. 'Her name is Nancy.'"

Harry paused to catch Nancy's reaction. She was watching him closely. He continued, "I realized then that he was trying to change the subject, but I wanted to stay on point. 'Seems to me, Dago,' I said, 'that you are the one fucking up the works. You're going into town an awful lot these last weeks. Are you meeting up with someone? I mean, why all the secrecy?'

"'Relationships gum up the works,' he said as if I had said nothing. 'Things get personal and then you fight and nothing gets done. I just wish you two would cool off a bit, that's all.'" Harry shook his head.

"That's just Dago," Nancy said. "You know Harry, I think he's jealous."

"Dago? Jealous?"

"Well," she said and cupped him in her lap as she lay next to him, "sometimes he acts like a schoolboy. He ignores me, or avoids talking to me or sometimes he talks about stupid things, just like an awkward schoolboy, you know?"

Harry couldn't grasp that Dago might be jealous. "Yeah, I'm not sure about that Nance," he said.

"Harry," she said toying with him, "never question a woman's intuition."

"Well that may be," he said, "but let me tell you what he said."

"What's that in your hand?" she asked.

"That's what I have to tell you about." Harry recounted his conversation with Dago. "I told him we could save a lot of time and money by going for supplies once a month, once every two weeks if need be. We haven't even found the site yet. 'And this is your gig, not mine,' I said to him.

"'It's not about supplies, Harry,' he said, 'it's about the Russian.' Then he said to me, 'Harry, it's this fucking guy I used to work with. I owe him a lot of money and it seems he found out about our expedition and came to collect.'

"I thought at the time he was lying to me.

"'But, I'll take care of that,' he said. 'You just look after things here and find that site.' Then he pulled this book out of his back pack." Harry showed her the book.

"What is it?" Nancy said.

"He handed this to me and held onto it. His hands were trembling, I swear. He spoke quietly, secretively, 'This should help, use it with the map while I'm gone.'

"I asked him why he was whispering, and he said, still whispering, 'Harry, I don't trust them.'

"'The others?' I said.

"'No, no. I don't mean like that,' he said. 'Just don't let them in on anything you find.'

"I tried to calm him down, but he wouldn't have it. Then he said, 'I can't really explain it now Harry. You'll just have to trust me. Still, it would be a good idea if you all carried side arms at all times.'

"He's gone out again," Harry said, dejected. "This time for I don't know how long."

"You two should stop fighting," Nancy said from under her covers.

"We're not fighting," he turned around and looked at her. "I just wonder who this Russian is. What he has to do with us—this site.

"He's lying."

Harry seemed surprised. "What makes you say that?"

"He seems worried an awful lot. Like he has something to hide. Like the sword of Damocles is hanging over his head. This Russian is obviously someone from his past and ..."

"What?"

"Nothing," she said. "The sun will be up in a few hours, and I think I hear Don getting breakfast ready." She stood up and pulled Harry up to her and held him close.

"Still," Harry said, "You had better put this on and keep it with you from now on," and he pulled her handgun out of the box, holstered and loaded. Their discussion ended there, and they both dressed and went to see what Don had prepared.

They ate Viscacha again for breakfast, and prepared for the day's search. Dago had already gone off on the bike, and the guides were off somewhere.

The Getaway

1978

When they were packing neither one said anything much. It was a rough night for Conner and he looked like shit. CJ had changed her mind about coming along, but Harry never thought it would actually happen.

"We shouldn't tell Conner," Harry warned, knowing he wouldn't like it much. But Harry couldn't leave her there after what had happened with Skinny. When they were at the car loading it up, Harry told Conner what had happened.

"Are you kidding?" Conner's face reddened and the veins stuck out on his neck.

"You weren't there," Harry explained. Then he chuckled. "Well, you were, but man you were out of it. You don't remember anything do you?"

"Hell no I don't. And now you want to bring her along? You've gotta be mad."

Trying to defend himself wasn't easy. Harry saw the flaw in his own argument and even knew it was stupid, but something inside him wanted this.

The Bug sat over by the trees, alone. As they talked, CJ came up to them bounding with energy. She carried a small bag of things and wore a warm winter coat. She was ready for travel.

Harry and Conner were on opposite sides of the car, yelling at one another. Steam poured from their mouths in the cold damp air. Frost covered the car. She ran up to Harry smiling at first, but soon had a worried look on her face.

"Harry, is it ok?" She tugged at his arm.

He looked at her, annoyed that she had to ask. "Look at her Conner," he said offering her enthusiasm to him as evidence that all would be fine.

CJ ran over to Conner and tried to explain, but he pushed her back and shook his head as he threw his pack in the back seat.

She ran around the car bouncing back and forth between the both of them as they argued with each other, squealing like a little pipette flying along the surf, trying to get her own words in, pleading to come along.

Suddenly Conner stopped and stared at the hotel, his mouth agape. Both he and CJ stood motionless staring past Harry, whose back was to the hotel.

"Shit, now you've done it," Conner said.

Harry turned and saw Skinny walking quickly toward them. Skinny grabbed CJ and started dragging her back to the hotel, but she jerked away and ran to Harry.

Skinny swung at Harry.

This time Harry was certain he was ready for it and ducked out of the way.

But Skinny surprised him with a left sucker punch to the side of his head and Harry went down.

Skinny grabbed CJ again, but she still refused and pulled free.

Conner stood beside Harry.

CJ helped him to his feet, cooing him, "Oh poor baby. That bastard."

Skinny ran back into the hotel leaving a trail of steam behind. Harry thought he had given up.

Conner got in the car and started it up. The car rattled to life. The passenger door was already open and he yelled at Harry. "Get in the car, man."

Harry, still a little dazed, stood facing CJ and wondered what he should do with her.

Conner repeated the cheer but this time with more gusto, "Get in the goddamn car. Now."

Just then, a loud crack echoed across the lot. The screen door to the hotel flew open and smacked into the building. Skinny stood in the frame holding a shotgun. He pumped it and fired into the air.

Conner cheered Harry on, with still more encouragement, who now had to make a decision to leave her behind and save his ass, or take her along and possibly get his head blown off.

"Get in the car," Harry said. "That man doesn't look too happy."

He threw CJ into the front seat, as the Bug started moving and then he dove into the car. Conner stepped on the gas, sending the wheels spinning on the gravel lot. It took off with the door still open. They had to make a U-turn to get out of the lot, and as the VW swung around Harry held on, almost sliding out from the pull of the car. CJ clung to his coat.

They found the road and headed away from the hotel as shots rent the air, scattering buckshot on the rear side and window of the getaway car. CJ managed to cling to Harry, the door still opened as they accelerated. Harry barely had time to pull his foot inside when Skinny let go with a couple more shots.

Conner drove that thing as if the breath of God was pushing it. The spinning tires sent a cloud of dust and stones back in retaliation. They hurried away from the Arapaho hoping to be long gone before Skinny figured out which way they went. They drove down the long driveway towards the gate that originally welcomed them, it read, "Thank You," in large white iron letters.

When he reached the road, Conner turned the wheel sharply, almost tipping the little car on its side.

Harry held his breath.

Conner's knuckles were white gripping the steering wheel.

CJ sat in Harry's lap pounding on his chest and screaming with joy.

Conner looked over at Harry scowling and mumbling expletives under his breath, "You beat all. Do you know that? You beat all."

"Don't worry. He's far too busy to be chasin' after me," she said.

After a while, CJ climbed into the back seat and settled in, grinning.

Conner drove aimlessly for about an hour, periodically checking his rear view mirror for Skinny.

Harry's leg started itching persistently and after a while began to hurt. He scratched it and saw blood on his hand. He turned to look at CJ who saw the blood on his hand.

"You've been shot." She already had her head between the seats ready to climb over, pulling at his leg.

"I'm alright. I don't think it's too bad," he said pushing her back into her seat. The car swerved a bit as Conner craned his neck to get a look. Harry urged him to keep his eyes on the road. "We don't all want to die." He slowed down anyway so he could get a better look at the wound.

"Not here," CJ screamed. "Keep going I'll tell you where to stop. I think there is a place on up ahead where's we can stop and take care of it."

Conner was still a little frantic, since they now had bullet wounds to worry about. "We should call a doctor or something," he said, looking in the rearview mirror at CJ. "Is there a hospital around?"

"No, no," she said quickly. "Don't do that. We can fix it up ahead. There ain't one round here anyway."

"It's just buck shot. No big deal," Harry offered.

No one suggested they call the police. Harry couldn't imagine the complications of that.

"Up ahead," turned into a twenty-mile drive. They were climbing in altitude. An occasional beam of sunlight peered through the murky clouds that highlighted the mountains in the distance. They passed through meadows rolling over fields patched with clumps of trees. Here and there, steam would seep out of the ground. The whole area, up to and including Yellowstone was one big volcano ready to explode.

They drove for twenty more miles with CJ guiding them from memory. Up ahead in the middle of nowhere they saw a motel. In the front was a set of gas pumps. The old oval sign, half lit, read ESSO. Its red letters were fading and the pole that held it had rusted and badly needed paint. It towered over two gas pumps that sat near the road; which were old, but working. Around the corner, there were rooms that extended in an "L" shape and ended snugly tucked into the side of a tree-covered hill. Blue neon lights lined the awning that followed the length of the rooms and flickered in a sickly pale and uneven pattern.

"Pull in there," she said. It was on the left side of the road, and the hill rose slowly up and disappeared into a murky fog. A sign over the diner read, "EAT." Conner drove up to the pump and stopped the engine.

"What are you doing?" said CJ.

"Outta gas. Almost." A man walked slowly over to the car. He stopped near the rear end as if to consider it. He was dressed for fishing; his waders held up by braces. His shirt was a green chamois, and over it all, he had a plaid and patched overcoat with several missing buttons. When he finally made it to the window Conner asked the headless body to fill it. He let CJ out of the car so she could go around and look at Harry's leg. The old man watched her. When he seemed satisfied what she was doing, he took the handle out of the pump and put it in the car's tank. His hoary hands were scarred and broad from years of manual labor; the cold and sun had baked them brown. His thick hands easily unscrewed the cap, lifted the handle, and flipped the switch to begin the pumps.

"What else do you sell?" Conner stood next to the old man now.

"Breakfast, lunch, dinner. The like," he said. "Best flap jacks. Make our own sausage too."

The man pulled a bluish cloth from his back pocket and in the other hand produced a bottle of cleaning fluid, which he squirted on the windshield, and gently stroked the glass in circular motions. "Package store in the back."

Conner leaned in the window and whispered, "Should we call the police?"

"No don't do that," CJ said very adamantly.

He looked at Harry and ignored the girl. Harry shook his head. "I'm fine. Just get stuff we need. He wondered if he was doing the right thing.

CJ went to work on Harry. She winced when she lifted his pant leg. Blood had already dried and the jeans were sticking.

"How's it look," he asked her.

"I only see two tiny holes," she said. "Looks like one passed through." She didn't tell him about the shredded flesh on the exit wound of one of the BB's. She reached in the backseat for something. "Ask him if he has liquor," she said to Harry.

"All kinds." The old man stood slightly hunched over as he pumped the gas, and peered into the window at CJ and Harry.

"There's a package store in the back," the old man said

Harry pulled out a twenty-dollar bill and handed it to CJ. She took it and ran off toward the store after Conner.

"Whiskey," Harry yelled.

She caught up with Conner, leaving Harry alone with the attendant. As he cleaned the window, he kept looking through it at Harry who was trying to hide the blood. He didn't want to draw attention to himself. *How close are people out here?* He wondered. *This old guy might call up Skinny and rat on us.* Skinny could come along while they were still there, and finish the job. The old man did not seem in any hurry, so Harry lay back on the seat. He stared across the valley at the distant mountains. The sun peeped through the thick white clouds. Jacob's ladders shone through here and there and dark storm clouds gathered to the east.

As a child, Harry would imagine that he could reach Heaven by climbing up those ladders where they touched the ground. He had also believed in leprechauns at the ends of rainbows.

The old man was still cleaning the windows when Harry looked at him again. He smiled. "Is it supposed to snow?" Harry asked.

"Eh?"

"Do you think it will snow soon?"

As if someone flipped a switch, the old man answered, "Na. Gonna start soon. Maybe tomorrow."

CJ came back, and pulled a bottle of whiskey form a bag she had. She opened it and poured a little on the wound.

"That hurt?"

"Not much. How does it look?"

"I only see two little holes Harry," she said wiping at it with a paper towel. One had gone through completely and she said nothing about the fraying it left. She wrapped it with a bandage she bought at the store and tied it together to hold it in place. Harry trusted that she knew what she was doing. "It doesn't hurt," he lied.

"Where's Conner?" Harry said.

"Taking a shit, I guess. I don't know."

The old man leaned down to look through the driver's window. He could not seem to take his eyes off CJ. He said, "four ninety-eight."

Harry paid him.

CJ stood up out of the car and walked around to the other side, the old man watching her. She got close to him. It was cold but she had her coat unzipped just enough to show her chest.

"You want a sip, Pop," she said, holding up a bottle of Jack Daniels.

He said nothing.

She took a swig and asked for directions.

They talked quietly with their heads above the top of the car where Harry could not see or hear. When they had finished, he just looked at her as she climbed back into the car and then he gave Harry the change.

CJ had the bottle in her hand and she put it into a large bag she brought from the store and set it on the floor.

"I thought that whiskey was for my leg," he said. She gave him the bottle and he took a drink. She looked back toward the diner, "Where the hell is he?"

Just then, Conner ran back across the parking lot with a couple of bags, shoved them in the car at Harry, and climbed in. "You pay the man?"

"Yeah, let's get out of here."

The Rock in the Road

The weather had already turned bitter cold. In keeping with the season, the sun would set early and much of the day would stay shrouded in darkness as the clouds hurried by, ushered in by strong autumn winds. For now, the sun was warm on the car. The leaves had fallen, and only a few reluctant oaks held on to their brown and withered vestiges. Pines and Aspen were everywhere. CJ said she knew the area having lived here for the last ten years.

"We need to get some water for the canteen," Harry said. "It's out and I'm parched."

"I'll keep my eyes open," Conner said. Then he turned to CJ and asked, "So, how long did you work in that place? How long did you live there?"

"I said 10, didn't I?" She looked out the window at the trees passing by. Harry let it go. He did not want to think how long she had been a professional.

Up ahead on the side of the road, they saw a VW Bug parked in an open area. A road led from the car downhill through an open glade and into the trees.

Conner pulled up behind the car, and turned the engine off.

A man with long hair had his head in the backseat. He stood up to look at them.

Conner got out and walked over to them before Harry could say anything. He and CJ got out and joined them.

"We're on our honeymoon," Harry heard him saying. They all followed his gaze to his wife who was walking up from below, near the trees where a tent had been set up.

They introduced themselves.

"We're finally taking a long deserved vacation," Harry said. "Thought we'd go camping and check out Yellowstone."

"So are we, but it's been a long day and we're tired. This looks like a nice secluded spot to spend the night."

Harry understood that they wanted nothing to do with sharing a campsite. "Oh, we just stopped to get some water."

"There's a stream down the way," the man with long hair said, and pointed up ahead along the road to where the stream ran close.

They got back into the car and drove on after saying goodbye to the young couple.

"I got an idea," CJ said. "This road ends into 89 in a bit. Go left there."

As usual, a bit turned into another 15 minutes.

"That sign says 191 and 287," Conncr said. "I don't see 89."

"Just turn left," she said and slouched, down stretching her feet across the back seat. Harry was getting hot and he rolled down the window. She told them about a landmark up the road a ways, a "big rock," she called it, "can't miss it."

They drove for more than a mile. By now, he expected her directions to be off and only followed them because she was so persistent. All the while after leaving the Arapaho, the roads had been climbing in altitude. They passed meadows and pastures. Distant mountains peaked through the trees predicting colder temperatures, snow, and ever more distance from the civilized world.

"Stop," she yelled. Sure enough, they sat dead in the middle of a crossroad. The gigantic Ponderosa had gradually given way to smaller hardwoods and spruce. To the left of the road, a forest of Aspen and Birch looked dead beyond mere winter hibernation. The leafless trees bore no resemblance to the living. The white bark peeled off in foot long strips, exposing dark black wood beneath.

"This is where we turn."

"Where's the rock?"

They were expecting a large boulder, but all they saw was what looked like a mountain jutting out of the ground as if it were cut away to make the road. They could not see the top for the windows of the VW.

"That's it," she said.

Conner backed the car up and turned down the road. It was mostly scrub brush covered. It almost looked like swamplands or some sort of boggy meadow. Over time, the road began to break down and quickly washed out in repeated floods eventually becoming gravel, and then mud.

A metal sign, weathered and aged, leaned back against a tree on the side of the road. The tree had grown around the sign. It read 'Fordh...Sta...Pa.k.' and in small print at the bottom it said, est. 1889.

"This an old park?"

CJ shrugged and said, "Now turn right at the first road."

Conner slowed a bit, but kept going stretching his neck looking out the windows on all sides looking for a road, any road.

If there were any roads, their integrity had been lost years ago. He tried his best to avoid any potholes, but they were numerous and nearly impossible to miss.

"Keep going," Harry answered. "Do you want psycho Skinny to catch up with us?"

They went slowly, dipping from hole to hole. Conner almost broke his nose on the steering wheel as he leaned so far forward to see better out the window.

CJ sat in the back, holding herself tight with the strap attached to the seat in front of her.

Harry lurched forward against the dash and hit his chin against it.

Just when things were looking like they might dissolve into utter chaos, the road smoothed out and began to switchback. At one point, CJ and Harry had to get out and push the Bug through a twenty-foot washout. Conner wanted to turn around but they shouted him down.

"Oh, please Conner. This is nothing. In Italy once, I remember driving the truck up a road that makes this look like the Autobahn. We had to hitch up a winch just to get to the dig. We had to do that every day for a month until someone found another road. It seemed the locals were having a joke on us and couldn't believe how stupid we were."

"This is a car, contrary to what you might want to think."

Another road connected to the one they were on from deep within the woods. It looked in better shape, but went back downhill. They wanted to go up. At that point, the road became smooth and wide, following a small stream that wove through the forest.

Eventually, the road ended in what looked like an old Park service campsite, but it had no office or gate. It looked to be an old park run campground, heavily overrun with shrubs and trees. One site had a twenty foot Alder growing directly out of an old fire pit. The rest of the grounds were just some old campsites laid out with a few sitting logs and stone circles surrounding the washed out remnants of black ash and cinders.

They parked the car behind a clump of trees and found a path leading up and around some boulders for about 50 yards. They got out and headed up the path to look around. Harry's leg hurt, but not enough to keep him off his feet or from keeping up with the others. After the boulders, the path opened into a secluded site next to a little stream. Past the campsite, the path continued, but it was blocked by a neatly laid log.

"This looks good," Harry said, and sat down on the biggest log next to the old fire pit.

Conner got started on a fire. He had to rearrange the stones, and fastidious as he was, he cleaned out the old ash and wood. Soon he had a roaring blaze.

Cold soon turned into bitter cold and they had to move in as close to the fire as they could to keep warm. CJ sat across from the two men, quiet and unresponsive to conversation. She was deep in thought, but of what, she kept to herself.

Harry felt safe now, here in the middle of nowhere. Conner and Harry talked about the day's events, though Conner tried to avoid the topic of CJ.

Harry coaxed her to join them on their log. "We'll all be warmer," he said.

They were beat, all of them. They were dead tired and they wanted to sleep, but someone had to set up the tent they had back at the car. Conner and CJ let Harry rest his leg and went back for supplies. They soon had the tent set up and Harry had a light meal ready for them.

CJ looked at the wound after they had eaten. Harry thought it looked fine, but she was not so sure. One of the pellets was near the surface and came out with the tip of a knife. To prevent infection, CJ poured whiskey on the wound, and Harry poured some into himself as well.

The Book

1976

Harry went into his tent after he ate and took the book from his footlocker where he put if for safekeeping. It was small, about 4"by 8,"and tied well with the twine. He set the leather wrapping aside and looked at the wrinkled leather bound notebook. It was obviously old, but how old, he couldn't guess. It cracked as he opened it. The scratched and weathered cover opened to pages stained and smudged with soil. The script was spidery, but legible, and small. Stuffed inside a pocket on the front jacket was a thin plastic magnifying lens. He scanned the book, reading quickly through the chapters. It told of the search for the lost tomb of some ancient Inca king high up in the Andes Mountains.

It was the tomb they searched for, and as he read on it told of the great wealth it contained, and of the violent end to which these people came at the hands of the Spaniards who had befriended them. *Nothing new*, Harry thought. But he read on. Towards the middle of the book, the spidery script stopped and a bold new hand took over. It looked like Dago's but Harry couldn't be sure. The pages were badly stained. Harry examined the stains closely, and thought they could be blood, black now with age. He showed what he had found to Nancy and Don and they all felt a new hope in finding the treasures.

Dago had been gone a week when Harry and the others found a large cache of precious stones scattered near an old drainage trough higher up in the mountains. They all gathered around and stared with amazement.

"There must be more," Don said.

"Let's make note where we found this," Harry said, "and I'll enter it later in the journal. But for now we should gather this up and take it back to the camp."

Harry later wrote in the notebook:; *The rain, what little comes to this high dessert, must have washed the stones out of the rocks. The thieves most likely hid them, intending to come back later. Time washed away the covering. They never returned for the stolen goods. When will Dago return?*

He entered the exact location, noting the time, temperature, and day. He knew then it wasn't mummies they were looking for.

It was late in the day anyway and they returned to camp to examine the find. Don put the tools and things away while Harry and Nancy ran into the tent and spilled the bag onto the table and spread them out. There was gold, and jewels all intricately worked, and figurines made out of precious stones and turquoise.

"Harry, I want to take off my clothes and roll around in it," said Nancy.

"The mules are gone," Don said. He stood at the entrance to the tent and walked back outside. Harry and Nancy stopped what they were doing and followed him outside. The camp was quiet, usually the mules were not far off tied to a post, and someone always tended the fire. In their excitement, they hadn't even noticed the changes. Harry went over to the where guide's tent were set up, and saw they were gone. The gear for the mules was missing also.

"They packed everything up," said Don.

"I never trusted them anyway," said Nancy.

Harry realized their dilemma. He walked over to the fire and aimlessly threw a log onto it. The embers were still hot and the fire took off again. He turned and looked at his two companions.

"It looks like we have been left alone out here," he said

The Old Man

1978

Skinny was furious about them running off and he vowed to get CJ back, but what was the hurry? Everything she owned was here at the Arapaho. They couldn't go far. He went to the office in the basement to get money out of his stash in the desk and noticed someone had gotten into the safe.

"No she didn't," he mumbled, his face reddening and his heart racing. He opened it and his jaw dropped. He ran to get Mouse from his bed and told him to meet him in the car, and they drove after CJ and the assholes.

"I know where they're goin'," he said.

Mouse drove silently and wiped spittle from the corner of his mouth. He looked at the seat next to him and patted the candy bar he brought along.

"Where we goin' boss?"

"Shut up and drive," he said. "Head for that little liquor store out on 61."

They pulled up to the Esso station and it looked empty. The diner had a few cars in front of it and there was Vet and an old Ford Fairlane in front of one of the motel rooms in the back.

"Pull up by the office," Skinny told Mouse.

Their '69 Brougham pulled up to the front of the gas station office and stopped with a jolt. Mouse got out and Skinny followed smoking a cigarette. He didn't see anyone in the office and he led Mouse into the open garage and to the car lift, which was up about three feet. An old man was on his back and his feet stuck out from underneath the front of the car at the back of the station.

A transistor radio sat on a cluttered table surrounded by old oil filters, tools, and an opened bottle of coke and played the local country station. Johnny Cash sang about a boy named Sue.

Skinny clicked it off.

Mouse chuckled, "Suzy boy."

"How's that," the old man said, and slid out from the car on his cart.

Skinny stood over him and the man looked up.

"Can I do you boys anything?"

"Car's makin' a knockin' noise."

The old man stood up with some effort and wiped his hands with the towel on the table. Mouse noticed the coke and drank it.

"Eh, that's been there for a good week," the old man said. He looked back and forth between Skinny and Mouse. Skinny walked around the car and looked at the things on the walls. There was an old girly calendar by the tire changer, and he stopped to change the month because it said July. He flipped through the months and stopped on one in particular and suddenly looked over his shoulder as if he felt the others were watching.

"Let's take a look at the car," the old man said. "Might be the bearings."

"I think it's the alternator," Skinny said, and they both followed the man out to the car. Mouse stood close behind him. He knew what Skinny wanted from him, how to do this type of thing. Skinny liked that about the big fat idiot.

"Turn on the car and pop the hood."

Mouse looked at Skinny who nodded towards the car, and Mouse did it. The old man stuck his head inside the hood and listened. "Can't hear nothing here," he said and stood up straight, but Mouse stood too close behind him to move.

Skinny looked around to see if anyone could see them. The large hood covered a lot. He smiled.

"Well," the old man stuttered a bit. "Let's take a look at the wheel bearings."

But Mouse had him pinned to the car, a large hand on his shoulder.

"What is it you boys need?" He tried to shrug it off.

"We're looking for a couple a friends. You see, my daughter came by here with two fucking boys, as had no right to be with her. You see them anywhere's?"

The old man thought about it for a second. He squeezed himself free from between Mouse and the car and walked slowly into the shop. He was scared and Skinny could see it in his eyes, in his actions, and he enjoyed it.

People were more likely to lie when they were scared. He liked it—it was a game with him—cat and mouse. It threw them off, and they weren't sure how to answer thinking they could fake their way out, like that asshole in Reno who used to fuck one of his girls without paying. Asshole thought he was real slick, a real free loader. He taught him a lesson about economics, then he tore him a new asshole with his stiletto and left him to think about his lesson.

Skinny faced him off then real close and blew smoke in his face. Mouse came from behind and stood like a barrier. Skinny was in no mood for games anymore and he got to the point. He'd just as soon beat it out of him than let this go on any longer. It was getting late, and he was hungry. He wanted answers.

They walked away without the answers they needed. Skinny wiped his knife off with a blue towel used to clean windows. They got in the car and drove off spinning stones on the old gravel lot.

Skinny looked over at Mouse, and lit up a cigarette. "You beat all," he said.

Mouse bowed his head, "I'm sorry boss. I thought he'd talk..."

"Shut the fuck up." He opened the window and let the cold afternoon air in, and inhaled his cigarette. "I didn't want to kill him. Christ."

"Where to now?"

"Keep goin'."

First Night

"I guess we're all sleeping in the tent together," Harry said.

"At least it's gonna be cozy. Boy, girl, boy," CJ said. A big smile on her face, she climbed into the tent first, telling Harry to sleep here and Conner there. She arranged the covers so that they would all share the same bags. Conner went in after her and came out immediately, blushing. He suggested that Harry might want to go in next and when he popped his head in, CJ was gleefully naked and waiting.

Harry also came out and looked at Conner. He smiled.

Conner opened the tent and told CJ that they might actually sleep better if they all wore their clothes. "There would be less distraction."

Harry agreed and tried to convince CJ that they really needed to sleep.

"I never thought about sex," she said. "I just know it's a lot warmer this way."

She dressed.

Sleep was difficult. After five minutes in the prone position, CJ and Harry were hardly able to contain themselves. They did wait until Conner fell asleep before CJ skillfully removed all of her clothing and Harry's as well.

Conner slept soundly, as usual, and Harry and CJ generated enough heat to form a frost on the outside of the tent by morning. Like a Homeric character, Harry was lured, unable to resist her charm, her beauty, and her narcotic call that cast all men eventually against the jagged rocks.

Hippies

The large Chrysler Brougham sped past a pair of hikers walking near the side of the road, spitting stones and snowy dust into their faces. Mouse honked the horn, not because they were in the way, but because he hated people with long hair.

"Look at em fall over," he said. "Long hair fairies." His thick hands gripped the thin blue steering wheel. The car swerved back onto the road.

Skinny slouched in the passenger seat nervously smoking a cigarette and chewing his fingernails. His comb-over had gone askew in his struggle with the old man at the gas station earlier.

"They were fucking broads, asshole."

Mouse said nothing. He turned to look at his boss, his mouth gaping. He knew all too well who paid his way and he would never cross him. He was big enough to crush a man's throat with his hands, but the Boss terrified him and was good to him at the same time.

It was Skinny's skill with the knife that saved Mouse from being killed by those bikers five years ago in Reno, and he was indebted to him.

"Sorry Boss," he said. "I shouldn't a said nut-in." He talked as if he had a perpetually stuffed-up nose. His large hands reached up to adjust the rear-view mirror. "All I saw was the long hair, and I thought."

"Fa-get-it, Skinny said, emphatically. They looked at each other and burst out laughing. Skinny's cigarette burnt his finger and he dropped it on the floor.

"Shut up. Keep your eyes on the road."

Mouse noticed the snow falling in the open fields around them. It was still bright enough to see well, but

Mouse always drove with the headlights on. "Snowin' Boss."

"Pull over here." He liked Skinny's accent; thought it was a New York accent, and Skinny gave up trying to explain that he was from Louisiana.

The car slowly came to a stop at a small cut off on the side of the road. Hunters had worn it away over the years parking their trucks to take advantage of a prime buck location. The locals called it the Marketplace. Deer gathered at the Marketplace in the evenings to eat berries and succulent grasses, and they made easy targets in the spotlight beams.

Skinny got out of the car and stood by the front end to urinate. Mouse got out of the drivers seat, walked to other side of the car, and did the same. He looked over at Skinny to make sure they were standing exactly the same way.

"Boss, I'm awful sorry about that old man. I didn't mean to hurt him." He took aim at the falling snowflakes.

"Shut up already," Skinny said. "I'm tryin' to think of what to do next. I can't piss with you yappin'." When he finished, he lit up another cigarette and leaned against the fender of the car. "That old man could have told us something, like where they were headed, or at least that they had been there." He looked over at Mouse who smiled back. "Fucking idiot."

Mouse finished peeing and hurried over and sat next to him on the car and it sank down a noticeable amount.

Skinny started to slide, stood up, and walked away from the lights of the car. "I don't know what I'm going to do with you sometimes. What's that?" There was something in the distance. It wasn't too far up ahead. Past that clump of trees, "A campfire. Bingo," he said. "Let's go."

They both got back in the car and Mouse drove the car down the road. They came to a small road that cut into the field and went into a large patch of woods about three hundred yards down into the gully.

"Stop here numbskull, and turn out the lights. Park next to the Bug." The car was a Volkswagen Beetle and to Skinny, they all looked alike. It looked identical to the one that CJ got into with those two idiots.

"See that down there?"

"No Boss. Where you looking at?" His mouth was partially open as he tried to see where Skinny was looking.

"That fire down the road. See it?" Skinny pointed, but his bodyguard was not looking anymore. He had already seen the fire and was opening the door.

"Hold it stupid, where the hell do you think you're going?"

"We're gonna get them like you said, Boss."

"And what the hell you gonna do with them when you get them?"

"Um."

"Yea, I thought so. Listen." He burnt his hand with the cigarette. "Turn off the goddamn engine asshole." Mouse turned the key shutting off the engine. It purred, hardly making a sound. Skinny opened the door and got out closing it quietly behind him. Mouse did the same, but let the door shut with its full weight. Skinny shook his head and mumbled under his breath. They walked down the lane toward the fire. "Just be quiet, okay? You got the gun?"

"Sure Boss." Mouse patted his right pocket where he had the pistol.

"Give it to me. I want you to do it quietly."

Mouse handed Skinny the gun and smiled. He did not mind killing for Skinny. The last time the guy was as big as a bear and his only crime was being two months late paying a month's worth of services at the hotel. Once Mouse got his hands on someone's neck, nothing would make him let go. His favorite technique was to dig his fingers into the flesh crushing their esophagus.

They walked slowly and stopped a hundred feet away. They watched and listened.

"Where the hell is the other guy?"

"He could be in the tent Boss." Mouse was rubbing his hands together to warm them up. He was breathing heavily.

"You look like a steam engine," Skinny said. "Will you stop breathing so much?"

Mouse just looked at him. He concentrated on doing a neat and quick job.

"You go on and make it good. I'll stay back and make sure nothing goes wrong."

Mouse moved along slowly, leaving Skinny behind. He turned to look at his Boss one more time and saw only his breath puffing slowly and methodically. The ground was snow covered and hard. The couple inside the tent, unbeknownst of any danger, made enough noise to drown out Mouse's ponderous approach. Besides, he was aware of the noise he made, and he stopped, and listened. He could be very quiet. *Like a fox*, Mouse said to himself as he crept up to the tent. *You can call me 'The Fox' instead of Mouse,*

I'm Killin' em Boss

Mouse stopped five feet from the tent and watched some more, then smiled. The fire made a silhouette of the couple on the fabric detailed enough so Mouse could see the girl on top. *She's goin' at it. That's her for sure*, he thought. *That's CJ alright. I know her moves by heart. Listen to the bitch moan. And her hair, she always hangs it down just like that too.*

He always wanted her to do the same to him one day. He dreamed of it often. Now he was mad because he remembered he was supposed to kill her and would never get the chance. Not now. *It's all his fault. This'll be fun. The fuckin' hippie.*

Now to it. They were not supposed to scream. He would just go in and take the man first. If the girl tried interfering, he would punch her good and hard. That should keep her quiet while he crushed his throat. *Him and his hair. I never liked him from the start, the moment they walked into the lobby.*

He stopped suddenly. He could not help thinking about what she looked like naked, how she moved, and groaned. A smile crossed his face and he looked back at Skinny standing not too far away in the middle of the road, tiny puffs of steam coming out of his mouth, mixing with the snow. He turned back to the tent.

The fire burned brightly, and it sat directly in front of the tent opening. He would have to move quickly. That is when he noticed the big branch half in the fire, burning. Everyone knew that Mouse was a bit dull—always slow on the uptake, never too quick to respond to anything—but when it came to killing, he was a machine. His mind would relinquish control to instinct. Few ever escaped him once he set his mind on his target. Without hesitation, he bent down, picked up the burning branch with one hand and opened the flap to the tent with the other. Sure enough, they were both naked.

"Fuckin Hippie," he said aloud and stepped into the tent, firebrand forging the way. The girl screamed. It did not sound like CJ, but he was really too excited to care. Before the man could react, Mouse pushed the burning limb into her face, forcing her to the ground, and held it there. The tent filled with the smell of burning hair and sizzling flesh. She would not stop moving so he went to clobber her over the head with it, but there was not enough room to get a good swing. So he kneeled on her chest, pinning her to the ground. By this time, the man was struggling to get up, but Mouse had already grabbed his throat.

He dug his fingers deep into his neck, squeezing with incredible strength. The man struggled. He reached up at his attacker and managed to grab onto his sleeve, but his hand quickly slipped away. Suddenly, why this was happening was not important anymore; survival was all that mattered.

One more time, he stretched out his arm feebly, in a weak attempt to stave off his giant attacker, but he didn't have Mouse's strength. He had not spent a lifetime 'struggling to fit in,' to be one of the 'normal kids,' only to have to use his physical superiority to defend the verbal and physical abuse of his classmates. He could not possibly know the rage and frustration that can build up inside a soul that spends a lifetime wanting friends. He would never know the twisted manifestation of this sick childhood that would create such a skill – the skill of the uninhibited ability to kill.

It took only a few seconds for Mouse to finish him off, for Mouse to feel superior and in control of his environment. However, the girl was still alive, and he could not resist the urge to get from her what she had always refused to give him. He took that poor creature, with its burnt and unrecognizable face, while there was still a bit of life in her. It did not matter. He could never know more pleasure than the act of murder, and as he took advantage of her nakedness, he squeezed the last bit of life out of her, keeping his distance from her bloody and oozing face.

The Strangers

1976

They had to dig their way out of the tents to build a fire. A cold front rolled in and dropped ten inches of snow on the camp. The entire area was under siege for three hours as the snow—hard and icy—bit into the stones that stood like teeth around the tiny dingle where they had made their camp. It was early. An eerie darkness hovered over the mountains, the snow stopped, and the little campsite remained covered in dense fog.

Don was the first to rise. He lumbered out of his tent and had to brush away the snow that covered half its opening. He found the equipment and used a shovel to clear the campfire. After starting a good blaze he rescued the others from their tents.

Harry got up and cleared away more of the snow from between the tents, leaving areas packed down by their movements. Nancy slept.

"I think we should take the day off," he said to Don. "What's for breakfast?"

"Powdered eggs and Viscacha, and some of that trail mix she likes." He stoked the fire and sparks flew into the damp air. The fog thickened.

Despite their recent discovery, Harry felt the mission would be lost if they couldn't find the tomb soon, and he was ready to call the whole thing off. Dago was only a ghost partner at this point. Even when he was there, he offered little assistance to their efforts.

Harry was in the tent with Nancy and suddenly he thought he heard an engine. Perhaps it was Dago returning again, this time with some new vehicle. Don was poking at the fire.

Harry stuck his head out of the tent and looked across the flat and up at the hill. He saw a man standing at the top of the ridge looking down. They hadn't expected anyone to visit, and if it was Dago, he'd have come from the other direction. Harry stepped out into the open and called at Don's tent. He came over and stood by Harry.

"We have visitors," Don said.

"At least one." They both stood together waiting.

"Can you make him out?" Harry asked. But the fog had rolled in thicker and the image disappeared into it.

Harry looked up and saw a dark figure standing there. It wasn't Dago. A field of snow stood between them and only Don's footprints disturbed it.

"Go get your Hammer," he said in a whisper. He was referring to Don's huge and cumbersome .357 caliber pistol they called Thor's Hammer. With its ten-inch barrel, it looked more like a rifle than a pistol.

Don went into his tent.

Harry waved hoping the visitor would come down, but the man had already moved down the hill and suddenly appeared on the other side of the fire from Harry. That's when another man walked up behind the first like he was trying to catch up.

Don returned with his Hammer and stood beside Harry.

"Good morning gentlemen," Harry said politely enough.

"Too much fog for me," said the larger of the two, the first to come down. He was tall and wore a Russian sable hat and a warm Parka lined with wolf fur.

Harry walked towards them and offered his hand. Don stood behind holding his gun in front of himself for all to see.

The big man smiled, a flicker of gold. He removed his snow goggles. His voice was deep and resonant and he grabbed Harry's hand and squeezed it like a vice, and that caught him off guard, and he smiled and looked directly into Harry's eyes.

"My name is Illya Romanov," he said. "They call me the Russian. This is Rudy."

Rudy looked as though he heard nothing. He was average height and stocky in a muscular way. He had a full beard and thick lips, but what stood out most to Harry was his missing ear.

"We are friends of Benicia," Romanov said. "Is he here?"

Harry was cold and hungry and felt the need to drink some coffee and eat, and didn't feel like offering them anything that would make them feel welcome. So he stood where he was. "Dago isn't here," he said. "Where did you say you were from?

"Argentina," he said. His thick voice was heavily accented with Russian.

Harry lost his patience. "Look friend, I just woke up and I'm cold and hungry, and I have to take a shit. Don here has made a lovely breakfast for the three of us, and I could really use some coffee. Now I suggest you get to the point and tell me why you are here, uninvited and without Dago whom you say you know, but who hasn't been here in almost a week." If they really knew him, they would know that. "Where did you come from?"

Rudy opened his mouth to speak, but the Russian cut him off. "That little town Vallicia. We arrived last night and came here right away. Dago wrote us all about your expedition and gave very specific detailed directions which enabled us to find you easily. We didn't see him in town and thought he would be here. I'm sorry he isn't."

Harry was curious about how they got here and the Russian must have read his mind. "We hired a truck, but the road only came partly here. We walked the last hundred yards."

"I'll make more breakfast," Don said. Coffee's ready."

"Let's go into the main tent and we can eat there." Harry led the way, and they found Nancy already standing there eating. She was dressed ready for work, and had her gun strapped to her side. Harry introduced them and asked her to get some coffee for everyone. "Sure Harry," she said and left the tent looking over her shoulder at the two men. The Russian took off his coats at Harry's request. Harry noticed on his right hand, he had a large bracelet with a bull image in gold, surrounded by blue serpentine and red ruby stones. His left hand had a thick scar that was bright red from the cold, and looked as though he had severed his finger at one point and had it crudely sewn back on.

While they ate breakfast, the Russian told them about himself and his relationship with Dago. He made no reference to his companion, who ate little and talked less.

"I came from Argentina," he told them, "to have a look at the things Dago's group," he paused and politely corrected himself, " you have found. I am sorry Dago isn't here, and I apologize for the intrusion. I'm a collector looking for museum pieces."

The whole thing seemed wrong in some way to Harry. Nancy sat off to the side saying little. She later admitted to Don that Rudy had *creeped her out*. Don, the suspicious one, kept himself busy—always within view of Harry—and packed the things for a survey that day just in case Harry should change his mind about taking the day off.

The Russian's presence made Harry feel uneasy, who moved in his seat like a child at church, and answered their questions with equivocation.

Nancy chimed in. "If you came from town, then you must have seen Dago," she said. "Unless he isn't there." She glared at Harry. *Why aren't you asking these questions?*

As if he suddenly woke up, Harry realized she wanted him to end the visit and send these two strangers on their way. Harry stood. "I think you had better go now," he suggested. "We have a lot of work to do."

The Russian stood and put his coat on. Rudy helped him.

Outside the weather had cleared a bit and visibility improved.

"I think if you try, you might be able to find Dago in Vallicia," Harry said. "It's not such a big town." He breathed deeply and let it out slowly. "I smell dry air coming. It should warm up too." He looked at the two and suggested they be careful on the way down. "The snow often makes it hard to see the path."

The Russian turned to leave and thanked them for their hospitality, and they walked back up the hill and disappeared over the ridge.

Harry stood with Don and Nancy watching as they left.

Don followed them to the top of the hill and waited until he heard the truck engine start up and the wheels skid out on the ground under the heavy snow.

Nancy stood close to Harry and put her arm around his waist. "It's cold," she said. The fire portentously sent plumes of black and white smoke into the air. The strangers disappeared into the snowy mountain pass.

Harry sent Don after them, telling him to follow on the dirt bike until he was sure they were gone, and then he should go into Vallicia to find Dago. "He's been gone too long anyway."

The Tomb

Two days later Don came back, the dirt bike's engine whirring with Dago on the back. Dago looked like he hadn't slept since he left the camp. He walked over to the fire and rubbed his hands together. "Fuck this cold," he said. "It shouldn't be snowing this early in the year."

"It'll stop soon and things should warm up enough," said Harry.

"Did you run into those two guys," Nancy said excitedly.

Dago looked at them and Don handed him a cup of coffee. He looked like he hadn't bathed since he left and his beard grew in thickly with grey sideburns.

"Yes, I did." He answered.

Harry leaned into his space "Did they tell you about our get together?"

"Who exactly was here?"

"The Russian guy and his minion," said Harry.

Dago sipped his coffee and ate a piece of meat Don gave him. "Goddamn it all to hell Don. Is this all we have to eat?" He threw the dried meat into the fire. "I don't feel like talking about it." He went into the main tent leaving the others outside.

Harry was sure things were not going the way Dago had hoped. He walked in after him and opened the chest where they had stashed the gems. He stood, looked in, and pulled the bag out and set it on the table.

"All that glitters is not gold," Harry said. He watched as Dago slowly ran his fingers through it. He picked a piece out and turned it in his fingers, and put it back. He looked up at Harry and smiled. "Yeah, but this sure does. Harry," he stood and wrapped his arms around him, "This is wonderful. This is what we've been looking for." The others came in and watched as Dago enjoyed himself. "Of course," Dago went on, "this will lead us to the Tomb."

Dago asked Harry for the book, and wouldn't rest until he had read Harry's entries. "This is fine," he said. "This is excellent," was all he uttered for the rest of the evening until he went to sleep.

Morning came and things soon warmed up. The others got ready to look for the tomb, but Dago didn't show up at breakfast. Nancy went in to check on him and found him lying in a damp and disheveled bed of sweaty sheets.

He had a high fever and despite his protestations, work stopped while his illness lingered.

Nancy nursed him back to health with a special broth made from the bones of the Viscacha and a local herb called Cumbiar.

Two days later he recovered enough to lead the others into the mountains and they found the burial site they sought: a small pyramid covered in icy snow and hidden from the sun between two large crags cleaved into the side of the cliff. At thirteen thousand feet, the air was cold and thin,

Dago and the others worked furiously, chopping through the ice and dirt piled around the entrance. His newfound health seemed to give him super-human energy and a single-minded focus on the opening of the tomb. "I'm afraid that those jewels were hidden where you found them by grave robbers and we'll find the tomb to be empty," he said. "But I see no signs of disturbance here. We might be in luck yet and our troubles will be over."

ThatAin'tThem

1978

Mouse stood back still holding the burning branch in his left hand. The tent collapsed onto the bodies and he was panting heavily when Skinny approached —cigarette in hand. He went up to the tent to have a look. He wanted to make sure CJ and the assholes were dead. Mouse looked proudly at his Boss as he approached the tent ready to take praise for a job well done.

Skinny lifted the tent off the bodies and immediately threw it back down. He turned and tossed his cigarette at Mouse. "You stupid moron," he said. "That ain't them for Christ's sake. He glared at Mouse, and lit another cigarette.

"I only did what you wanted me to, Boss."

"Shut up." Skinny paced around the campsite kicking at loose snow and stones. "Did you even think to take a look at them first?"

"Aw Boss. I-I didn't even think it weren't them. Honest I didn't."

"Shut the hell up. Let me think." He went to the edge of the firelight and looked up at the starless sky. The snow had stopped. "You know we can't go leaving a trail of bodies all over the countryside."

It wasn't the bodies that bothered him, but that he didn't want the complications of police involvement. He only wanted to catch up with CJ and her two friends. He tried thinking of their names, but it didn't matter. He knew them by sight and that's all that counted.

"Double crossing bitch," he said quietly.

Then he looked at Mouse who was mumbling something unintelligible, wringing his hands together.

Fucking moron, he thought as he considered the kind of people he surrounded himself with. On occasion, Skinny wondered what his life would be like had he never gotten mixed up with smuggling and prostitution. However, things had gone well for him regardless.

He sat down on a large log and took out another cigarette and smoked slowly, thinking about what he had to eat that morning.

When CJ and her friends drove away from the hotel, Skinny had figured it wouldn't be too hard to find them. So, he went back into the hotel and had one of the girls cook him some ham, a slice of toast, and coffee. That was it. By the time he and Mouse left the hotel, it was nearly lunchtime and he let that meal go. Now he was starving.

"Drag them bodies into the trees and hide them good." He searched the goods lying around searching for anything of any use, or value. "Then hide the rest of this shit." When Mouse had done away with the bodies, he came back for the packs. "Give me that pack," Skinny said, pointing to the smaller backpack. He figured it must be the girl's and would have something in it to eat. "I'm starving."

Mouse picked it up and gently handed it to his boss, who promptly searched through it, digging deep until he found a hunk of cheese and a can of sardines. There was a canteen filled with water next to him and he decided it was enough. The can of sardines had a little key glued to the lid. He struggled a bit with it, dropping the key in the dirt a few times. He used his switchblade to slice the cheese and dig out the fish. The can slipped out of his hands, spilling sardine oil on his pants, and he cussed under his breath.

When he looked up to drink from the canteen, he saw Mouse sitting across from him with another pack in his lap. He was eating an elaborate sandwich on a roll that dripped with cheese, onions, lunchmeat and what looked like sprouts of some sort. He seemed to be enjoying himself. He had also found a bottle of wine, the kind with the wicker basket woven around the bottle. He paused, as he was about to take another bite, and noticed Skinny staring at him. He held the sandwich out to Skinny.

"Where'd you get that Poorboy, numb nuts?"

"Uh, it's a sandwich Boss."

"I know it's a sandwich moron. That's what we call them where I come from."

Mouse repeated the word, "Poorboy." He smiled.

Skinny threw the empty can of sardines into the fire and wiped his hands on his pants. Then he snatched the food from Mouse's hands, tore it in two, and gave half back to him. He took the wine and sat back down with his share of the food. Mouse finished his half in two bites. He remained where he was, quietly looking at Skinny, a guilty look on his face. His hand was in his pocket.

"What you got there?"

"Nothin."

"Come on. What you got?"

Mouse knew when he could lie to his boss and guilt had gotten the better of him. Skinny did not release his gaze until Mouse finally pulled it out of his pocket and unfurled his huge paw. In it was a half-melted chocolate bar already unwrapped.

"Goddamit Mouse, that's disgusting." He took another swig from the bottle. Then he stood and had a look around. "Finish up there and bring that bottle along," he said. "Then make sure those bodies are hid. There ain't nothin' connecting us with these two. Let's get the hell outta here."

There was a noise somewhere up the road toward the cars. Skinny froze to listen.

"Wait. You hear that?" Mouse started to say something, but Skinny raised his hand to hush him. The darkness lay all about, but the snow covering provided some reflection of the ambient light and it was there that they saw them coming. Up by the car, two people were walking toward them, or was it just one? "Shh, do you hear that?"

"Sounds like someone Boss."

Get'em

"There's two people at the car, Goddamit," said Skinny.

"Whatta we do Boss?"

"We gotta get 'em. They can't know what happened here." Suddenly everything was going wrong, and Skinny was not pleased. Things usually did not happen like this. He always tried to maintain control of everything he did. It was how he managed a successful business, how he had come from the ghetto in Lake Charles to here: his empire. He had built a good business smuggling stolen art into the country. Anything hot he could fence. Even in Reno, he had a reputation as a trusted businessman. He had been doing it for thirty years and he could not jeopardize it now.

"Get em," he said.

Mouse understood what he had to do, and took off toward the car. Skinny followed staying back a bit to let Mouse do what he did best. Mouse ran full specd up the long road toward his victims and growled as he neared them. His arms outstretched. He went for the fastest one first, the skinny one, but she slipped out of his reach and ran like lightning down the road. "Shit, Boss is gonna be mad." That left the fat one standing dumbly like a deer in headlights. He reached for her. Even as she tried to run, he had her in seconds. He grabbed her by the arm. She struggled feebly, but was easy to subdue. He took her by the neck and shook her hard. He did not want to kill her right off, only shut her up, how she screamed. Skinny would have to talk with her first. But when Skinny arrived, panting, the girl lay on the ground slumped into a heap, quiet and still. "I didn't kill her boss."

"Dammit all to hell," Skinny shouted. "Where the hell is the other one?"

"Um, she took off thatta way," he said pointing down the road.

"Get this one into the trunk, hurry."

Mouse rushed over to the car, and opened the driver's door, reached in and pulled the trunk lever. Then he ran back to the body of the girl and picked her up as easily as if it were a bag of flour, tossed it over his shoulder and ran over to the car, opened the trunk, dropped it in and closed the lid. They got in the car and started the engine. He knew what to do. They had to look for the other girl before she got away. He stepped on the gas and the heavy car sped off into the night.

The road was empty. Skinny chided Mouse for that. "She ran off this way Boss, I swear."

They drove a short while, and then headed back. They would go back more slowly and look. If they had to, they could use the spotlight and look deeper off the road. Skinny suddenly had a better idea. He knew that the nearest place the other girl could find help would be the gas station fifteen miles back. She would probably swing around and head for that, and they would be waiting somewhere in between. Still, they crept back to the place where it all began and hid the car. They stood along either side of the road and walked slowly east.

These were skilled hunters in search of easy prey, and they knew they would find her.

Skilled Hunters

Mouse walked back to the road. Skinny waited for him.

"D'ya see anything up there?"

"No Boss," he said. Mouse had not looked anyway. He was too busy trying to spell his name in the snow.

"She's gotta be around here somewhere, we just aren't looking in the right places. Let's get the hell out of here and go back a few miles and wait for her."

It was late afternoon when they killed the old man. That was earlier. No one saw them do it. Now, in the dark, they drove back to the gas station confident that when they returned to look for the other girl no one would recognize them. Skinny's position at the hotel afforded him some influence in the area. His business depended on word of mouth from the locals, yet still very few people would actually talk in public with him.

The local police had only one car that shared a fifty square mile territory. They often counted on Park rangers for help when seeking derelicts and scoundrels. An occasional robbery popped up now and then. If things got too serious they could call the state police in.

They sat in their Brougham at the edge of the parking lot watching as people came and went. Such excitement they seldom get. Two hours went by and no sign of the other girl. Skinny grew impatient. His mind moved in circles thinking about everything at once and his head began to hurt.

"I'm thirsty," he said after a long period of silence. Mouse sucked on his teeth and dug his finger into his mouth trying to dislodge something.

"Will you quit sucking on your hand," he said. "Do you have any idea where those hands have been? And go get me some vodka."

Mouse got out of the car and walked slowly towards the store. Skinny looked after him shaking his head as he lumbered slowly like some monster from a science fiction movie.

"Fucking ape," he said. Then he slowly got out of the car and walked towards the commotion, keeping his eyes on the crowd and constantly looking for signs of some sort of recognition. Nothing. As he approached, he heard the police talking with the old lady he figured to be the owner of the place. She told them about, "these three kids" coming in and out of the store getting gas, whiskey, and food.

"But that's nothing unusual round these parts. They just seemed to be in a big hurry, is all."

She casually glanced over at Skinny for a second, no more. She had seen him often enough to recognize him, though not enough to know who he was. He would not stay long enough to give her a second look and turned to leave. Mouse stood directly behind him and blocked his way. He stood dumbly eating a box of Twinkies.

"That's disgusting," he said. "You get the booze?"

"Yeah, Boss, he said, crumbs flying from his mouth. "It's in the car, over there."

"I know where the goddamn car is," he said lighting up another cigarette. "Let's get the hell outta here," he said. "That chick ain't comin back."

With or Without

The fire did not stave off the cold much. They stood close together drinking coffee while the bacon sizzled and CJ slept.

Conner had slept soundly despite Harry and CJ's heated exchange, but he was clearly annoyed.

"I don't suppose you two got any sleep last night," Conner said. "Look Harry, I don't care if you want to knock off a few with a prostitute, I did, but I didn't bring one along. This puts a damper on the whole vacation. You take the cake."

"You've already said that. Look, like I said, we'll get rid of her and go on from there. Screw Yellowstone. I've been there before and it's not that much." He avoided eye contact. "You think I'm being irresponsible, don't you?"

"Man, you kidnap a prostitute, get yourself shot by some goddamn lunatic, and now we are lost in the middle of God-knows-where. We're supposed to be having a vacation. Not an adventure."

CJ stirred in the tent.

"Why don't you get her up and we can eat and then discuss what to do," Conner said.

Harry went inside the tent.

"Just wake her up, will ya?"

Conner finished cooking the bacon and fished out the black bread they picked up somewhere. He found a tiny branch with two tongs, whittled them to points, and stuck the ends into the crust of the bread. It held firmly enough so he could toast the bread over the fire. Harry and CJ emerged from the tent and he was in no mood to talk to her.

"Why don't you have CJ slice some of the bread and toast it on those twigs," he suggested. "And get some of the cereal too."

"We're out of milk and besides we don't know how long we'll be out here before we come to another Safeway," Harry said. "We ought to keep that for another meal." He took the plates they had and dished out food for the three of them. CJ said little, and Conner thought it might be because she overheard them talking.

"You ok, CJ?"

"I don't talk much first thing," she said. "It takes me some time to warm up."

They ate silently staring at the fire. The stones were glowing red at the bottom of the pit beneath the black and white chunks of wood that now turned into charcoal. The fire danced in the cold morning air. Conner tried to follow one flame as it flickered, furiously licking the grey morning like a snake testing the air. He tried to count the tips of the flames.

"Maybe we should get more wood for the fire," he said.

Harry sulked and stared at the fire.

They felt safe by their fire, their car just down the path, a warm fire, and food. "Growing up," Harry said, "my father would take us to the east side of town on occasion, just to see how other people lived. We'd look at the river below the waterfront and see the hobos. They would sit around a fire built inside an old washtub or some sort of can. Anything to keep warm." Harry gazed into the fire lost in his memory for a moment. "Father wanted to show me how tenuous life is. One's situation can change at a moment."

CJ had stopped eating and stared at Harry. Conner knew she was infatuated with him, but he couldn't get over the feeling she was using them. He knew they could always go home, forgoing the rest of the trip. The memories of Skinny and CJ and the Arapaho incident would vanish.

Most likely he would use those memories in one of his plays: *The Damned Diner*.

CJ ate slowly. She looked into the fire and remained quiet. On occasion, she would look up and give Harry a smile, as if to reassure herself she was not alone and that she was safe.

Conner watched her eat. Her blue cheerful eyes looked around at everything. She glanced his way and he found himself smiling at her. Then he noticed she was flirting with Harry: a wink and a curled lip. She squeezed her breasts together and opened her legs.

It pissed him off that he was ever put in this predicament.

Conner drank his coffee. CJ looked at him, threw her arm around his shoulder, and kissed him on the cheek.

"Here, what's that?"

"Thanks," was all she said. He got up and flittered around, picking things up and making sure they were ready to move at a moment's notice.

CJ watched him as he did.

Her mascara had streaked, and Harry noticed it for the first time. "Are you wearing make-up?"

She turned to him holding a piece of bacon, thick and crisp, crunching it. "What'd ya think? I look this good without it?"

Conner took the dishes to wash them in a snow pile near the stream, but not in it. He didn't want to pollute the water. The scraps would make a snack for some creature.

"You'd be feeding the fishes," Harry said. Then he turned to CJ and said, "I hadn't given it any thought. You look good with or without."

She ate more.

Harry got up, grabbed his toothbrush, and headed for the stream. He looked for a flat spot and cleared off the snow so he could kneel down and lean over the water and began brushing.

CJ appeared next to him.

Without looking he said, "I don't suppose this will do the fishes any good."

"Fuck em," she said.

Dago Dies

1976

Dago was right. The whole trip took a bad turn when they finally opened the tomb. It was empty. The mummy, including the sarcophagus, was gone. Beeny had left the camp and was never seen again. But Suno would come and go with no explanation of where he and Beeny had gone.

Dago had been working inside the tomb when he became feverish again. There, he spent the last hours of his life alone. The others figured he must have woken sometime during the night while they slept and returned to the tomb.

The next morning, they found him inside the empty grave. He looked peaceful lying on his back with his arms folded neatly over his chest. Nancy stood next to Harry and looked down at their leader. "I knew he was sick. I never thought he would come up here during the night."

Harry hopped down into the hole and examined the body. "He must have found something important to come here after we all went back to camp. I didn't think he was that sick."

They buried him there, near the site of the mummies, in an unmarked grave. Harry felt it would be best to leave Chile immediately.

Closed for Winter

1978

Skinny and Mouse arrived at the cross roads around foredawn the next day while Harry, Conner, and CJ slept soundly. Mouse turned the car into the park road and drove until they came to the original park entrance sign. A few years back, federal funding ran out and the road disintegrated. Fordham Park had once been a very popular camping place for locals and travelers.

"This the way to the park Boss?"

"Yeah, yeah, that's right Mouse." He lit another cigarette. It was the last one. He crumpled the empty pack and threw it out the window. "Damn it," he muttered.

"What's that Boss? You say something?"

"Shut up," he explained.

The road wound on for about a half a mile until clearer signs of civilization appeared. Signs pointing to the visitors center went this way and signs for Campground East that way. Dining area to the left. A splintery wooden post held a sign they couldn't make out. Skinny told him to make for the visitors center first.

When they arrived at the abandoned center, they parked the car near the entrance and made sure there was another way out.

Skinny and Mouse got out of the car and walked up to the front door and pushed on the handle. It opened easily. A make shift sign hanging on the door said, "CLOSED FOR WINTER." Skinny walked inside.

"They cleaned this place out."

The building stood empty of anything of value since the park closed years ago. Litter, which was scattered all around, marked the years of transient use. As time went by, lone campers and travelers looking for cheap room had stayed, taking less care of the place than they would if it were still open. Because of its remote location, local school kids would party there. Empty bottles of booze, candy wrappers, and used condoms were everywhere. In the corner was an old chewed up sleeping bag that looked as though someone had blown it to pieces with a shotgun.

He turned to see Mouse standing in the doorway with a non-filtered Camel in his mouth, unlit. He had the pack in his huge hand.

"You don't goddamn smoke," he said as he grabbed the pack out of his hand. "Where the hell d'ya get this? Give em here." He fumbled with the pack. Mouse had gently closed the foil neatly in place. "Got a light?"

"It's in the car Boss where ya left it."

"Go get it. I have to figure what the hell we are gonna do tonight. They ain't been here, for sure."

Mouse walked back to the car. His stomach growled, and he stopped to look around, "I'm awful goddamn hungry," he said, and muttered audibly as he went, "that's for goddamn sure."

Skinny followed him to the car. He opened the trunk while Mouse searched for the lighter. He had forgotten about the girl. "Oh Christ," he said, throwing his head back. The body had emptied itself of its bowls and bladder.

"Whatta reek. I guess she's dead alright."

Mouse came back with the lighter and handed it to Skinny. They both stood looking at the body.

"I'm still hungry Boss."

"Hungry, you're always hungry. How can you eat at a time like this, with that fat thing stinking up my trunk?"

Skinny lit up the cigarette, took a long drag, lifted his face to the sky, and blew out a stream of smoke and frozen breath. Mouse took the lighter from him and lit his own cigarette, puffed, but did not inhale. He looked up also.

"Let's get this stiff out of here. I got an idea where they are."

Mouse put the smoking cigarette in his mouth, reached in, took a hold of the body, pulled it half way out and then hoisted it over his shoulder, crushing his cigarette in the process.

"Where do ya want it boss?"

"Over here." They walked back to the building. Skinny found a loose stone and broke the window on the door, which had amazingly survived unscathed all these years. Once inside, Mouse dropped the body on a bench in the inner room. Skinny gathered as much debris as he could find and scattered it around the body.

"Wait here," he said to Mouse. He walked back to the car, opened the passenger door, and leaned inside. He reached in to the cavernous glove box and produced a full bottle of vodka and a flare he had for some time. He wondered if it still worked.

He opened the vodka and took a long drink. Then he lit another cigarette and walked back to the hut. He took two cigarettes, laid them on the body, and covered it with newspapers. Then he poured the remaining vodka on the papers and lit the whole thing with the flare, which sputtered at first and then took off. The pyre flared into life.

Skinny and Mouse stepped aside for a moment to make sure it took well enough to burn the body and the building in which it was entombed. When the heat became too much they turned back toward the car. The air coming in through broken window would help feed the flames.

They Leave

1976

They made it safely back to the same hotel they started from, and sold the gear for a fraction of the cost to the hotel manager's brother. They sat in Harry's room after a restless night. Unwilling to be seen in public, they had their meals delivered to the rooms, and dirty dishes littered the table. Don knocked on the door, and Nancy let him in.

"Did you do it?" she asked him.

Harry came out of the bathroom wrapped in a towel, and drying his head with another. "It feels good to shower finally."

"That's the second one you took since last night," Nancy said.

"Well," he said, "you never know when we'll be able to take another."

Don was sitting at the table picking through uneaten toast. "Did you get us a car?" Harry asked.

"They want two thousand dollars. We don't have that kind of money, Harry."

There was a knock at the door, and Don opened it. The maid entered with their clothes, cleaned and folded. She smiled and handed them to Nancy.

"Sus ropas estaban muy sucio, Señora."

Harry walked over to her and handed her a tip, "Sí. Muchas gracias."

As Harry was closing the door behind her, she stopped and told him that the manager would like to talk with them.

"Sí, gracias," he told her and handed her another tip.

"Don't spend all our money Harry," said Nancy.

"I had better see what he wants," said Harry. He walked down the hall and Nancy closed the door.

He came back moments later and leaned against the door. His face was flushed, and his eyes were dilated. "Fuck," he said.

The others stood around him. Don's eyes goggling. "What the hell is it Harry?"

Harry avoided Don's eyes and walked over to the window, and lifted the thin veil that covered it. "I have good news, and bad news," he finally said.

"No games Harry," said Nancy.

"Armand said that the reason the car is so expensive is because the tall man with the accent has procured the only cars available. I suspect he meant the Russian. We fought, but he insisted he could do nothing. Then he gave me this note."

"Read it," said Don.

Nancy grabbed it out of his hand and read it aloud, *"Since I am a procuring partner with Dago Benicia, it is my right and duty to collect all materials and documents obtained during his expedition. Should you withhold any item, I will be forced to have you arrested and imprisoned."*

"I intend to turn this over to the University and have them negotiate its return to the government of Chile. The manager insisted he could do it, and would." Harry sat on the edge of the bed and pulled Nancy with him. "The good news is I found transportation. The bad news is it is a motorcycle. I'm afraid if we buy it only two can use it, the other will have to take a train leaving tonight to Peru, and from there," he stopped and threw his arms in the air. Nancy looked at Don, and then Harry. "I'm not leaving you Harry. Can't you find another bike?

"No, don't," said Don. "I can take a hint. I don't mind the train. It'll give me some time to think, and write in my journal."

Harry felt like he was abandoning his friend and said so, but Don insisted it would be all right. "What can happen? What time does it leave?"

"One hour."

The Fight

1978

Harry took a deep breath and looked up at the grey morning sky. The air was crisp and smelled like pine. The threat of a Skinny reprisal seemed less of a reality with each passing hour. They had a discussion earlier about where they were and how accessible the park was, if in fact it ever was a park and not some private campground.

"I guess if you two aren't in any hurry to leave this beautiful park," Conner said. "I'm going back to the car and get some booze, and more food, maybe a book." He took a step and turned, "You want anything?"

Harry was poking at the fire, trying to maintain a good burn. He looked up and saw CJ come out of the woods and pass Conner. He watched her turn the corner past a crop of hawthorns.

Getting back to normal won't be easy, he thought. *She could never go back, could she?* Harry quickly got up and ran after Conner, but he had already disappeared.

Harry made for the latrine himself and then headed back to the camp. He wanted to have coffee alone with CJ. Have a little talk. As he neared the fire, he heard screams, and muffled grunts.

His ankle hurt, but he ran and saw what looked like a bear attacking CJ. When he got to the clearing he saw that there was no bear, but a huge man. She fought him, kicking and screaming, as he dragged her out of the tent.

The big man backhanded her, sending her crashing to the ground. Harry grabbed a large stick from the woodpile and ran to help.

As the big man bent over, Harry swung the club at his head. But he caught him between the shoulders instead and that was enough to drop him to his knees. Now the goon was aware of Harry, and he quickly got to his feet. CJ had scratched his face from lip to ear. *Good for her.*

The man stood a good head taller than Harry, who felt that the stick in his hand was far too inadequate for the task, but there was no backing out now. He braced himself for the inevitable. He called for Conner knowing he probably could not hear him anyway.

The goon grinned and lunged at Harry, his hands reaching for the throat. Harry got out of the way just in time. His leg didn't hurt now because adrenaline coursed through his veins.

Harry jumped aside as the goon lunged for him, twisted around, and planted the club firmly across his attacker's skull. The stick cracked in two and had the effect of shooting a Grizzly Bear in the rump with a . 22.

He stood up and rubbed the back of his head. "You're gonna be awful sorry you little turd." His beard was wet with saliva and his nose swollen.

One good blow from this man's hand and Harry would be done. This was a killing machine. He seemed distracted. It was as if Harry was not the main target, but just some annoying fly getting in the way of his dinner. However, a fly he would relish killing.

He wanted CJ, and glanced over his shoulder at her. Harry would have to use that against to his favor. If he could only keep him aware of her he could use her presence to distract him.

He called out, "CJ, you ok?"

"Yeah," she said, and popped her head up from where she was hiding.

The large man turned in her direction, distracted by the motion.

Harry lunged at him, taking him out by his legs, and together they collapsed into the tent and poor C.J. The man stood up slowly this time. Harry reached from behind him, grabbed his beard, and spun him around.

As his opponent bent over in pain, Harry thrust his thumb into the man's eye and forced him to lose his balance and together they stumbled on the tent peg and fell over backwards into the fire, where the giant's head struck a large stone. The giant took the brunt of the fall with Harry's weight still on top of him.

Harry rolled off and jumped up onto his feet. He was ready for more, but it was over.

CJ in the meantime freed herself of the tent.

Harry stared down at the fire and the man who nearly killed the both of them. He wasn't sure if he was dead or unconscious. As he looked, CJ bent over and rolled the man off the fire. His hand had started to burn.

CJ lifted her coat shreds up over her shoulder, only to have them drop. Goose down fell like snow.

"Shit, Harry."

Harry knelt down next to the body; the coat had caught fire and was smoldering. "If that didn't wake him up," Harry said, "nothing will." He pressed his fingers against the carotid artery and felt for a pulse. There was nothing.

"He's dead," he said. "Where the hell is Conner?"

Sweat poured down his face. He had no idea what to do. *Hide the body*, he thought.

CJ just sat there looking at it.

"Shit," she said. "He's dead."

Harry stood motionless looking at the body. The sound of a distant engine played dully in his ears. CJ had turned white. He helped her down next to the fire. Her pallid skin contrasted with her hair and made her look like she, too, was dead. Her lips were nearly bloodless.

"I'm alright," she said. She looked over at Harry.

"Who the hell is this guy CJ?"

She said nothing, only looked into the fire.

"CJ. I just killed this man and he seemed familiar with you. Now tell me."

Slowly, as if drawing from some long ago memory, she said, "He works for Skinny. Mouse. He's his body guard."

Harry heard another engine, or was it the same one?

Get in the Car

Skinny waited. He made sure this time that he had the right car. That was definitely his double ought buckshot holes in the tail of the VW. Now all he had to do was wait for Mouse to do the right thing, and bring the girl back—alive.

Lighting up another cigarette, he leaned back on the VW and inhaled slowly. Exhaled. The air was cold, mixing smoke with heavy steam from his breath. He looked down at his boots; the silver caps were scratched. "Shit," he said.

He took out his knife, and stabbed the two front tires. Air escaped slowly as the car settled into a lower position. Then he took a swig of the whiskey he had found in the back seat of the Bug.

"Damned nice of these fellas to provide for my needs."

He heard someone coming down the path. It was probably Mouse. *That was quick*, he thought, but something told him it was not. It sounded like only one person; CJ would be shouting and putting up a fight. *Unless he killed her. That would be just like that stupid shithole.*

He decided he had better hide, just in case, and ran to the edge of the road, stepped behind a tree, and waited. Before long, Conner appeared, casually, and too unconcerned to be running away from trouble. He must have left before Mouse got there. *Now I have to deal with him*, Skinny thought.

Conner came through the opening to the path as if he was entering someone's gated yard, strolled to the car, opened the door, and leaned into the vehicle.

Skinny moved quickly toward the path entrance.

Conner was looking for something, and was moving things, reaching further into the back of the car.

Dope hasn't seen the mess yet, Skinny thought. This was a good time for him to move in quickly and clobber him. He would do it neat and clean. Skinny thought of how the knife sounded, how it felt as it entered the flesh. No bone, no interference, just a clean slice, and then a quick jerk and twist, and sever the artery. His element was surprise. *This guy looks big, so I gotta get right on top of him and do it quick. I don't want no fighting.*

He moved quickly, one-step, two steps, three, and snap. He stepped on a twig, and the damned thing sounded like a gunshot.

Conner jumped out of the car. When he realized who was behind him and saw the stiletto, he took off down the road away from the camp.

Skinny ran after him, but stopped when they passed his Brougham. He got in and drove after his prey. He could not get away from the road, because on one side there was a steep bank and the other a river. Conner was still on the road running at full tilt, looking back every few feet.

Skinny waved, smiled, and waved. *Follow him slowly, let him get tired out, and then it'll be a cinch to kill him.* Then he thought about the situation with Harry and his bodyguard Mouse. Maybe he would need a little assurance. Maybe it would be better to keep him alive, take him back to the hotel, and hold him hostage, just in case.

"That's it."

He had stopped running. He just stopped and stood there looking around. Skinny pulled up the car in front of him, and got out with his knife in hand.

"Now you be a good boy and get into the car and we'll go for a nice ride." He thought Conner would cow, but he put up a fight, more of a struggle.

Conner deflected the knife out of Skinny's hand and threw a punch, knocking him to the ground.

Skinny was up quickly, almost before he hit the ground it seemed, and with a branch in his hand. Before Conner knew what had hit him, he was out.

Skinny ran to the car and opened the trunk. There was rope in the back, and he used it to hog-tie his captive. That done he got him into the trunk with some effort, and closed the lid just as Conner was waking up.

"You be a good boy, and stay quite now, ya hear?" Then to himself he said, "We're going back to get Mouse, and the girl."

He found his knife in a small pile of snow-covered leaves over by the river. Wiping it off, he made sure it was dry and then folded it up and put it into his pocket. Then he stepped over to the car and relieved himself, pissing into the snow. A plane flew overhead and slowly drifted off into the distance, leaving only the sound of the river trickling over the rocks and gullies. He stepped out onto the pebbled flats and dipped his shoes into the water, washing the mud off his boots.

Someone was calling. It was a voice from back at the other car. He listened. "Conner," he heard it say.

It was the other one. The one he really wanted. *How the hell did he escape Mouse?* Yet, he did, and that was not a good thing. His body heated, and he started to sweat.

"Shit," he said. "Goddamit." Skinny got into the car and turned the key in the ignition. He pulled the stick into gear and drove off down the road, throwing stones, gravel, and snow into the air behind him. The car drove over potholes and bumps. He could hear Conner hitting the sides of the trunk, but did not care enough to stop to see how he was. He swerved to avoid the holes as best as he could, but it was no easy task.

He was screaming now, his muffled voice coming from the huge cavernous trunk. When he felt safe and when he thought Conner was subdued enough, he stopped the car, got out and opened the trunk.

"You're not dead, are ya?"

He did not look too well. Blood pooled on his face where he scratched it on the jack in the trunk.

Skinny helped him get out, half dragging him to the back seat, and then pushed him in. He was certain that Mouse didn't do so well in getting CJ and he was pissed that Mouse had let this one walk away from the fight. He had to do something, but more fighting wasn't the option. He would find a safe place to stuff this one for now and go back to the campsite and see what happened.

"You an' me is goin' for a little ride back to the hotel."

"What did you do with Harry and the girl?"

"I'll take care of them later. But for now we're leaving this hole."

Conner tried to kick the door open.

Skinny showed him the knife and put the tip of the blade to Conner's nostril, letting him know he would not look too pretty after Skinny was done with him. "Now you gonna shut the hell up?"

Skinny turned the key in the ignition but nothing happened. "Shit." He tried again. This time it started. Black viscous smoke poured out of the tail pipe. The engine raced and the rear tires spun wildly as the car took off down the pitted road.

Where's Conner

Harry and CJ ran back down the path to where they had parked the car. Harry's legs were weak and shaky from the fight. Why didn't Conner answer? Something must have happened to him.

The Bug was there, but no other car. *How did they get here?* He figured there must have been someone else with him. There were many footprints shuffled about in the snow. By the looks of things, Conner had his own trouble, but no prints led away from the immediate area.

The snow had not really settled much on the gravel, the wind had blown it into patchy spots, but he could see tire tracks coming into the cul-de-sac and leaving.

Who drove the other car and why did he leave the bodyguard alone? It could have been Skinny. Maybe he took Conner as hostage.

"They could be waiting up the road. Oh hell," Harry said, "this is too fantastic."

He yelled again and listened for a reply.

"He's probably gone by now, the fuckin' coward," she said. "Lets go."

In the distance, he heard an engine of some sort. It distracted him. His mind raced with dizziness. He looked toward the sky and saw a tiny plane passing overhead. He imagined two or three people inside the plane. *Touring the mountains*, he thought. His lips were moving as if he had been speaking that thought aloud, and he looked around to see if CJ heard him.

His head cleared. The clouds began to break and patches of blue sky were scattered here and there. Large dark vultures circled overhead on the warm updrafts slowly scanning the ground for food, gliding in a ceaseless vigil.

He put his hands to his mouth, and yelled, "Conner!"

CJ joined in the yelling, but Harry shushed her. "Listen," he said. "See if you can hear anything."

No answer.

He listened carefully, turning his head from one ear to the other. He heard something down the way. People talking, but it sounded like they were yelling. Up about fifty yards or so the road bent in a rapidly curving series of S-curves. The sounds were coming from that direction. The hills and snow dampened the noises.

"Stay here by the car and don't move," he told her. He looked her in the eyes sizing her resolve in what must surely lay ahead for the both of them. Then he trotted toward the commotion and saw no one when he turned the corner.

Further on.

A car had stopped in the road. Someone had urinated in the snow. Steam still rose, just barely. He heard the babbling sounds of running water. Mirroring the road past some huckleberry hedges was a stream. He walked onto the pebbled flats and listened. One more time he called for Conner.

Still no answer.

He ran further on down the road, hoping to find them.

Gone.

Harry stood in the middle of the empty road feeling hopelessly lost.

The rifle.

He darted back to the car. He should have brought the rifle along with him. Stupid fool. He barely survived the first guy. Surely, Skinny would have some sort of weapon. Then he thought about CJ, hoping she was still safe. What happened to Conner? He felt the urge to vent, to yell out, but he did not.

When Harry returned, he saw CJ rummaging through the Bug.

The car appeared to be in good shape, until he noticed that the front two tires were flat and the driver's window was broken. He opened the door, pulled the latch to the trunk, and lifted the lid. He leaned inside and searched around until he found what he was looking for. He closed the lid, looked back the way he came. He saw nothing, just leaves and snow blowing in the wind along the gravel road.

"We have to get the hell outta here," he said. Start getting things we need to go on from here."

"You mean we are goin' to hike it outta here?"

"That's what I'm saying, this car is useless, come on." He reopened the trunk and dug through it. Somewhere in the trunk, they had a Mosin-Nagant M91/30 rifle Harry's uncle snatched from a dead German in Poland during the Second World War. It had an old shoulder strap that smelled of musty canvas. He clipped it to the stock and barrel and then looked for shells with the rifle slung over his shoulder. They had ten boxes of 7.62X54R shells, just in case, in a leather hip bag along with some oil and cleaning rags. That was hard to find underneath all the shit they had brought with them, but he managed without wasting too much time.

CJ was moving things around looking for her own possessions.

"Come here," said Harry. "There are some things you can wear. Take off your clothes and put these on." He handed her a new shirt. "It's Conner's. He's closer to your size than I am." He found a sweater and an overcoat for her.

She held them up, and looked at him, "Are you kidding?" she said.

"Well, you didn't bring anything warmer, did you?"

Harry thought it wise to pack light, so he left the whiskey and only took any dried food, clothing, and water containers he could find. A few blankets would come in handy. CJ found another box of cartridges for the rifle and stuffed them in her pack.

"We can repack these back at camp. You ready?" Harry scanned the area one more time, hoping to find something, but what? Conner? The keys?

CJ was close to Harry and she took his hand. Their foggy breaths mixed slowly between them.

"Do you think we should put on our long johns?"

"No. We had better pack them away for when we really need it. We'll be working up a good sweat soon." He pointed up the hills toward the mountains.

"Up there?"

Harry felt that her psycho boyfriend might come back that way and finish the job the big man was supposed to do.

"Mouse," she said.

"Mouse? Is that his name? Mouse?" He paused a moment thinking of his options. "Still," he said, "we do have this rifle. Maybe we could pick him off when he comes back."

"No way, Harry," CJ said rather forcefully. "He's comin' back with resources. Skinny don't like to lose, and he isn't used to losing. He's gonna bring others. We gotta get the hell outta here.

Harry had already resolved to that situation and agreed without too much discussion.

"Well, we'll have a better chance getting help skirting around the hill. It shouldn't be too bad."

They had not passed any town and Harry really had no idea where they were. He was hoping CJ did. He asked her where they should go. "Well, this area don't look too familiar to me."

"You brought us here."

"Yeah, but I made a wrong turn back at the old sign." He let it drop. There was no use arguing. He suggested they go back to camp and rearrange their bags so they could carry them. It took a short while, but when they had gathered everything—the clothing, food, and two backpacks, they headed up the trail.

The snow had started to refreeze and became crunchy. The wind picked up and blew around any loose snow. It felt cold against the face, and Harry was glad he had some extra clothing.

CJ clung to Harry looking around as if she expected Skinny to jump out at any moment. Harry half expected it himself.

"He's gone," he said, reassuring them both. She said nothing until they got back to camp. At first, she just stood by the end of the path. She looked lost and pathetic in her torn clothes. She looked like some fire victim at the end of her wits looking at what used to be her home.

"That bastard," she finally said, and plopped herself down.

Iquique

1976

Don had left Vallicia immediately. Before they split up Harry insisted they each take a share of the gems with them to insure at least one third arrive safely back at Ogden Sumner University.

Harry and Nancy were already deeply in love and they vowed to marry as soon as they could find a place to do it. They figured Iquique on the northern portion of Chile would be most romantic by virtue of its name alone. They rode fast on a 1960 Triumph Trident T150T that was badly in need of new leather seat, stopping only for gas and at the end of the day for a quick meal and sleep. Nancy was obliged to wear a sizeable backpack while sitting tightly between Harry and a bag strapped to the back end of the bike. After the first grueling day of travel and sleeping outside, Nancy insisted on renting a room, no matter how modest.

"If you want to marry me," she said rather jokingly, "you had better see to it I get a bed."

After day three, the chain broke in the middle of the desert highway and they were lucky to hitch a ride on the back of a flatbed Ford. The driver wanted money from the "rich Americans" as he was only going to within 50 miles of Iquique. They wanted to conserve money and so they traded the bike instead, and he let them off at the outskirts of the city.

Evening of day four found them in a small hotel on the fringe of the port there. From their room they could see the fishing boats pulling in to dock. Nancy had just finished taking a shower and stood wrapped in a towel at the window looking out when Harry came up behind her drenched from the shower. He put his arms around her waist.

"Harry, you're all wet,"

"You took the only towel," he said and tore it off her body throwing it over his shoulders. She jerked away and turned to face him. "They can see," she said coyly.

He looked over her shoulder and out the opaque window, which had no curtain. "We are two floors up and at least 100 yards away from the nearest fisherman. They can't see a thing." He held her tightly and squeezed her close to him. "I have a raging hard-on," he whispered.

She smiled. She reached down and stroked his penis. "Oh," she said and giggled. "I should have ridden this instead of that damn bike. Turn off the light."

"I like it on," he said and nibbled on her ear, and caressed her neck.

"Your beard itches," she protested, but wanly, and Harry threw her onto the bed and it squeaked wildly for a while.

The next day, they walked the piers and visited the local taverns, enjoying the sights. A large twenty-crew boat was leaving for Panama in two days. It was a fishing troller that didn't mind taking on a few passengers, and Harry managed to find room on board. They discussed getting married on board and thought that would be most romantic. They made their plans, and ended the day with dinner at a small restaurant.

"Dinner was great, don't you think?" she said, shrugging.

"The wine wasn't bad, but I think there was too much garlic in the linguini."

"You're an ass Harry Thursday. My fish and chips were just fine." The waiter came over and asked if they would like anything else, and behind him the man playing a Concertina wooed a nearby table where a couple sat caressing each other's arms.

"I didn't know sailors could be so romantic," she said looking over at them.

"There's an old saying in ocean ports. 'Seamen and women don't mix.'"

Their world seemed to be sliding into normal. The grueling and dirty work in the field was now something they boast about to their fellow collegians. "Ah, the gold," they would say, "and the mysterious men." And of course, "poor Dago."

Harry felt happy, and well. Nancy looked different to him, she looked more at ease and he could now see that she put work ahead of pleasure. Her shiny brown hair had grown measurably and she let it flow long and free, as was the fashion. When they made love it was wild, whimsical, and as Harry often said, "It would be illegal in nineteen countries."

They paid the bill and walked back to the hotel room stopping at the dock where people tied up small fishing boats and pleasure craft. They gulls flew overhead, and squawked, dipping down to snatch at anything edible. When they realized Harry and Nancy had nothing to eat, they flew away. Only when a family arrived, did they return.

Nancy climbed down the ladder and sat in a small boat there. It had two oars and a tiny troller on the back. She looked up at Harry who didn't follow. "Why don't you come on down?"

The boat rocked in the swells, and she had to hold on. A large yacht had just gone by leaving behind its wake.

"Nah, I think I want to stay here and watch you get into trouble."

A young man looked over the seawall at that moment and began yelling in Portuguese to Nancy. He looked at Harry for answers, who tried in limited Spanish to explain. "I think you had better come on up," he said.

Nancy climbed quickly and showed her reddened face. "Lo siento mucho, señor."

Harry lifted her over the wall and they headed off with the man still yelling. Harry stopped suddenly and turned to glare at him, and he stopped and put his attention to his boat.

At their door, he fumbled for his room key and she toyed with him, putting her hands deep into his pockets before he could. "Let's not go in just yet," he said.

"But why Harry? Besides I'm tired, and I've got the key," which she pulled out of his pocket

"I could use a drink."

"You won't need it," she said, and she rolled her shoulder against him and backed herself against his crotch, and she opened the door. They stepped inside and standing there was a man. At first, he was in the ambient light of the window – a shadow. Nancy let out a small scream, and Harry instinctively stepped between them. He flicked on the light.

"Turn out that light," the man said. His voice higher than you would expect from a menacing intruder. He was shorter than Harry and impeccably dressed for a thief. His image would haunt Harry for years to come. He was a strong man, dark skinned like some half-breed, and he was stocky and looked very athletic. His nose was bent like a hook, and his one ear was bulbous and deformed. "Cauliflower ears," he would later tell Conner when he relived the experience. His lips were full and he sounded like he had a perpetual cold, which made him sound stupider than he was.

"Where is it?"

He knew immediately what he wanted, and was determined to make it painful.

"Where's what?"

"Harry give it to him," Nancy said. She held tightly onto his arm. "He's got a gun for Christ's sake."

Their bags were a collateral mess. He had been busy, and even the bed was thrown over. Harry was pissed, but not enough to be a hero. He knew his place. Who the hell was this guy? Was he in Vallicia all the time, and if so why hadn't he seen him? Did he follow them? And how the hell did he find them?

"We turned them in to the authorities back in Santiago," he said. *Convincing enough,* so he thought.

"I was with you in Santiago," the wrestler said. "You have them and I want them." He walked toward the couple and Harry prepared to fight.

"He creeps me out, Harry," she said quietly to Harry's ear. "It's under the chair."

He stopped and looked over at the chair by the far wall. Harry did something else that night that he would regret, but that would make great conversation fodder for future gatherings. He reached out for the gun in the man's hand to knock it away, but the wrestler threw his free hand up to block Harry's approach, knocking Harry off balance. He came around with the pistol, planting it firmly against his temple and dropping Harry quick as that.

Hiding Mouse

1978

It looked like it could snow at any time. The sky was active with heavy clouds, birds, and wind. They looked again at the body by the fire, half expecting that it would not be there and that he would come charging out of the bushes—quite alive—to finish them both off.

It looked like it could snow at any time. The sky was active. Heavy clouds, birds, wind. They stood silently watching over the body when CJ said, "Creepy, huh?"

Harry said nothing. His mind was too busy with everything that happened that morning. What started as a beautiful, peaceful day ended so violently.

To become a victim was an affront to everything his father had taught him. He used to say, "Harry, if you chip your tooth on something hard while eating an oyster, it might be a pearl, but the chances are it isn't. But, don't stop eating oysters."

CJ packed everything and would not let him help pack her bag. The packs weighed a good fifty pounds apiece.

They were ready.

"Where are we going?"

"I want to stay off the road in case your friend comes back with a posse. He must have realized Mouse wasn't coming back and took off with Conner. Why, I don't know."

"Why are you looking at me like that?"

"He's your boss. You tell me." He kicked the snow and soil onto the fire to make sure it was out before they took off. CJ helped Harry drag the body off into the bushes. They felt it would be safer, and maybe give them more time to get away should Skinny come back looking for them.

Mouse was a big man and there was a lot of dead weight to deal with. It was almost as if his body worked against their efforts and resisted them.

Just past the clearing were some bushes clumped together with young Hawthorne trees that were nesting on the edge of a deep gully. After some concerted effort, they pulled the body over to the edge and rolled it down the hill.

"There is a path over there," he said, and pointed to where they stood earlier. "We'll follow that, and see if we can't find something."

Aren't You Coming?

Harry had not felt the pain in his leg all this time, but the adrenaline had stopped coursing through his body. Now it itched. CJ had reapplied the bandages though it had stopped bleeding. He was unsure of what to do next. He was in the middle of God's country with a prostitute and buckshot in his leg. Conner was missing, there was a dead goon, Skinny would no doubt come calling soon and expect remuneration, it looked to snow any time soon, and maybe, just maybe, they had two days' supply of food left, at best.

CJ watched him pace back and forth, muttering to himself, scratching his head, and working out every conceivable plan of action. Then CJ said that if they had only gone down the road they used to get there and turned left, they could have come to a visitor's center, which was three miles further down.

"Spilt milk," he said. "What we have to do now is find safety, a town, a house, and other people, anything soon before the weather turns really bad. One thing is certain; we can't go back to the hotel. And if we stay with the car, we'll freeze and Skinny can just collect his debt in the spring."

He looked at CJ a long time.

"I feel like you're undressing me, Harry, are you mad?"

"I am, I must be, and you look worried," he paused. "What are you thinking about?"

"Nothin', much." She avoided his eyes, fussing aimlessly with the ground, brushing dirt into little piles with her feet, and kicking snow onto the fire.

The sun came out and provided some warmth, melting the snow that clung to the trees. But, in the distance, the sky looked crimson under heavy clouds.

"Boy," said CJ rather slowly, and with that heavy southern accent, "it sure is gonna snow sometime soon. Look at that sky over there."

As she pointed east, Harry felt a chill run through his spine. His head began to spin. He stopped pacing and stood straight up breathing heavily through his nose, and forcing the air out quickly through tightly pursed lips. Cold and purified fresh air filled his lungs and fed his brain.

"Why ya doin' that?"

"It helps calm me down and it warms the face." He looked around one last time making sure he had cleaned up all evidence of their presence. He hid whatever they were not taking with them in the bushes nearby. Then he straightened up the pit, arranging the stones, looking for bloody ones, and tried to make it look like a very old fire.

Then he turned his attention to the path ahead. At the opening to the path were two old and tired red tag markers nailed to the trees on either side. The path had been marked some time ago judging by the rusted condition of the nails and the wear and tear on the plastic strips.

He hoisted his pack and started walking.

After ten feet, he noticed she was not with him and he turned to see her standing with her pack at her feet. Her eyes were downcast and her arms limp at her side.

"You coming?" Harry asked a bit emphatically. He walked back to her, picked up her pack, and tried to place it in her hand. "We have to go. Now."

She shrugged her shoulders.

"I think I'm making a mistake." She looked up at Harry. Her face twisted with doubt. She bit the edge of her lip. "I haven't ever been away from Skinny b'fore. It don't seem right somehow. Ya know?"

Harry felt the steam rise up inside his head, and he held it there a while rather than blowing it off at CJ. He could not blame her after all.

"I don't know why I even came along. Dumb-ass move."

"You did, though," he said, his voice strained. It grew higher as he talked. "And now he wants to kill you."

He had to remain calm. Losing his temper would help no one and only harm things from here on out. Harry had to show authority and take charge. Of course, he didn't want her to do anything against her will, but she had gotten them into this mess and he was damn sure she was going to see it through. He calmed down, and in a quiet determined tone, he added, "And he'd like to see me dead, too, I don't doubt. I don't even want to think what happened to Conner. Now you want to go back to him. Well I need you right now, and I know you need me. We're going on. Now, come on."

CJ stopped and looked behind. Harry thought she was still hesitating, but she was looking back at the fire pit and beyond. Suddenly, Harry saw it too. The body that they dragged across the ground and into the ravine had left a flattened path looking akin to crop circles.

"We gotta fluff that up a bit," she said, and started back, but Harry stopped her.

"The snow will cover it soon," he told her. "Besides, if Skinny comes back he'll find what he wants to. He has to know Mouse is not coming back anytime soon. Don't you think?"

Harry felt suddenly sick to his stomach. The shock of killing the fat man finally came home. He fell to all fours, shook violently, and vomited. He got up afterwards and went to the stream to wash up and drink.

"Ready."

Skinny Returns

Skinny drove along the road on his way back to the Hotel, but something told him not to abandon Mouse just yet. He wanted Conner out of the way, but felt that he would come in handy. He turned off towards the Visitors Center.

Conner sat quietly for a while, but when Skinny turned the car off the main road, he spoke up. "This isn't the way back," he said.

Skinny looked in the rearview mirror and said, "Shut the fuck up." Snow began to fall thickly with small flakes. He turned on his headlights and wipers.

He pulled up to the center's entrance and stopped the car to look at the burnt out building. He smiled at his work and turned the car into a side parking lot now almost covered by weeds and small trees. A shower house stood alone at one end of the complex. Thick brakes and vines crept over it, breaking through the windows and looked almost as if it was trying to lift the building off its foundations. He skidded to a stop, threw open the door and got out. He stood for a moment to light a cigarette, and then opened the back door, reached in and pulled Conner out onto his feet.

"Oh thanks Skinny, but I don't have to go just yet," he said.

"Asshole." Skinny half dragged him inside using a rope from his trunk, tied him to the door passing the rope through the broken window. He tied him in such a way that little room was left to allow Conner to sit down.

"I'll be back." And he got in the car and started it up.

"You won't find him there," Conner yelled after him.

Snow began to fall harder and a thick blanket covered the ground, where moments earlier there had been little more than a dusting. He pulled up to the Bug and saw that they had ransacked it. He got out of his car and looked inside, then headed up the path towards the campsite. It was quiet.

"Fucking asshole better not be dead," but he knew what to expect even before he said it. He came out to the open space and saw the tent collapsed in a heap. The fire had been put out and as he inspected it he saw blood under the snow, but no signs of Mouse. He searched the site, walked around its parameters, and stopped where it sloped off.

That's where he saw him.

He climbed down the little gully and saw Mouse's huge boot sticking up from under the leaves and snow.

Skinny usually looked at life through a detached view, but something made him take a closer look at Mouse's body. He brushed away the snow and leaves.

"Fuck," he yelled. "You goddamn moron. You let that twerp get the better of you."

He could not imagine how it happened and felt a little bit of a loss for the man who had served him well for so many years.

Mouse had just strangled one of the longhaired pigs with his bare hands outside a bar in Reno, when they first met. The other two bikers arrived too late to save their friend, but they were going to pay Mouse back. They had circled him, sizing him up, probably surprised at his agility for such a big man. Just what their friend should have done, but it was too late for him.

As they circled, trying to distract him, one of the thugs threw a chain around Mouse's neck and pulled him to the ground. The other took advantage of his prone position and kicked him in the stomach, and in his crotch – hard. Mouse managed to free himself from the chain. He would have gotten up too, given a chance. Blood oozed into his eyes from a gash on his forehead. He wiped it away and that is when the chain flew across his head. Mouse fell for good.

Normally, Skinny would not involve himself in other people's disputes. They might have a good reason for pummeling him, but Skinny had seen the big man before. He caught him peeking in on one of the girls having sex with her John in the shed behind the train-yard fence. He sensed usefulness in this giant man, whom he would later name Mouse, and decided to wait and not stick him on the spot.

Skinny quietly approached the fight, pulled out his 6-inch bone-handled stiletto, went up quickly behind the one with the chain, and sliced his neck. That was easy. Then the other one wanted some, too. He came at Skinny unafraid, or stupid, it made no difference to Skinny. As he stooped to pick up the chain, Skinny rushed over, stepped on it, and kicked his right boot up into his jaw. Blood poured from his mouth, but he quickly got to his feet and braced himself against the alley wall. He lunged at Skinny, dragging the chain behind and throwing it in his right hand. But Skinny never lost a fight. He ducked under the sweeping chain and moved to within a foot of his opponent and shoved the stiletto deep into his eye. He held it there until his attacker dropped.

Skinny took mouse back to his apartment, cleaned him up, fed him and clothed him. Mouse was better off than he had been for a while and pledged fealty to his new Boss. Within a year, they had moved into the Arapaho and set up shop.

But that was then and now the big goon was dead.

Skinny let his emotions take over and kicked the snow around the fire. He lifted the tent and looked for clues as to what CJ and Harry did next, where they went. The cold air froze the wet hair around his mouth. He stopped to run his knuckle through it and felt the ice-covered mustache crackle. He looked over at the posts marking the path into the mountain.

"That's where they went," he said. Then he yelled as loud as he could, "I'll get you, you assholes." Then, he took off, fetched Conner and returned to the hotel.

The Hike

The path sloped lazily, at first. So, in the first few hours, they made good time. As the day wore on, the climb became more difficult and the hills steeper. The path started as a graduated climb through the woods instead of a switchback, as Harry would have expected, and wound around the hills in wide turns. It took little out of them at first. Soon it became harder and, as the path led them deeper into the hills, he focused only on the thought that it would lead them to safety.

"I wonder who made these paths."

"Hunters, likely."

He wondered how she knew that and found himself looking for signs that hunters did indeed use that path.

They took several breaks that first day and lunched in a large clearing somewhere in the middle of a mixed grove of pine and oak, where the leaves fell so heavily that little grew but mushrooms.

They sat under a large oak nibbling on dried fruit and leftover bacon. Just above their heads, an old arrow was sticking out of the tree. Its four-pointed tip, still oiled and razor sharp, was three-quarters buried into the bark. The shaft was old and dry, the feathers gone.

CJ rested and eventually fell asleep.

Harry sat silently in thought.

The forest was eerily silent except for a distant creaking sound of two trees rubbing together. He doubted that their luck would hold out and went in search of the path that had disappeared when they reached the grove.

Very little snow lay on the ground, it was covered instead with a thick and soft bedding of compost. There was a musty smell, a rich earthy odor that permeated the air, even in the frigid temperatures. Across the clearing 10 feet up, a blind sat wedged in a Tupelo.

CJ woke up. "Did you rest?" she said.

"Not tired," he said. "This place gives me the creeps. Like we're not alone. Something lives here."

"Shut up Harry, you're just trying to scare me." She looked around just to make sure they were alone. "What lives here?"

"Bigfoot."

They packed their things and hurried on the way. As they walked, the path began to tighten up into a clear route for them to follow. It wound deeper into the hills and thickening forest. Soon the sun lost its will to fight and hid behind lofty grey skies.

The sense of urgency trickled off after a while and they both became more relaxed. They walked slower and then stopped altogether.

"I'm tired," she said, "let's camp here."

Harry looked around and found no better shelter than where they were.

"I think we're lost. I don't see the path anymore, do you CJ?"

She dropped her pack and Harry walked back the way they had just come, trying to find the path. Even that way was unclear. "Might as well camp here," he said.

CJ went to work getting things out of the packs they would need. First, she produced a bottle of Jack Daniels from inside his pack. "It's chilly," she said.

The kindling was damp and they had some trouble starting it, but CJ got on her hands and knees, bent down until her chin touched the ground, and blew at the embers—slowly at first then harder as the flames grew— and the fire sprang into life.

"You've done this before."

"Once or twice," she said, and gently stacked wood on top. "Now we need more wood." She went in search of suitable wood while Harry rested his now throbbing leg.

"Did you remember to pack food with that whiskey?"

"Besides the bacon? Yeah. There's dried fruit, that bark you like, and freeze-dried dinners in here."

"How 'bout cooking gear?"

CJ looked nervous, and hesitant. "Um, uh."

"Um uh what?"

"It was making so much noise a while back that I took it out and forgot to repack it."

"We're screwed. All I have is this tin drinking cup."

She passed the whiskey after taking a few nips herself. "Let's have a look at that leg," she said.

Harry stretched out his leg and winced.

She lifted the pant leg over the wound. He winced some more. She looked long at it, but said nothing. She boiled some water in the tiny cup, washed the wound with it, and then applied a new bandage.

"Let's hit the sack. Maybe things will look better in the morning."

Harry added the largest logs to the fire while CJ got the beds ready. There was no tent. Instead, they used plastic ground cover. They weighed the corners down with stones and used a stick to prop up the middle. Sharing the bags, they could make enough heat to stay warm through the night.

They woke up to snow. Heavy dark clouds dropped about an inch of fine soft powder. They toyed with the idea of staying put but thought the better of it. They made no fire, but got up, quickly packed, and moved on.

CJ said mournfully, "If we are where I think we are, it will be hard to find the path, and it'll be even harder if we're not where we need to be."

The Storm Cometh

Dusting off the snow proved easy. Once packed, meagerly fed, and toileted, they headed on toward the sunrise. After an hour walking, they came to a clearing. The sun shone through the trees as it peeked over the tops of the distant mountains. There was a cliff overlooking a small steep valley that was part of a larger system of rifts and river valleys of the foothills of the Grand Teton ranges. The river that fed the lake at the base of those mountains ran straight and swift, cutting deep sheers into the sides of the hills. It hurried toward a fall-off that was blocked from their view by three granite overhangs that jutted in cantilever from where they stood.

In the distance, the sun lit up the jagged tops of the snow covered peaks that looked one dimensional, razor sharp and fragile, as if they might flake or chip should something hit them.

"Listen," Harry said. He could hear the waterfall for a moment, but the wind interfered and the snow covering the ground acted like insulation, dampening any sounds that might travel toward them. "Can you hear it?"

"I think I know this place," CJ said.

"How would you?"

"Every year I act as a hunting companion for a bunch of guys from Pittsburgh. They come here to these mountains to hunt and fish. It's supposed to be great Elk and Griz country. Bighorn over yonder," she waved her hands carelessly toward the peaks. She stopped talking, and sat on the rocky ledge kicking her little legs back and forth over the edge of the cliff.

"Can you get us out of here?" Harry said. "To someplace safe?"

He walked over to another ledge to get a better view of the waterfall below. He could smell a change in the air. The moisture felt like a cold sauna.

As he looked over at CJ, who was sitting on her own ledge about thirty feet away, she looked tiny. She was whistling some indecipherable tune, seemingly unconcerned and carefree. She dangled her legs over the precipice as she leaned back on her arms, and looked at the valley below, like a diminutive elf waiting on the threshold of some giant's doorstep. She was talking aloud, and must have said something that amused her because she chuckled at it. Harry could not hear her clearly, her voice seemed to drop off immediately, and fall down into the river below.

He yelled across to her, "I smell snow."

"Those clouds are headin' south," she said. "We've got time."

"Did you happen to look back that way?" She looked at him, and he pointed behind her. She twisted her body around, and stared at the on-coming storm. The sparse trees at the edge of the valley heralded the forest, as it loomed behind, as if they were afraid of falling into the canyon. The black sky lay open and broad. It looked as turbulent as a deep mountain lake just before a storm. Dark burnt clouds swirled and quickly shifted shapes like those same giants were stirring them using mighty oaks as paddles.

The soundlessness was deafening, like the tide pulling out to sea before the onset of a tsunami. Harry pondered their predicament; it did not matter to him at this point, how they got there, but that they were there. Harry had been hardened to the effects of Nature over the years. Though, as a young child, he would venture into the forest thinking it was a vast and unexplored jungle. It was an adventure to him at the time, but it never required courage. He always had the certainty that when he wanted he could turn around and go home to dinner and a warm fireside.

But summoning the courage to jump headfirst into a black pool of water not knowing what, if anything, lay beneath the smooth surface, required steel nerves. Life is incalculable and death is the only certainty we are given. But the question of when death will come is the question that keeps most people from taking chances.

CJ came un-noticed to Harry and stood beside him, slipping her hand into his. She squeezed gently.

"How well do you know this area," he said, not looking back.

She took a long look down river. Her body shook quite suddenly, involuntarily. She said, "I think there's a cabin bout a mile away, or two from here." She pointed in her usual vague manner, back into the forest. "Up in them hills."

"Who lives there?" Harry imagined a roughly built log structure with thickly laid mortar, smoke coming out of the chimney, and a little hippie family laboring hard to make a meager living off the land.

"No one now, likely. This is too high for anyone to live in year round. The owners use it as a huntin' lodge. But once snow hits, it's too dangerous."

"Your Pittsburgh buddies?"

"Yeah." She turned to walk back to the bags, Harry followed. His leg was throbbing, though he had not paid much attention to it recently. The rim of his boot touched the wound and sent raw pain to his brain. All he could think about was getting there and taking off his boots. He felt feverish, and sick to his stomach.

CJ seemed to sense his condition and her mood fell. They gathered their things, hoisted their packs, and headed off toward the cabin.

They walked, saying little for some time. New snow had fallen and Harry listened to the sound of their feet scuffling over the leaves and humus beneath them. CJ found it hard to remain in a black mood for any length of time and that spread out from her like a candle at the end of a dark hallway, and soon she began to jabber away, often about nothing at all. Her mood lightened and she quickened her pace, unaware of how it affected Harry.

He concentrated on CJ walking, pushing the pain out of his head, and looking at her tiny figure bouncing in front of him. Her ass filled out her pants and he enjoyed watching how her cheeks moved rhythmically back and forth.

She talked on, her hands darting out now and again. All of a sudden, she stopped and turned. "Four people died out here last year in September." She spoke vigorously and with great use of her arms, "When a storm came over them in the night. No one ever found the bodies."

"How do you know they died then?"

"One of their cars was found at a ranger station over in Flag Canyon. They put on their itinerary they was headin' this way." She looked sad as if she had known them, and then changed her mood suddenly. "Fishin's good here in this river."

"Pittsburgh?"

"Oh no," she said dismissively. "Didn't know these fellas."

Half-hour later they came to a meadow with a river meandering through it. Two small mountains met to form a valley that spread out to expose a view of some larger mountain in the distance. Trees carpeted the hills, and the grass was brown and dormant for the season. The stream ran dry in many parts, its wide alluvial flats showed signs of frequent flooding. Sands had gathered where eddies had formed. An old oak fell across the creek a little further downstream from where they stood, its roots exposed by quick powerful waters washing out the sandy soil beneath.

They crossed into a large open space filled with wintered cat-o-nine-tails and willow reeds. Thick hedgerows of chokecherry, and hawthorns spiced by wild vines of honeysuckle, and aspen bordered the meadow. Game birds frightened perhaps by some hungry fox shot up into the sky, and over the treetops.

They drank their fill of water from the stream and rested until their headaches left them. A small break in the chokecherry across the way looked like a path through to the other side, and they headed for it. The ground here was flat and boggy, and finding a firm foothold proved difficult. After several unsuccessful attempts at crossing where they were, they agreed that the edge of the meadow would be dryer and firmer. The streambed was better ground, so they followed that until they reached the edge of the open bog.

Here the stream cut back, diverted by a large outcrop of rock, and dropped steeply off, almost becoming a waterfall.

"Five minutes," Harry said. He felt the need to rest against a tall white stone that had a natural seat cut into it. He took off his pack and leaned back against the cold frozen edifice. CJ climbed to the top and planted herself there, smiling, but Harry did not want to stay in any one place for long fearing that he would become unable or unwilling to move on. They filled their bottles with fresh water, packed them away, and headed off and kept to the outskirts of the greenery.

This proved disastrous, as the ground was far spongier than they thought. CJ stepped into one spot, and sank nearly up to her knees before Harry grabbed a hold of her and pulled her out, making an odd almost cartoon-like sucking noise. They stepped carefully from there on out, following the thick ancient row of hedges. After a quarter hour of painstaking travel, there came a break in the vegetation, a passage perhaps formed by years of passing deer determined to find a way into the rich marsh and beyond.

Once through the break they walked a steep climb with a few switchbacks. At the top of the climb was the path. Two red flags like the ones back at camp, marked that they were on the right road. Harry had been sweating profoundly for a while when CJ stopped and turned to look at him. She pushed Harry down onto a rock and lifted his pant leg. He could tell by her face that it was not good news she had to tell him. So he didn't ask, and she didn't offer. And so on.

The Fatal Snow

They trudged through the dry sunless land. It seemed to them sullen, and hostile, made more so by the lack of wildlife, especially birds that seem to have left before the pending storm arrived, or perhaps they knew where to hide, and so avoid the brunt of Mother Nature.

The air seemed to be getting thinner with each step. A light breeze picked up in the treetops. They could hear it in the pines as they whispered and swayed, passing the wind along like a wave. Then it came with great force through the forest, bringing with it cold and damp air. Some snow had already fallen there. It lay thick in spots on the ground. Harry's head started aching, and he found it hard to go on.

The wind sounded like a freight train and with it came the snow, which fell heavily from the first flake.

He was hot and began to sweat. The cold wind felt good. He shivered and grabbed onto CJ and pulled her over to a clump of trees that offered no protection, but seemed better than standing where they were.

"Are you sure this is the way?" He had to yell for her to hear him. She nodded, wincing from the cold air and snow in her face. She had already pulled the hood over her head and tied it tightly around her chin. Harry pulled her to his chest, and brought her face close to his so their lips almost touched.

"Just over the next hill," she said. She was lying. When he tried to kiss her, she pulled back and said, "You look like shit."

"You're so tender. Let's get this over with," he said, "I hope there isn't anyone home."

"No," she paused and slowly said, "You don't look too good Harry."

The snow fell so thick and heavily that they could hardly see one another, though they were only inches apart. They trudged on toward safety.

After a while, the fever gripped him hard and he pulled off his hat and hood to cool down. His head spun, and his feet were numb and heavy. He looked down and saw only stubs wrapped in tattered cloth strips where his feet should be. He let go of her hand and fell to his knees, too tired to hold on.

He fell face down in the new fallen snow, now already a half-foot thick, and felt himself melting through it and into a pool of water. When he opened his eyes, he was floating in a warm ocean, snorkeling, and looking down at bright blue waters filled with fish, plants, and a coral reef. He was about to dive down to have a closer look when he felt himself being dragged out of the water by his feet.

He heard CJ calling him, "Harry, Harry, what are you doing?"

He was suddenly in boiling water, and he tried to swim free—back to dry land, only it was not dry. It was wet, cold, and snowing.

"Harry, baby wake up, we have to get out of the snow." She was terrified, thinking of the possibility that if Harry should die suddenly, she might be alone.

Slowly, he made it to his knees and with CJ's help stood. She held on as he stumbled along, following her to an eroded wall of earth surrounded by bushes and partly covered by spidery roots that jutted out of the ground above them. Perched on top of that was a young spruce hissing in the wind, bent over from the burden of snow in its leaves.

Harry had fallen into another dream as soon as they hit the ground. CJ took their packs off and placed them at their feet, took out a sleeping bag, and covered herself and Harry with it. She drew him close and held on. He was shivering. She called to him. He did not respond. They waited.

It could have been hours or days, but CJ waited until she heard the wind stop blowing. She must have fallen asleep herself because Harry had slipped down into an awkward fetal position at her feet, but safe in the bag that covered them. The snow had fallen so thickly on them that it appeared to be nighttime in their little cave; it pressed down and kept them warm. If anyone were to pass by, he would not have seen the two blended into the earth, until they shook the snow off and emerged from their shelter.

The wind had stopped, but the snow had not. It was a beautiful sight: white, silent, and fatal.

CJ emerged first and smiled, moving her limbs to warm her hands and feet. She found a branch lying nearby and picked it up. It was just long enough for a walking stick. She snapped off the branches, leaving the end with one large "Y" like a crutch. It felt sturdy when she tested its integrity, and she put it in his hand. Harry stirred and slowly got to his feet.

"What the hell just happened? Where are we?" Although he stopped sweating for the moment, he still looked ill, his hair matted, and his eyes red like bleeding wounds. His wan face made him look like a carved tallow figure.

"I'm trying to figure that out now Harry." The snow deadened their voices.

"We came from that direction," he said pointing to his right. How would he know?

She said, "I don't think it's too much farther on." She looked back, and he was on to the ground scooping up snow, and eating it.

"You shouldn't do that baby. It's not good to eat icy cold snow."

"Should I eat warm snow? My head is killing me. I need to drink." He looked up at CJ and added, "I don't mean whiskey either."

She helped him with his pack, took the rifle he had been carrying, and handed him the walking stick.

Then she tucked her tiny frame against him, wrapped her arm around his waist, and began walking.

With each step, Harry winced from the pain, but said nothing.

"Hold on Harry, it ain't that much more. Lean on that stick."

He tried, but his fever renewed and he trembled violently. His teeth chattered, and he fell to his knees, and buried his face in the snow. She ran to his side, and tried to lift him out, and turn him.

The snow fell relentlessly, still unyielding.

She pulled his head onto her lap and stroked his forehead. She began to cry. Tears streamed down her red frozen cheeks. They dropped off her face and froze into tiny balls before hitting the snow. The temperature had fallen to below freezing. This, at least, kept the snow light and dry, and so it was easier for them to move in it.

CJ cradled Harry's head and rocked back and forth. This is not what she had expected. She counted on Harry and Conner taking her as far away from Skinny as possible. By now, she thought she would be in some warm hotel on her way south, not stuck in the goddamn freezing hell she was in now. If she knew how to, she would have prayed, but she never learned. Her fate was to live with the hand dealt to her, accept it, and survive.

Suddenly he opened his eyes and sat upright. Harry got to his feet as if attached to some unseen strings, and he trudged on, often stumbling, but he kept going. CJ tried to keep up with him. She ran to his side, held tightly to his arm, and steered him back onto the path from which he had veered. She asked him questions and tried telling him to follow her instead of wildly going nowhere. He said nothing, but followed blindly, walking like a drunken sailor.

Harry was in a world of white. Everything blended into a whirling blizzard, a blank canvass, and he was lost. He felt something urge him to get up, that lying in the snow would kill him, and he found somewhere inside himself the strength to stand up and walk. Painfully he lifted his leg, sodden with the weight of snow and blood. His legs were senseless limbs touching the ground he could not feel.

What drove him, he could not tell. Some terror following behind threatening to take his life away, so he struggled on not even aware that CJ was there. He felt the wind lift him up and push him along. Where? Forward, even though he took as many steps sideways as ahead, to him he was moving and that meant staying alive.

He felt as though his head had cracked open, exposing his brain to the elements, and blood poured from his eyes. His mouth had become a parched cracking hole. His throat crusted over, and he found breathing difficult, as if he was turning to stone.

A hand grasped his arm firmly and pulled him roughly. It hurt, and he felt unsure of where he was going or who was hurting him. Instinct told him to sit down, to lie down and sleep. When he did, his head stopped spinning, and his mind cleared as if he was coming off a terrible cold, and his sinuses finally cleared allowing him to breath.

The thick flakes seemed to part, opening up to him a clear view of the quaint structure. The fifty yards went quickly and then in no time they stood at the house's feet, staring up at the welcoming sight. The chimney was huge and stretched a good fifteen feet across the north side of the cabin. Smoke poured out thick and grey. The windows, covered with steam, shone with a warm amber glow. The door opened and out came a fat old woman wiping her hands on her flour-dusted apron. From behind her came a cozy inviting light and the smell of bacon and corn bread. A bathtub full of steaming hot water sat beside a fire deep inside the house.

"Well," she said placing her hands on her hips, "dinner's ready. Come 'n get it." She turned and went back in the house, closing the door behind her.

Marry Me

1976

Harry woke with a terrible headache. His mouth was parched and he had been breathing in dust particles from the floor. His nose itched and that's what woke him up. He rolled over and suddenly remembered he had been hit on the head. He shot up, but stiffness had settled in and he fell back down.

"What the fuck," he said. Slowly this time, he got up off the floor and sat rubbing the side of his head. His hair was matted with dried blood and it smelled like someone had vomited.

"Nancy," he said. "Are you alright?"

He looked around the room. She was sitting in a chair tied with the bed sheets. Her mouth had been stuffed with underwear, and she looked mad as hell. He got up, but slowly, and as he did he stumbled. He made his way to Nancy and untied her.

"Who the hell was that?"

"Harry," she said. Her eyes reddened from crying. "Are you okay?"

He rubbed his temple. "Peachy."

Nancy got up and led him to the bed and sat him down on the edge. She looked at his wound. Blood had dried over the gash.

"Did he get them?"

"Well," she began slowly. "Good news and bad."

"Just get to the punch-line."

"He took only my share. We still have yours." She walked across the hall to the bathroom and came back with a wet towel, and began to clean his head.

"What time is it?"

"We have three hours to get on board."

Harry stood up and undressed. "I'm going to take a shower," he said. He wrapped the towel around his waist and headed for the bathroom. Nancy came with him.

"I want to come along," she said.

He smiled at her, and caressed her head and held her chin in his hand. "As much as I'd like to, I don't think I got it in me this morning."

"Funny, Harry, but I want to see you don't fall."

"I'll be fine," he assured her. "You had better pack our things and be careful with that bag." He pointed to the ceiling lamp where they had hidden the other bag of gems. "Good thing he didn't turn it on."

An hour and a half later they were climbing on board the troller that was to take them to Panama.

A crewman showed them to their cabin. The boat was big enough to have three rooms, but today it was only the two of them, and they gave them the biggest one. The sailor that carried their bags was a large hulking man, broad shouldered and clean-shaven. He spoke English and Spanish, and although the boat was Brazilian the crew had a mix of three or four nationalities. He threw open the door and ducked down to enter.

"La Suite nupcial," he said proudly, and gave Harry a jab with his elbow. He left and closed the door.

They laid out the bags and Harry suggested that one of them carry the bag of gems at all times, "Especially if we both leave the room. I may be paranoid, but we got some strange looks from some of the crew members."

"I think they may have been looking at me Harry," said Nancy, and she wagged her hips and stuck her breasts out. "Did he say Nuptial? As in wedding?"

"Well, we did agree to get married somewhere, and I thought it would be nifty to do it on board a ship. So I made arrangements with the captain to marry us on board."

"Nifty? And this is a boat not a cruise ship. Can the captain of such a small boat even do it?"

"Sure," he said. "Absolutely. And besides this isn't too small. There must be twenty crew members."

"Twenty three," a voice said from the door. The captain stood at the entrance and smiled. "I knocked, but you didn't hear." He introduced himself to them. "I'm Captain Ramon Pineda, at your service. You are lucky we are not going fishing, just yet. Señor Harry made sure that you would go directly to Panama." The captain looked less like a tough sea captain and more like an intellectual. His greying beard belied his age and he had a thick head of hair that brushed back. His blue eyes smiled when he talked and he had a heavy Portuguese accent.

"Come now, please," he said, beckoning them to follow. "We have little time before we set off and I would show you around." He introduced them to his Chief Mate and other members of the crew, especially the cook who told them about meal times, and that there were no leisurely activities on board fit for a cruise liner, but the crew meets after dinner for a few drinks and socializing.

The boat set sail and Harry and Nancy stood on the stern from a safe vantage point and watched as the deck crew managed the sendoff. It started as a beautiful day, but the sky quickly darkened.

They saw little of the Captain that day and into the next, and stayed mostly inside their cabin, making love. They tried to be quiet about it, and she would call out "My little Viscacha."

At midday of the second day, the Captain performed the ceremony in front of selected crewmembers, including those they had met on the first tour.

The sky turned black and the clouds rolled across the sky like waves, and the wind soaked anyone that walked outside. The seas were rough and dinner was no easy task for Nancy, who had never gotten her sea legs.

"This is not normal," the Chief Mate said in perfect English. They had been drinking, and celebrating with the crew after dinner, and he noticed Nancy's pallor. "We have a squall brewing, so you might have to stay close to your quarters tonight and make the best of it. It could get rough."

Nancy felt the best way to make the best of it was to get drunk. The alcohol was flowing and both Nancy and Harry took advantage of it. But they soon went back to the cabin and Nancy threw up on the way.

They went to bed and Harry slept like an old salt, while Nancy struggled if not for the motion, then for the constant creaking of the structure.

Conner & Jackie

1978

He cracked an eye slowly peering around his immediate field of vision, and took inventory: Table – poorly painted and chipping; a chair – old and dirty, with a tear in the side; a desk –which looked like a desk a teacher would have used; and a couch with a girl on it.

He was lying on the floor, head on a pillow, looking up at the girl in the room with him.

She was already sitting up with her knees drawn to her chest. She was chewing on a strand of hair and looking at him contemptuously.

Conner cleared his throat, and lifted off the blanket that covered him, and ran his hand through his thick head of hair. His arm was stiff, and felt a bit numb from lying on the cold and dusty floor. He sneezed.

"Are you okay?" he asked her, but she didn't respond. She seemed frightened of him and he had to let her know they shared the situation.

She did not take her eyes off Conner. She just sat with her head resting on her knees, hugging her legs, and chewing her hair. He sat up and stretched.

Her eyes followed his every movement like a hungry dog watching its master eat.

He looked over at her and said, "What was your name again? You never said." She looked like she had been through a lot, too, and he felt bad for her.

"Conner," he offered. He waited, but she said nothing.

"Did they give us anything else to eat besides your hair?"

Her eyes crinkled, and she let the hair drop out of her mouth. Then she dropped her legs to the floor, and put her hands palm down on the couch. She flicked her eyes over to a corner of the room and he followed them to a table with a jug of water, and some cheese sandwiches, which were neatly cut diagonally and stacked on a plate with pickles. Next to the jug of water were two glasses wrapped in paper.

Conner got up and walked over to eat. He poured himself a glass of water and took a sandwich. "Hmm. Swiss," he said, and held the sandwich up as proof. "You have a name? No huh? Well I'm sure it will come to you, honey."

She said nothing.

"Look, I'm not the bad guy here, okay? Girlie girl?"

"Jackie."

"Well hello, Jackie," he walked over to shake her hand, but she pulled back. He continued around the tiny room looking behind the dusty boxes with papers sticking out askew and taped on walls as he went. Suddenly he jerked his head around and said, "No window. There are no windows here."

"Touché, Sherlock," she said. "And there is only one door, and it's not the bathroom. I already looked."

He pulled back an Oriental room divider and said, "Then this must be the other door leading to a bathroom."

She jumped up and rushed to the newly discovered door saying, "Move," and as she passed him she said, "I gotta go."

She closed the door and he heard the lock click.

He took another sandwich and sat down to wait. After a few minutes, he heard the shower running. He waited for what seemed to him ten minutes, and while he waited, he tried to open the door to the hallway. "You never know," he said, and tested its integrity by shoving his shoulder against it. It held solidly.

The door to the bathroom opened and out she stepped dressed only in a towel. Conner was a bit shocked. Why would this girl, who seemed so shy and frightened, come out of the bathroom with only a towel on?

"Um," he said, "you work here?"

"It's hotter than hell in there, there's no fan and no window." Conner was staring at her with his mouth open. "A minute ago you couldn't even tell me your name," he said.

She went back into the bathroom, closed the door, and emerged a few minutes later fully dressed. "Better?" she asked.

"How long we been here, do you suppose? Did you sleep?"

"Not too long I guess, couple of hours," she looked at the top of the wall and said, "No windows."

"Yes, but luckily I have this handy wristwatch to tell me the time and day." He looked at it quickly and looked at her, then looked at it again. "Course I haven't any idea what day it was when all this started. But, it is three o'clock anyway, on the 25th. So tell me about yourself. Why are you here? You don't work here. How did you meet Skinny?"

"I didn't, exactly," she said. She withdrew to the couch again, and curled up into another ball. "He killed my girlfriend. He tried to catch me, but I ran." She began to tear up, and shook her head. With her face buried in her knees, she told Conner what had happened to her and her friend Paula from the beginning when he tried to run them off the road. When she had finished, Conner sat silently unable to provide her with anything consolable, with any comfort.

"Are you sure she's dead? Maybe he has her somewhere."

"She's not here. I am. I heard her scream, they drove off and left me alone."

A chill ran through his body. He was unable to answer questions about his own ordeal, but he tried by piecing together the things that happened to him since leaving the campsite.

"I guess that Skinny had sent someone to do away with us, or at least to take back CJ. From what you are telling me, his regard for human life is below his regard for garbage. I am sorry for your friend though.

That's horrible," Conner said. "You must have stumbled onto something they were doing. I mean it's not like you are part of all this."

Jackie shook her head. "We were just walking along enjoying life. How am I going to tell her parents?"

"You may not have to. Well who knows what he has in store for us? Oh, don't worry, I'm not going anywhere soon, except out of here." Conner walked into the bathroom, "Did you leave me any hot water?" He closed the door.

When he was finished, he came out of the shower in only a towel just as she had, but they were not alone. There were two other girls with them. One of whom he had met before: Sylvia.

"Well," said the second girl, "looks like you two have become acquainted—real cozy like," she gave a coy smile to Sylvia. "Maybe we came back too soon, huh sugar?" She looked over Conner's body, looking long at his well-defined chest and stomach.

"I'm surprised he got the best of you," A wink and a smile

He walked over to the door, not intimidated by their presence, and opened it. Outside in the hall stood a man about six feet tall with a hooked nose and cauliflower ears. He put his hand up and pushed Conner back into the room and closed the door.

The first girl to talk was Sylvia. She was tall and slender with smooth skin and a high-pitched voice that was almost like a little girl's. She said, "Skinny isn't gonna let you out that easily." She had on a short skirt and tight fitting blouse, no make-up, and her hair was up and rather messy. The other girl went about straightening up the room and Conner noticed there was more food available on the table, a bottle of whiskey, a box of saltines, cheese, and apples.

"Last meal Sylvia?"

"Sorry Conner, nothing personal you know."

The other girl said nothing.

"You sure are taking good care of us," he said. "Why don't you just let us leave?"

The other girl came out of the bathroom with wet towels and Conner's clothes.

"Whoa, whoa, where are you going with those?" He went to stop her and the door opened. In came the man from the hall. He held the door for the two girls and out they went.

Conner was angry, and blushing. "Great. I get to be naked."

"Well don't get any ideas," Jackie said folding her arms across her chest.

"I hope they clean them at least. It appears I am not going anywhere soon. This is awkward." He looked at Jackie and smiled. "Might as well make the best of it."

"Back off bud," she said and looked around quickly for something of a weapon. She picked up a ledger and held it threateningly.

He turned to sit down on the couch, but changed his mind at the last instant and took the chair. "Don't flatter yourself sister, you're not my type."

Jackie huffed indignantly, "Good." Then she crossed her arms and fell onto the couch in her usual spot.

They were in an old smokehouse in the back of the hotel. They spent their time quietly. Conner sat on the floor with his legs stretched out uncomfortable that he had only a towel to cover him. He took the time to tell her why he was there, what had happened to him and Harry, and CJ. As he talked, she listened intently and asked questions at one point or another to clarify things.

"And that is how I ended up here, in wonderland." He was sitting cross-legged, now forgetting he was naked under the towel. Jackie glanced down at his lap and quickly turned her head. She went to the bathroom and emerged with a white cotton robe.

"Where'd you find that?"

"On the back of the door. I hadn't noticed it earlier. I must have put my wet towels on top. I just noticed it hanging there while I was..."

"Wonder why the hostesses didn't say anything about it?"

"I wonder why they took your clothes."

"Oh, I'm sure they were just having fun." He did not tell her what he thought; that they most likely had a peephole in the door or on one of the walls.

Sick Harry

Death creeps unawares upon its victims. But Harry no longer feared death, not after a near fatal experience with malaria, not after so many bar fights, not after being arrested and held for three months in Ecuador for smuggling diamonds, (a charge that was later dropped), and certainly not after three failed marriages. Death was something his father said was as much a part of life as living, like marriage and taxes.

"If you're not afraid of living, then don't be afraid of dying," he would always say. Dying meant an end, an end he was not willing to take lying down. However, fever was ruthless.

For almost an entire day, he lay in bed. Luckily, he had CJ to convalesce him. He tried to open his eyes, but the light in the room was blinding. He finally managed to open just one eye and after some struggle keep it open. What caught his sight immediately was a large stuffed grizzly bear mounted at full height with its mouth wide open and front paws attacking. He closed them.

When he opened his eyes again, the room spun and his stomach swam. He sat up and the covers fell from his bed. He was naked. He fought back the urge to vomit. CJ was prepared and handed him a small pail.

"I'm okay," he said. "I think."

He sat on the edge of the bed, and tried to cover himself with the sheet.

CJ gave him a bathrobe instead.

He looked at it. It was thick, soft, and blue. He had only seen the like in very expensive hotels, like the one in Santiago. The thought of his Nancy came back to him. He smiled, but then he remembered her sudden death, and the smile dropped. Harry let the bathrobe drop to the floor, and he fell back onto the bed.

When he awoke again, he opened his eyes, and the room spun. He closed them quickly. He stomach churned. His lips were hard and cracked, and his tongue felt as big as his foot. He had crashed into awareness. His eyes hurt, but he opened them slowly again. "My brain must be swollen," he said to the ceiling. "What time is it?"

"I guess eight," it said back, "seven maybe."

CJ's face appeared where the ceiling had been. She smiled. Her hair hung down and bridged her to Harry. He brushed the dangling strands away from his face. "Where's the old lady?"

"Who?"

"With the apron," he said, "On the porch." He vaguely remembered reaching the cabin and was certain he'd seen an old lady earlier, beckoning them inside.

"You don't feel too good. Do ya?"

"No. I do not. Water." He tried to get up, but fell back to the pillow. Later on, he woke again. CJ sat next to him lifting his head up to help him drink.

"What time is it?"

"Why the hell do you want to know the time for anyway? You expectin' someone?"

"You never know. Where are we?"

"In the huntin lodge. You had a real bad fever Harry."

"That explains all the dead animals." He sat up, and this time he stayed. "I'll take that robe now."

She looked at him and smiled, but didn't move.

"The robe?" he said.

"You look fine without it."

Harry got up, and looked around the room. A fireplace took up one whole wall. Leaning against it were their backpacks. The actual pit could fit a full-grown buck dressed, and skewered. Indeed, there was a long iron skewer in there as well as a pot hanger, and grate. On either side were two black bears mounted, one standing, and one on all fours. On top of the mantel were two very large stuffed river otters, posed as if they were sunning themselves leaning up on one elbow, and staring out over the room. He saw dozens of animals all over the place.

Next to the cot where Harry lay were two large comfortable overstuffed leather chairs flanking a wolf.

He turned, and walked toward a hallway.

"Where are you going?"

"Nature calls." He walked back toward where he hoped the toilet would be. When he turned the corner, a large grizzly bear startled him. "Who the hell owns this place? Madame Tussaud's demented cousin?" he said as he closed the door to the bathroom.

CJ sat on one of the overstuffed chairs waiting for Harry, one leg draped over the arm of the chair, her thick blue velvet robe tied at the waist. She had a drink in her hand, and the ice clinked as she sipped it.

"Is it time for cocktails already?"

" You want cocktails, or somethin' else?" She stood, and let the blue robe drop to the floor as she walked over to him. She draped her arms around his neck.

"A cocktail would be great," he said as he pecked her on the lips. She dropped her arms, turned back to get her blue velvet robe, and then went to the bar against the far wall.

She pulled a bottle of wine from under the counter, "Would you like this instead?"

He wondered who owned the place.

"No one lives here this time of year," she said, "it gets too cold. They lock it up for winter."

Harry found the robe, and looked around, and out the windows, then at the front door. CJ answered his next question before he could ask.

"I been here before, Harry. I know how to get in."

"Oh," he said, "the Pittsburgh boys. Now I remember."

"I'm sorry Harry, but you're not my first." She had made coffee and breakfast while he was in the shower, and asked if he would like any.

He walked to the fire to check on his drying clothes.

"Why don't you go sit down in bed, and I'll bring it to you. You don't need any clothes just yet. You can dress later."

"I feel exposed, naked."

"Just the way I like you," she said as she dropped the tray on the bed at his feet. She placed him back on the bed and fluffed up his pillows. Her breast fell out of the robe, and she pressed it to his lips.

"Food first," he said ignoring her for the moment, "I could eat one of those bears." He dug into the sausage, and eggs.

"You are."

He stopped chewing, and looked at her, "Bear?" He pointed to his plate. "Not bad."

"We need to eat while we can."

What did she mean by that? "How's that?"

CJ walked to the front door, and threw it opened. The wind gusted through her blue velvet robe. Snow flew in the front door, and Harry could see a good three feet lying outside.

"I don't think there's enough food here to last the week Harry."

"A week?" He thought for a moment. "How long have I been asleep?"

"Since yesterday afternoon when we got here." She said that up here it wasn't anything to get 5 to 10 feet at a time. "And by the way it's falling, we ain't going nowhere." She closed the door pushing hard against the wind, and clicked it shut.

"Get me a gallon of water, will you. I am parched. It's hot in here."

"The boys built this place good. They are loaded, and they love to hunt. And they don't like to bring their wives." She filled up a pitcher with water, and set it on the table next to Harry. "I'm going to clean up a bit, and then take a shower. You should join me."

He watched her as she moved about with a feather duster, and put things to order.

"You're cleaning up like you expect someone to visit."

"You never know."

"You don't have a maids outfit do you?"

"Not on me. You just rest. We'll get down to business later."

Harry slept the night, and woke in the morning to more wind and snow. The fire had gone almost out, and he got up to re-stoke it. It was dark although the sun had been up for several hours. It would not appear that day.

To save on energy, the owners from Pittsburgh had installed a cold storage room that extended off the back room. The house nestled against the side of a hill. In one corner sat a huge rock on top of which stood a large blind used for armchair hunting. They built the room from cleanly shaped stone, and natural logs mortised to show little or no seam. It used the cool of the earth to refrigerate without electricity. In here, they found various animal parts that looked like small hams, and smoked briskets.

CJ appeared suddenly behind Harry with one of these briskets. "Look what I found," she exclaimed holding up the meat for him to see. It was big enough to belong to a large deer, possibly a moose. She had it cooking over the fire in minutes. It smelled as good as bacon.

"They smoke this meat themselves," she said. She squatted by the fire still in her blue velvet robe poking at the meat on the grated spit. "The fire's gone out in the hot water heater Harry. Could you look at it? It's in the room at the end of the hall."

Harry was by no means a technical person; the outer limits of his knowledge in these matters might have been distinguishing the heater from the hot water heater. Looking carefully at the unit, he figured that the pilot must be behind the little door at the base of the heater. On it were two tiny ribbed hand screws about the size of a pencil eraser. He grunted and struggled, but he emerged from the back room victorious.

His leg throbbed, and he hobbled over to the kitchen.

CJ knocked over the backpacks. One almost fell into the fire, but CJ lunged for it and cradled it like a baby. Then she gently put it back and wedged it into a corner of the stones. She came back to what she was doing, and smiled at Harry. He put his arms around her slipping inside the robe, and cupped her breasts in his hands

. He pressed his mouth against her ear, nibbled it a bit, and whispered, "My leg is killing me."

She turned slowly, keeping her body pressed against his, and let the blue-velvet robe fall.

"I can fix that," she said, and ran her hand along his abdomen. She knew he liked that, she had done it before, and he was hers. With that, she slid out from under Harry as he leaned against the counter.

Her soft breath brushed against his ear as she whispered, "I'll get the whiskey."

The Storm Taketh

1976

Harry woke up just before dawn; the storm had subsided. He reached over to caress his bride and found her not there. He sat up quickly and shook the drowse from his head. He dressed and went to the head hoping to find her there, but she wasn't. He performed his ablutions and headed back to the cabin. *She must be waiting,* he thought. And still she wasn't there. Alarmed, he ran to find the Chief Mate.

They searched the entire boat, twice. Harry walked the decks with Captain Pineda, whose concern grew with each room. He barked orders at the crewmembers he found not involved in the search.

The Mate approached, his eyes reddened – he had taken a fancy to Harry's wife and found her quite capable of drinking with him. "We've searched everywhere, Captain."

"Did you search the other rooms?"

He hesitated and shook his head.

"Then I suggest you search those," said the Captain. "And even his."

Harry wondered what he meant by that, *I thought we were the only ones onboard,* but the Captain ushered him away and towards the galley. They sat together for a while, Captain Pineda trying to calm him down, trying to sooth his guest. He had a bottle of whiskey brought to the table. Harry could see the emotional state Ramon was going through, and that even he cared a great deal for his wife.

Every few seconds a crewmember came in with no results. Finally, Captain Pineda stood at the other end of the room with his Mate. They whispered, but Harry knew what it was they said. He fought the tears, sick to his stomach, and hung his head.

"Señor Harry." Ramon Pineda stood above him, the Mate next to him, other crewmembers off to the side. Pineda waved them to leave.

"I'm afraid she is nowhere to be found. Did you notice her leave the room last night during the storm?"

"No. I slept." He threw his glass across the room, and began to pace.

"Think. It's important."

Harry held his hands over his eyes and tears started. "No, she must have gotten up. But why?"

"All I can figure is she went to the head in the middle of the night and the storm washed her over."

Harry thought about what he said. It made sense, but the thought of her falling overboard in a storm, alone, and in the dark, frightened him and enraged him at once. The Captain reached out to Harry and gently held his shoulder from behind.

Harry turned quickly and in one motion swung at Pineda hitting him squarely in the jaw. The Captain fell back and into the Mate who caught him.

Two of the crew who had been watching from the kitchen, came up and held on to Harry, who wanted more.

"What kind of boat is this?" Harry said, and he struggled to free himself, but they held him firmly.

Pineda stood in front of Harry rubbing his jaw. "I can understand your anger, señor, but I assure you it is highly possible for this to happen. I'm sorry." He motioned for his men to let Harry go, which they did cautiously. Harry relaxed, and turned away from him more embarrassed than anything. He leaned on the table with both arms, "I'm sorry, Ramon."

Ramon came over to him and handed him another drink, patting him on the back.

"You have every right to be mad. I know I would want to kill someone, but who? She takes what she wants and gives less."

Harry looked at him confused.

"The sea. She is in control and we can only hope she allows us to sail her."

Fever

1978

The tiny snowball floated to the top of the glass. A little iceberg bobbled on the surface, spinning as it absorbed whiskey. It looked like a snow cone, and then dissolved. CJ looked at the glass with reproach, and took a drink. "It must be too hot in here. It melted. Now the whiskey is watery."

"Put the bottle in the snow, and it will stay cold and the snow won't melt."

"You're so smart Harry, but it won't last that long."

Harry drank his and poured more. The wolf's snout sat between them. It snarled, baring its teeth, and its prosthetic tongue stuck out to one side just a little bit through a slightly opened mouth, and he offered it a drink.

"He's not thirsty today. Says he's stiff enough." Harry laughed so loudly that the shillelagh leaning against his chair slid off onto the floor with a loud thud.

The wolf found nothing to laugh about, but stood erect and alert, ears facing forward. Its large yellow eyes with black slits looked more like windows into some fiery crucible than something it once used to see. The inscription on the footboard told the story of the wolf's demise. It said they found this beast walking in the forest surrounding the Lewis River Valley that feeds into Jackson Lake, and they used a 270 Winchester 30 – 06 / 250 grain.

"It's how they first saw the dog before they shot it. They like to keep things natural looking."

"Poor fella."

"You drunk, Harry?"

"Not as stiff as these bastards," he said, waving his arm around the room. His eyes stopped at the rifle leaning up against the far wall near the front door.

The storm was beating the house senseless. The wind had been increasing hourly, rocking the windows as if it was trying to pull them free from the walls. For the moment, they were safe from the elements. They sat in silence listening to the howling wind and the bang, bang, cu-thump thump of the house. Harry grabbed the shillelagh and hobbled over to the front window to look out. His leg felt better.

CJ got up to stoke the fire to keep it alive.

The logs sparked and sizzled. One of them rolled out of the fireplace and onto the rug there. It smoldered a bit and sparked into flame. CJ looked frantically for something to extinguish the fire with and finally tore off her robe and threw it on top of the small flame. As she pounded the floor, she reminded to him of some naked Aboriginal woman pounding grain into flour.

She finally looked over at Harry standing against the front window smiling at her. "What are you looking at?"

He did not answer. The aboriginal pose took him back to his wife Nancy.

"Just thinking about another adventure I had once a while back. You want to hear about it?"

CJ looked as if her teacher in class asked the question, and she needed to come up with an answer or look foolish. "Nah."

The Howling

"Harry, Harry," he heard her saying, as he crept out of his reverie, "you wanna join me?" She was naked and heading for the sauna in the back.

Why not? He followed her and watched her as she stripped for him. He joined her in the steaming tub. She wasted no time in straddling him, trying to rouse him to perform.

"I feel sort of weak, CJ, I think my fever is lingering."

But she looked alluring, the soapy water glistened off her breast as she bobbed in and out of the water, and she wasn't the kind of girl to take no for an answer. He knew that, and why should he refuse such an invitation?

"Come here, you," he said. He pulled her to him and kissed her deeply, passionately, and she slid onto him.

The water splashed onto the floor, and they laughed.

Harry felt tired afterward, and got out of the tub slowly and put on his robe.

He dreamt he was in a house he shared with seven other boys in college. He had been drinking all afternoon, when a knock on the door woke him up. He was in the chair of the cabin, sitting by the stuffed wolf. He got up to answer it. When he opened the door, he was in the tomb in Chile. It was a dark cave with an empty grave inside a tiny pyramid, but in the grave was Dago, laying face up as if someone laid him there. He had pulled back the stone covering the entrance and gone inside. He was dead, frozen solid. He had fallen into the hole, and his torch was cold and dark on the floor of the tomb above him.

But the sun was beating down. It was hot, and the flies were everywhere. He could hear the buzzing of flies, and monkeys screeching in the distance. Then he took a sip of an icy drink beads of water dripped down the sides of the tall tumbler, and the sound of the ice clinking in the drink woke him up.

But he was still in his dream, and noticed that his feet were cold and numb, frozen in two blocks of ice. They were bleeding, and the blood ran like lightning through the ice.

Dago said something about someone very bad. He said that Harry should be careful and that he would be next. His feet burned. They began to itch. He had the bag of jewels in his hands, and threw them down into the grave on top of Dago.

Then suddenly Skinny appeared, painted in blue azure and looking like a sacrificial slave, his eyes were covered with red beetles and on his finger was a great ring of rubies, and black onyx shaped like a snake. He stood over the decaying body of Mouse, whose face was half-covered with rotting flesh. Dago's voice told him to run, and he turned with great effort, as if he stood in a pool of mud. He panicked, and his heart raced. It was hard for him to breath. He was drowning.

He woke hours later on his back in the bedroom. CJ was wiping his head with a damp cloth. "Not again," he said.

"No. You conked out pretty fast afterwards, and didn't sleep too restful. Then you were sweating so I hadda cool you off a bit." She looked concerned, worried. "You can't have an infection anymore. I think you have a cold or something. How do you feel?"

"I'm hungry now."

"Good," she said, "have some more beans."

"I need meat. That brisket would be nice."

She went to the fire and took the meat off the spit where it had been resting and sliced him some.

"What do you think he'll do when he finds out about Mouse?"

"He ain't gonna be happy, I can tell you that."

Harry's head still hurt. Water was the only cure for that, and they at least had enough of that. His leg throbbed and it felt damp under the bandage, but he said nothing.

"We don't have to worry about that till the snow stops anyway."

Harry drifted off to sleep sitting in his chair with his leg up, there was little else to do. CJ brought a plate of brisket, and beans over to him. She set it on the table next to him, and gently nudged him awake.

He ate in silence.

"You must be starvin'," she said, "I ain't never seen anyone eat my cooking without complainin 'bout it."

"Oh, man," he said, and handed her the plate, "that hit the spot." She took the plate to the kitchen.

"Is he in trouble?"

"Who?"

"Conner."

CJ considered the question, and slowly said, "Nah. Most likely Skinny will drop him off somewhere, and send him packing."

"You really think he'll do that? He came after us with that goon of his." Harry didn't say more, because he wasn't sure how Skinny's mind worked.

"He wants me and..." She did not finish the sentence.

"And what? Me?"

"Yeah. He wants us both," she said. "He's a nut, I tell ya, Harry."

"Still, I don't get it. Why all the trouble over a..." He stopped short. "But he knows that Conner will want to find me. He's not going to let him do that."

"Ya know Harry, they're snowed in just like us."

Outside the wind had not let up; it still shook the windows and blew through the eaves. "Listen to the wind howling," she said.

It howled long and mournfully. "That sounds like wolves, not wind."

"No Harry. Don't be silly. It's gotta be the wind. What would wolves be doing out in this weather anyway?"

"They have to eat."

They howled some more. It was quiet for a few moments, and then they heard dogs outside the cabin growling at each other, more than one, and they were close. Harry hobbled over to the window and looked out. It was darkening, and he could not see too much. So he opened the door and stuck his head out enough to keep the lights from the house behind him. A howl died quickly, and he thought he saw them scuttle away.

"I'm going to bed." He walked back to the bed, took off his robe, and climbed in. CJ dimmed the lights in the main room and came after him, took off her robe, and climbed naked into his arms.

Tired and happy, she slept contentedly. Their lovemaking always made him tired, but he had had enough sleep for a while. He lay next to her for some time watching her until her breathing slowed. She lay on her back, facing away from him, the thin covers draped loosely over her prone figure. Her breasts were at rest, and her firm stomach lay flat falling to her abdomen as it disappeared behind the slight rise of her hipbones where the sheet rose like a tent supported by the center pole. Slowly her chest rose, and quickly it fell as she breathed in and out. As the minutes passed, her breathing slowed to a soft, almost imperceptible rhythm.

Harry realized at this moment that he could be feeling an emotion richer than simple lust.

Sara

Two days must have passed, and no sign of Skinny. The first two girls disappeared and were replaced by Sara, the girl from the diner. Conner was pleased, although a little surprised.

Jackie could not have cared less, and seemed annoyed by Conner's familiarity with the new hostess.

Sara came into the room with two servings of the house special – meatloaf with potatoes and glazed carrots. "It's a specialty of Skinny's," she said, and plopped it down on the table. She pulled out a bottle of whiskey, and sat that next to the food. "This is a specialty of mine."

"How'd you get that past the guard?" he asked. "D'ya bribe him?"

"Shithead doesn't bribe that way," she sighed. "We wonder about that boy."

"So, does Skinny own that diner too?"

"Yeah, that's where he gets his girls. Well most of them."

"CJ?"

Jackie was getting annoyed. "Who's CJ?"

"This chick," Conner said. He was about to say more in the way of an explanation, but thought better of it.

Sara sat with them for a while, and talked of the day Conner and Harry came into the diner.

"When are we getting out of here?" Jackie said with a tsk.

Sara looked at Conner to answer as if Jackie was not even there, "Skinny isn't done with you two yet. You pissed him off and gotten got in his way. He'll be down to visit soon, wants to ask some questions. He likes answers that fit his questions."

"How old are you?" Jackie asked.

"Old enough."

"Seems to be the standard age around here."

"Well, let's just say that I'm not as mature as you are lady." Then she turned to Conner, "Your mother here seems a bit nosey."

Jackie stood up and looked at Conner, who had been sitting back and watching up until now. He was smiling.

"You enjoying this are you," she said.

"You two are doing fine. I have nothing to say."

Sara turned toward to leave, "Skinny will be here shortly. He wants to find out how much you know. My advice to you is to play it stupid. He doesn't like it when people get too close. He's really pissed about CJ."

"I could really use some clothes," he said, "My own preferably."

"I'll see what I can do."

She knocked on the door, and it opened. She smiled at Conner, ignored Jackie, and turned and left. The door closed quickly behind her. The bolt clicked.

Conner listened at the door as soon as it closed. She was still there; a shadow covered the peephole. They spoke in soft-muffled tones. Then she walked away down the hall, but the bodyguard remained. Conner could hear him breathing heavily through his mouth. He paced back and forth slowly on his soft padded sneakers. When he had taken four steps, the floor creaked, and he turned back the other way, passed the door three steps, and turned. This went on for five minutes.

Conner turned to look at Jackie. He looked long at her sizing her up. She seemed strong and sure-hearted, yet frail and vulnerable. Talking with her and watching her strut about in just a towel, he concluded she was not shy and could take a good joke or two.

Sara was attractive too, and that complicated things. Always, in the back of his mind he thought about her as a character in one of his plays: a heroin for sure. The bizarre situation they were living through may be okay for Harry, but it was not acceptable to Conner. But it gave him new energy. He wanted a typewriter, or at least a notepad and pencil.

His creative juices were flowing like a spring river. He had been working on a new play about two brothers—one is a Harvard professor and the other a grill cook—who go on vacation to a dude ranch outside of Las Vegas Nevada.

Conner looked at Jackie. He smiled.

"She could be useful." He thought there might be some attraction between them. Men and women in tight places and stressful situations often find sex relieves tension. He used that scenario many times in his plays.

Jackie still had a sour look on her face, "Do you think so?"

"Do I think so what?" He had forgotten what he said. "Something is wrong here."

Jackie rolled her eyes. Conner continued un-phased, "Have you noticed anything unusual about the girls here?"

"They're all whores?"

"Yes that too, but they are all young, very young. Under 20 young."

Jackie sat on the couch arms folded over her chest, pouting, her head turned away from him. "Oh, I don't think they are that young. Sara isn't so young."

" She turned her head twirling her hair in her left hand. "I thought you would notice her. Don't you feel that something terrible is happening here?"

"You mean aside from this being a whore house?"

"You're joking, but you know what I'm saying." Her hands were on her hips as if she were scolding him.

"Look, Jackie," he said. "This isn't lost on me. I understand that this place shouldn't be here. Normally, I don't concern myself with how people make a living, but this asshole seems very bad."

"Seems?"

"Yeah, he's a criminal and I'd like nothing more than to see him behind bars, but I didn't ask for any of this. I was on vacation."

"And now here we both are against our will. And what about your friend's little whore? CJ? How much of this is her doing?"

"What do you mean?"

"From what you said about her, she has more to offer Skinny that her services. She's either really good or she knows something about him that he's afraid of."

Conner thought about what she just said, surprised that he hadn't thought it himself. "Huh. You think so?"

"I'd say so. I mean he has plenty of girls working here. What's one more or less?"

"What do you do?" He wanted to change the subject. He would have to think about that some more.

"Meaning?"

"For a living. You look like you are in good shape. What do you do when you're not hiking?"

"Meaning what?"

"Wait, don't tell me. Let me guess. You work out of doors. No? For an outdoor company. No?"

"I work for a sports marketing company. We represent players in the media. We get them advertising gigs," she paused. "Billy Jean King."

"Oh," said Conner, "You know her? So you're an agent."

The deadbolt sounded, and the door opened quickly and with force. Skinny entered, smelling of gardenias and wearing a new black studded shirt with mother of pearl buttons. He wore the same boots and clean jeans. He had slicked his hair back, and applied fresh grease. He entered the room, and smiled. Conner could see the gold teeth gleaming between his lips. He looked over at Jackie to see what her reaction would be.

She stared at him with a steady gaze, lips curled in a slight snarl, and eyes wide open. Before today, she had only seen him in the dark.

"What did you do with Paula?" Jackie wasted no time in starting in with him. Conner looked surprised but realized she was passionate.

Skinny ignored her for the moment, and looked around the room, his boots clicking on the hardwood floors.

"I hope you two are happy." He looked at how Conner was dressed in a robe and towel. "But then I see you two got acquainted." He looked at Jackie and leered. "Maybe I should put that on his bill hey sweets?"

Jackie didn't flinch. "Where's Paula?"

"I don't know no Paula," he said. "Who's that?"

Conner stopped her before she said anything else. He knew it was fruitless, that Skinny was toying with her and she couldn't win. "Hold it Jackie. He can't hear you."

"Oh, I hear her fine, stud." He exhaled in overly dramatized exasperation, "What am I to do with you two?" He took a pack of Marlboros out of his shirt pocket, took one out, and lit it, and before he put it away, he offered one to each of them. "No? Could be your last wish."

"Do you have a firing squad outside?" Conner said sarcastically.

"Well, it's snowing outside so I guess you two are safe for now. Looks like we're all stuck inside for about a few days anyway. No school. Except you and her ain't goin' outside to play in it." He turned to leave. "As to you missy, you and your friend were in the wrong place at the wrong time. I'm afraid Paula screamed a bit too much. Mouse didn't mind though, he got out of her what he wanted before he killed her." He opened the door a crack. "I wouldn't get your hopes up any, leastways not 'till I figure what to do with you. I'll be back," he said as he closed the door.

Jackie stood stiffly looking at the door for what seemed like ages. Her face was tense and her fists clenched.

He said nothing and watched her color turn red. Then she burst out crying like a kettle whistling.

One of Many

His leg swelled, and puss formed around the tiny holes. It hurt him like the devil.

"When is this Goddamn snow ever going to stop?" she said.

"Well when it does the fun will begin." He watched her prance around the cabin darting in and out of the rooms. She had found some clothes that fit her, clothes she kept there for the pleasure of the Pittsburgh clients, clothes that accentuated her ample bosom and hips.

What the hell can she be doing?

"You're making me nervous sit down will ya?"

She was lifting a huge pot of beans around, and setting it up next to the fire to cook. "It's an old family recipe," she said. One of the few good memories she had of her childhood was before the old man took to molesting her sister her mother was actually a good cook, and used to make all sorts of Mexican meals.

"That's where she came from," she told Harry. She didn't talk much after that, but started banging things around.

Sitting around drove him crazy, he hated inactivity and always had to be doing something. There weren't any books in the house. The owners came to hunt not read. And if they were not hunting, they were enjoying some of Skinny's girls.

"Sit down, will you? You're driving me crazy," he said to her.

"Do you want to eat or not?" she said and came over, grabbed a glass and the bottle, and poured herself a drink.

"You drink too much, you know that?"

"You're no amateur yourself," she said. She fussed with the pot in the fireplace stirring the beans, taking the lid off and putting it back on. Then she picked up the bottle to pour a drink, forgetting that she had already done that, and then put the bottle down.

Her hair was disheveled and could have used a brushing. She reminded Harry of Elizabeth Taylor in "Who's Afraid of Virginia Wolf," and he liked it.

"I like what you've done to your hair," he told her. "Why don't you come over here and let me brush it for you."

She smiled at that. Her mood changed instantly and she sauntered over, swinging her hips wide and slow, one side to the other. "Boom-chic-a-Boom," she said with each swing. She looked at him with alluring eyes, and a smile, sucking on her finger and then running it down her chest into her cleavage. She opened her blouse and let her breasts fall out.

Harry, still in his robe, could not hide his reaction to her performance.

She ran over and jumped on his lap, accidentally brushing his wounded leg with her foot.

He pulled back and winced in agony.

"Oh Harry," she said. "Did I hurt ya?"

"Ya, a little," he said pushing her off his lap, and rubbing his ankle. But she was undaunted in her desire, and she mounted his lap once again and moved in a slow circular pattern. "Let me make it feel better," she said in her best to please voice.

Harry held her by both shoulders and stopped her from moving, "Don't you understand? I've lost the moment."

She pulled back his robe still smiling and unsure if the playing was really over and checked for herself.

"I can fix that," she said and started rubbing him.

Harry stood up abruptly and let her fall onto the floor. "Cut it out, will you." He walked over to the fire, picked up the poker and started playing with the logs and hot embers, and pushed the arm that held the pot of beans to the other side.

CJ ran over and took the poker out of his hand. Then she pulled the pot back to where it was. "It'll burn over there." She looked hurt, and walked into the back room and slammed the bathroom door.

When she came back out, Harry stood by the front porch window. He looked over his shoulder at her and she tried to avoid his stare. "I'm bored Harry. Tell me a story."

"Fresh out of stories," he said. "Look at that snow, will ya?"

She came over to him with a new drink in her hand and held it out. He took it and sipped at it. "Were you ever married?" she asked.

"I told you before I was, three times. Two were for the wrong reasons."

"Did ya get a girl pregnant?"

"You'd like that wouldn't you?" He looked down at her standing next to him. He felt something just then, a disconnection, not necessarily from her, but from the moment. "No, the first time was in the Amazon. I was fifteen and with my father. We were visiting this tribe called the Yeshret. We helped them out a bit and they took a liking to us. They looked up to my father as if he was a god or something. They gave me a bride—the chief's daughter."

"Was she cute?"

Harry put his arm around her neck, and pulled her to him and kissed her passionately. "She looked like you, but only brown, and her tits were smaller. She wanted babies. It was expected of me to provide her with them. That night she nearly raped me. She couldn't take her eyes off me."

"Ya can't rape the willing Harry."

"She tried. It worked."

"What were you doing in the jungles?"

"My father owned an aircraft company and he was always looking for new and better parts. He wanted their secret for making a rubber substitute. It killed him."

She looked surprised, and frowned, "Ooo, how'd he die?"

"He had made a flying body suit: a wing suit. He thought it would work given the right amount of upward draft.

"Later, he put on his suit, which was white and black, and when he spread his arms, the chief laughed and said he looked like a flying squirrel. He gathered everyone around him on the precipitous ledge of this waterfall. He spread his arms and made a little speech, which I recorded on 8mm. His last words were, 'If I do this Harry, I'll be famous, which should suffice as I am already rich beyond belief. Now watch this.'

"He turned and leaped into the misty air and disappeared instantly into the loud waters below. The Indians cheered him on, inspired by his magnificent flying suit. I think they expected him to come soaring back up and into the trees. It was pathetic and I cried, knowing he was dead.

"Later, back home, the National Geographic Society honored him for discovering a new natural waterfall by naming it Alfred's Fall."

"Gee, I'm sorry, Harry. That kinda sucks. Did ya stay with them?"

"Only for a little while until the chief's three sons took me back to the big city two-hundred miles away San Carlos de Rio Negro, I think it was called."

"Do you miss her?"

"Never really thought about her much, you know. I thought about going back to visit once long ago, but I got busy with college and Italy." He drifted off, and walked over to the door and tried to open it, but it was stuck from the cold and snow piling up on the porch. Then he walked over to the bar and sat on a stool and she sat next to him.

"Bet you got a little Harry running around with his own kids now and all that. A whole tribe of Harrys."

"Then there was Sunny." He thought about that experience in '69 during the Woodstock concert. He would rather leave that one alone too, but CJ persisted.

"Sonny," she said, "I knew a guy named Sonny once. Twice't actually."

Harry smiled at her when she said that. He loved the way she talked, making up words, or her own versions of them. He knew it stemmed from a terrible lack of an education, but she was intelligent under her ignorance, and was pretty sure she knew it, too. "Well my Sunny was all girl, boy was she all girl, but sex didn't mean the same to her as it does to you. Do you understand?"

"There's not a whole lot I do understand when you talk," she said. "You mean she didn't charge."

Harry laughed a little at that. "All women charge for that, in one way or the other. No, she didn't charge, but she gave it out freely. We made love just an hour after we met, and later that day she was with someone else doing the same thing. At least, I'm pretty sure she was. But she came back to me and stayed until the end of the concert later that weekend."

"What did she look like? Was she tall? Or short like me?"

He held up his hand a few inches above CJ's head and said, "About here."

"I bet she had red hair."

"Blonde." He was looking towards the ceiling thinking about Sunny, like he was trying to remember her attributes.

"Well," CJ said, "Small titties, and huge ass?"

"Is that how you want her to be? Then that is just what she looked like, buck teeth and freckles."

"Good, that sounds just fine, go on."

"Go on? You mean there's more?"

"This is your story Harry," she giggled and shoved him, almost knocking him off his seat.

"Oh," he said rubbing his face. His beard was growing, and it began to itch. "Later we headed off to the dark trees to make love while hundreds of people sat around the bon fire casting great shadows onto the trees that surrounded the grove. Some were dancing to the music coming from the stage.

"Where did she go?" CJ asked.

"The Dead played, 'Dark Star,'" Harry said without answering her question, "and no one moved, even the bonfire seemed to quiet down and listen. After a while it flared back to life as if someone had thrown more logs onto it, but no one did. The fire fed vicariously on the music just as the people."

Harry expected CJ to be bored, but when he looked over at her, she had a gleam in her eyes. "He was wrong in one sense," he said to her green eyes, "the things we do last for more than just the moment, even throughout history, and the future, beyond the machines, and the technology that records everything we do. People will remember as long as there are people. We will remember. Let's have some more whiskey."

"There you go again Harry. I don't understand what you are sayin'. How's your leg? Maybe you shouldn't. It says in that book that alcohol is bad for infections."

"To hell with the infection."

"What ever happened to the girl, huh Harry?"

"I spent a month in hell in some commune in Vermont."

The trees that surrounded the snowbound cottage opened out onto fields, and meadows that in the spring give birth to thousands of varieties of flowers. Snowcapped mountains with bare and jagged crests rose up in the near distance like walls of a giant keep. The world glowed under the red sunlight as it cast long gray shadows on the wet snow, and soon everything was half in light, and half in dark, and then all dark. Like a silent sentinel the darkness watched against intruders, but who could reach them there?

It promised to be warmer. The tiny rivers formed by melting snow the previous day had frozen overnight, but soon began to carry the melting snow downhill again. Harry slept on the large leather chair, and opened his eyes as the light hit him. He followed the beams that were visible in the dusty air of the cabin as they shone on the wolf. In the bright light, the dust particles looked like swarming black flies, and the wolf looked alive in the dancing dust. Its eyes gleamed.

Harry had a presentiment of death awaiting him, if not from his wound, which did not hurt anymore, then from something. He knew Conner—if he were still alive —would try to find them, but that Skinny would be the first to arrive.

Suddenly, as if still dreaming he heard the howling of a lone wolf outside the cabin – he looked over at the stuffed wolf. Then the howl was answered by another, and then another. They were loud.

CJ had been up for a while, and made coffee, and a small breakfast. She had found some kind of sausage in the freezer, cooked them up with powdered eggs, and fried withered potatoes. Then she tried to open the front door, but the screen was blocked. It was packed tightly with snow and it took some doing to open. She had found a shovel in the storage room, and used that to plow a path toward the steps so the sun might melt what remained. When she heard the wolves howl, she ran back into the house, and slammed the door.

"Did you goddamn hear that?"

"They're drawn by death," he said. "They can smell it."

"No they can't," she said.

"They aren't here for the beans."

"They can smell the meat cooking." She looked frantic, and ran over to the fireplace for the shotgun breaking it open to make sure it was loaded.

"Stop," he said, but she had thrown open the door, stuck the barrel out, and fired. It fell from her hands. Harry got up quickly, lunged for the rifle, and held it close to his side. He opened the barrel to check on the shots. Both barrels were empty. "They're gone now."

"What happened to the hippie girl?"

"Don't you let anything go? Sunny? I married her of course."

"How long?"

"Oh that didn't really count though. After the concert, she went back to Vermont with the people she came with and moved back into their little commune. I tagged along for the time being, not wanting it to end. That is when I married her. The clan leader performed the marriage

"They shared everything, even each other. I didn't like it much, besides I had obligations in college. Sunny soon found other distractions besides me. She could hardly keep her mind on one thing for more than a day. I walked away, and that annulled it."

"It did? Are you sure Harry?"

"As far as I was concerned, it did."

CJ looked away. She had never told Harry or anyone about her past, about her father and mother, or about her sister. Skinny knew. He had seen her story a hundred times before. He used to listen to them go on about their lives until it did not matter anymore, and now he just tuned it out.

"Did I say something wrong?"

She shook her head, "No."

"It something about marriage," he paused waiting for a response, but there was none. "Give me something here."

"I was twelve," she said. "It ain't nothin' so great anyhow." She walked away into the corner of the kitchen, and fussed with the coffee she was making. Then she sat down and looked him in the eyes, and after a long pause said, "You really want to know, don't ya?"

Things That Go Bump

Later that night they slept as before, Conner took the floor and Jackie on the couch. But this time, Conner laid out cushions and tried to balance on them as he slept. He gave up, and rolled over onto the hard dusty carpet. His watch said 2:00. The dark made sounds louder than they would be otherwise. He heard a little scratching, which he took for mice chewing at the walls. They scuffled and squirmed inside the wall. They sounded very busy. He could hear them better if he laid his ear on the floor. Then they stopped. Outside he could hear a bird call. *Probably an owl,* he thought.

"Can you hear the owl?" Jackie asked.

Conner did not expect her to be awake. "Yes how long have you been awake?"

"Just now, I can't sleep." Then he could hear movement outside in the hallway. Someone was walking toward them. Whoever it was stopped and retreated. Now the footsteps returned quickly, trying to be quiet. They were tiptoeing.

"Shh."

The person stopped outside the door. Conner had acute hearing. He could hear the person breath. It was a female by the sound of it. The dim light of the peephole disappeared, replaced by a shadow, the click of the deadbolt. Conner's heart raced. He sat up and so did Jackie. The light from the hall returned. They waited for someone to enter the room but no one did. They heard no sound of footsteps.

Conner went to the door and peered through the peephole, but could see no movement. He went to the chair, and sat down to dress, but remembered he had nothing to wear.

"Shit."

"What?"

"Get dressed, we're leaving."

"But you don't have any clothes."

"I'll find some." Putting on the robe, he took her by the hand, walked to the door, and slowly opened it. No one was in the hall. He looked left, and did not like that way; there was a dim light at that end of the hall from around a corner. He stood still, and considered which way to go and Jackie without hesitation headed toward the dim light. He grabbed her by the arm and gently pulled her the other way. He looked her in the eyes, shook his head with a frown, and then tossed his head in the other direction.

They walked lightly down the hall into the darkness. He could see light slipping out into the hall from a door at the end. He paused to listen. There was no peephole, but there was a keyhole. He slowly bent down and had a look. The light remained unchanged, and the room appeared to be empty, but suddenly the door opened. A hand reached out, taking hold of Conner's shoulder and pulling him in.

Jackie quickly followed.

Sara quickly closed the door and turned to display a man, who was tied and gagged on the floor behind her. It was Ronny, Skinny's bodyguard. He was dark. He had a large curved nose and his hair tied in a ponytail. He looked to Conner to be a Native American. His ears stuck out and one of them was bulbous and deformed, the signs of a long time wrestler.

Sara kicked his head, and he fell to the floor and moved no more. She threw Conner some clothing. It was his. "Here get dressed. You can thank me later."

"He looks tough," said Conner, "how did you subdue him?" He dressed quickly. Sara clicked her tongue and waved her hips.

Jackie giggled.

It took him a moment to figure it out and said, "Touché." He looked around the room searching behind the other door. It was a toilet. "We have to get the hell out of here fast," he said.

"I'll help you as much as I can."

"But why?" said Jackie. "Why would you want to do that?"

"He's going to have you killed in the morning. You're in the way."

"What the hell did we do anyway?"

"You both stumbled onto something, Jackie," Sara said. "You, and your friend obviously came along too soon, and now he means to finish the job. When he came back, I overheard him talking to Shithead here about how he went looking for you, and everything started going wrong."

"Paula," said Jackie.

"Yeah, 'Collateral damage,' he called it, and it seems that your friend," she turned to Conner, "Harry, killed his favorite man, Mouse. He's pissed."

"Way to go, Harry. I hope he is alive out there. It snowed pretty hard. If they get caught in it, it could be dangerous. Although, Harry's been in tough spots before."

"Skinny isn't taking any chances. He came back here to regroup and wait for the storm to pass. He was going to take this turd along to finish them off."

Conner was confused. "All this for CJ? She must be really good at what she does."

"She's a small part, but it goes on deeper."

Jackie had been quiet until now. "So, what's in it for you? Why stick your neck out?"

Sara did not answer. She seemed preoccupied. "We have to get you out now." She moved toward the door, opened it, and stuck her head outside into the hall. She must have been out there for a full minute, before she came back inside. "Follow me." She opened the door and slipped out as if she had been doing this sort of thing for a long time. Conner pulled her back in and said, "Answer the question."

She looked at them both, and then at the man on the floor. "I'm not a whore," she said, then turned and walked out the door.

They Smell Death

As night fell on the cabin, CJ told Harry about the abuse she endured in her past. She told him about her short life, about how it was she ended up with Skinny. CJ never made the connection between the abuse and her chosen profession. To her, there was no emotional tie between the lecherous father and prostitution. Being a whore was something she found she could do well.

Harry had been with loose women before and enjoyed their company. Never had he considered their past, or the hell they lived through that made them do what they did. Now, listening to her, he understood that it wasn't their choice really—the profession chooses the girl. He took her in his arms, and held her for a long time.

"Harry."

He said nothing.

"Harry? You okay?"

He felt a surge of emotion, something more than passion. He tried to put a name to it. Empathy? Maybe. Or, it could have just been a sincere concern for the girl's wellbeing. It was a warm feeling, more like anxiety. His heart fluttered in his chest

The wolves resumed their residence around the house. They were howling to one another, and on one occasion sounded as though they were at the front door. There was no moon, so he found a flashlight and opened the door to have a look. He spotted a pair of eyes some twenty feet from the door. They reflected back unblinking, and looked like luminescent globes of mother of pearl, cold, and frightened.

But they held behind them the power of the Teton Mountains.

He turned leaving the cold outside, and stood with his back to the closed door. CJ stood before him holding a cup of coffee, which she rarely drank.

"There is a culture," he said, "that believes that, in the beginning of the world, wolves were gods from the heavens sent by the Great Wolf to Earth to carry messages to the creatures that shared their world. And people, who were primitive and ignorant, learned much from the wolves. They prayed and gave homage to wolves for their beauty, and power, their grace, and stealth, everything they worshiped in themselves."

"Where?"

"Here," he opened his arms as if to offer the cabin they were standing in as the answer to her question.

"Here?" she said demonstratively. "Right here where we are standing?"

"Here in these mountains. The Grand ol' Tetons. Thousands of years ago before any recorded history took place in Greece, in Samaria even. Before time was counted."

"Go on then, 'bout the wolves."

"And the wolves believed the people when they said, 'we love you, we will worship you,' and they allowed themselves to be worshiped. The people made friends with the wolves, and took them into their homes, and nurtured them, cared for them, protected them. But after many years of this, the people grew jealous of the untamed wolf. Those that they did not domesticate, they hunted and they used their hides for clothing and shelter. Many years the wolves endured this from the people, until one day, the Great Wolf called them back to the stars."

"But they are still here, they never left."

"They still came to earth, but avoided the people they once loved. Their messages now told of a creature that went about on two legs and ate voraciously. They warned that this creature would soon devour everything in its path leaving only darkness. That it would even consume the heavens that were the stars.

"And so the wolves have withdrawn into their own world, and when they brood, they howl to lament the prophecy they themselves have foretold."

CJ looked at Harry seemingly mesmerized by his story and said, "Get out."

"No, it's true."

"Who are these people?"

"They are long gone now overcome by time. Now, those that remain live in small reservations, or villages in the mountains of the Canadian Rockies. They drink, and fish, and make bobbles for tourists."

"Y'all are creepin' me out Harry. Shut up, will ya?"

The stuffed wolf that Harry had made friends with stood unmoved, staring back at him. "He understands," said Harry.

They both looked now at the stuffed creature with its large teeth framing a prosthetic tongue that stuck out just a little bit through a slightly opened mouth. It was panting and fully alert with ears facing front and head held high. Its bright yellow eyes nearly halved by large black slits – curtains veiling a fiery soul.

Inside the Wall

Sara led them down the hall and through a maze of short hallways. They came to a tunnel so low that they all had to bend over to enter. It looked like an old brick bread oven like the kind you would find in an adobe home. It was a long archway that was lit only at the entrance. They ducked down and walked along a dirt floor with damp spidery walls of crumbling brick. When they reached the end, they had entered a long dark room that looked older than the house itself.

Sara stood up and lit a lantern. The walls were thick, heavy logs, and the floor was polished mahogany. It smelled of cedar.

"Where are we?" Jackie asked.

"This is an old wine cellar. During the Civil War, it was an underground railroad for a short period. Skinny uses it to store his valuables. We don't have much time before he returns."

Jackie walked up and down the dark room touching the walls looking for a door. "Where does that smell come from?"

Sara pointed up at the walls. "Cedar. It protects the wine, papers, and valuables.

"He runs his whore house out of here?" Conner asked.

"That's just a front," said Sara.

"Okay," Jackie said. "Explain to us what you said back there. If you are not a prostitute, then just what is going on here? Who the hell are you?"

"And why are you helping us?"

"Doesn't it seem odd that someone would kill all these people for a runaway whore?"

"Just how many has he killed?"

"Besides Jackie's friend: three others, all just innocent bystanders. Wrong place at the wrong time."

"Who the hell are you," said Conner.

"Listen," said Sara, "we don't have much time."

"I'm not going anywhere until you spill it. Who are you, and why are you helping us?" He and Jackie were pawns in some sick deadly game with real consequences, and no one knew the outcome.

"I've been working undercover as one of his girls for a year now." She was moving about the room while talking to them and moving small pieces of furniture around. "I work for the Bureau of Audits and Reclamation." She looked at their faces. They needed some explanation. "We originated in the Second World War. You see, after the war there was a huge displacement of property, art mostly, and money and even real estate that our government wanted to recover before it fell into the wrong hands."

"But that was thirty years ago," Conner said, "and you're still looking?"

"That figures," said Jackie.

"Look, there isn't time for that now. I am getting you out of here before he kills more, and I am coming with you. My cover is blown."

"Okay. So what does Skinny do, actually?"

She reached behind a cabinet and pulled out a small envelope. "It's in here. Help me put this back." And they helped her move the furniture back into place. When they finished, Sara walked down to the other end of the room and began to feel the wall rubbing both hands over it. "Here it is." The wall slid open on an axis breaking at natural and unseen seams.

She turned to the others. "We've been on to him for several years. It started when he moved from Reno to here but the more we learned the more we realized he was bigger than a pimp. That is when I got involved. This is all a front, a lucrative one at that, but a front nonetheless." She put out her hand in which she held the envelope. Skinny has been smuggling for years, and I have enough here to put him behind bars for good.

"Years ago in South America, in Brazil and Chile, he began smuggling jewels, people, gold, guns, whatever he could get his hands on, whatever made him money. But mostly it was valuable artifacts. I'm not sure, but I think that Harry and CJ are carrying a large stash of these jewels. At least CJ is. And that's why he's on rampage."

Suddenly, they heard noises down through the tunnel that led back to the hallway. Voices screaming.

"Trapped," Conner said. Jackie shrank away from the tunnel and hid close behind Conner.

"This way," Sara said as she picked up a lantern and slid through the opened wall.

The Jewels

Harry was as bored as she was and kept fussing around the fireplace and opening his backpack and rummaging through it.

"What are you doing?" CJ asked, annoyed.

"I'm just looking for more shells for the rifle."

"They got plenty in the other room to go with that rifle over there."

He walked away from the fire and into the back to the bathroom.

CJ rushed over to the fireplace, took a small black satchel out of her backpack, and hid it behind the otter on the fireplace mantel, hoping Harry wouldn't see it. And then she stepped outside to look around and check on the weather. The trees blocked out the sun, but it was certain that the blue sky had turned red. To her right, the ground sloped down and then rose steeply in the same direction.

The cabin actually sat on the side of the mountain. The snow-covered road leading to the cabin was part of the terrain as it dropped off steeply toward the north. To the south, she saw the mountains veiled in falling snow. A plane traveled out of the southern storm toward her. She turned and went back into the cabin.

Harry walked over to the fireplace and set his drink on the mantel.

CJ watched him intently. As he drew near the backpacks, she went quickly to stop him but he was reaching for the shillelagh. She stopped suddenly and sighed. Still he would not move from that spot.

He turned to see her and asked her what she wanted. "You look like the sword of Damocles is hanging over you."

She looked up, and he chuckled. "I mean you look nervous, as if you expect something to happen."

She turned away, stumbling for words to say. "No, no. I'm okay. Well, it's just that it stopped snowing, and the weather is clearing up and all. You look a little better, ya feel it?"

Harry looked down at his leg as if he had to see it to talk about it. He lifted his knee, and dangled his leg back and forth a little. "Yeah, seems to be getting better. You sure are a good nurse." He put his foot back down and pretended to fall. "You're worried about Skinny finding us, is that it?

"Oh no, no."

But Harry stayed where he was this time and stood very close to the otter. He put his drink down, and it moved.

CJ could not help hide her tension. She knew he suspected something. She moved her hands as if she was trying to move him away, like a puppeteer.

He turned around and nudged the otter again with his elbow.

She jerked again.

"You're hiding something here."

"No, why don't you come over here and sit with me." She threw open her blue-velvet robe to entice him.

He turned around, lifted the Otter, and saw the leather bag.

"What is this? Look CJ. Look at what I just found."

She tried to take it, but it was useless.

Harry tossed it up in the air and caught it.

"Sounds jingly."

She protested, but he ignored her, holding her off as he made his way for the bar. He opened the bag and spilled its contents. Out came dozens of precious stones—some tiny and some large—all very expensive. He sifted the stones on the counter, examining them briefly. He noticed one of the stones carved in the shape of an Inca god.

"What the hell is this CJ?" His face turned crimson, and he held some of the gems in his hand and looked at her.

"These are worth a fortune. Where did you get these?"

CJ stumbled on her words, not sure what to say.

"Come on CJ, I'm on your side. Did you steal these from Skinny?"

She nodded her head unable to say anything.

Harry looked long at the stones.

"The last time I saw anything like this was in Chile. I mean I never thought I would see their likes again."

"Yeah," she said. "They're his. He won't miss them. He's got plenty."

"Are you kidding? This is worth a fortune. These gold coins alone could buy and sell a small country." He examined them more closely. "I recognize these stones. These belong to me, to my expedition. To Nancy." He put them back in the bag, and put the bag back where he found it.

She went for it, but he stopped her. "They'll be fine there," he said keeping her away from the stones.

Harry told CJ about how he and the others found them in Chile and how he was certain that these were the same stones.

"Dago died while we searched for the tomb where these came from. Some sort of fever. Have you heard of Montezuma's revenge? No?

"In Mexico, when you visit, and drink the water, most everyone gets diarrhea. Montezuma was the King of Mexico City when the Spanish came and destroyed their civilization for the gold and gems they possessed. So legend has it he takes revenge through diarrhea."

She stared blankly at him as if he was speaking Greek to her.

"Never mind. These gems cost the life of Dago and my wife, Nancy. Do you want to tell me what's going on?"

The Precipice

Conner and Jackie followed Sara closely as she led them through the ancient walls that wove through the outer building. Finally, she took them to the back of a structure that was historically a barn for horses, then later converted into a garage for cars, and even used for a while as a distillery. It sat empty now, unused and derelict.

"This is where the slaves from the old railroad would be led through the woods to a waiting wagon, and to freedom, if they made it this far west."

The wind was bitter, and the snow fell nearly parallel to the ground. They ran through a thickly wooded area and made quickly for the parking lot in the back of the hotel where the employees kept their cars.

"Skinny's car isn't here," said Sara. She opened the doors of her Ford Pinto, and they got in.

"This is all the FBI gives you?" asked Jackie.

"B-A-R," she sounded each letter. "I had to look the part of a poor prostitute."

As she started the car and threw it into gear, she looked at Jackie sitting next to her and Conner at the door.

"Stay low," she said, "just in case we're spotted. They'll think I'm just heading out somewhere. But if they see either of you, we're screwed."

Then she drove slowly away from the hotel. The sound of the gravel beneath the tires seemed to resound in the open lot at night. The sun would rise in a half hour, and there was barely enough light to navigate away from the hotel without using her headlights.

"So, who was that in the hallway? Maybe they aren't onto us just yet."

"You could be right, but that Shithead is a pretty resourceful fellow. He just looks stupid. He could have freed himself and come after us, if he knew where we went."

"He could figure it out."

"Not necessarily. I'm not sure anyone here knows about the secret passage, not even Skinny."

"But you do?"

"Well yeah, but that's because I got the floor plans from the archives back in DC. This house is a historic site because it once housed the governor of Wyoming. All of the records for it went to Washington after he lived here. I thought it would be helpful to know everything about the place."

"How thorough," said Jackie.

She drove her rust colored Pinto skillfully through the lane to the main road. Once out of the hotel property altogether, she turned on the headlights and navigated the curvy mountain roads, taking the exact turns that Conner and Harry took when they left the first time with CJ in the Bug.

Conner looked in the back of the hatchback and saw sleeping bags, hiking boots, and somewhere under it all, he thought he saw the butt of a rifle.

"Where are we going? Turn here."

Sara drove in the other direction, heading away from where Conner and Harry had gone.

"If we are going to catch up with Harry we have to follow him," Conner said

"We need help. I have a chance to close in on the whole operation. There is a ranger station up the road here a ways, and we need them. I'll call the office when I get there, and they can advise us."

The sun crept over the horizon, but barely enough to make it through the trees. In the occasional breaks, there was a view of the distant landscape: a hill, a valley, the sun's red light shining along the surface of the world.

"Well I know what to do."

"We need their help Conner," said Jackie. "Daddy can help." She told them both that her father was a police officer in a town about 40 miles away.

They drove on. The road tightened up as it wound through the trees. A car came toward them from the opposite direction, its headlights still on, driving slowly. It was a large Chrysler Brougham complete with Skinny in the driver seat. He was alone. They could do little to hide their faces and he passed them before they could react.

"Did he see us?" said Conner. Sara was looking in the rearview mirror for some sort of reaction from Skinny.

"No I don't think he saw us. At least he didn't stop the car."

Jackie was looking out the back window the whole time.

They all began to breathe again when the car Skinny drove disappeared over the rise and into the forest. They placed their attention on the ranger station.

"How much more is it to the station?" asked Jackie.

"It's been a while since I've seen it, but I think it should be another ten miles or so."

At that moment, the Pinto lurched forward with a sudden jolt. They turned to see Skinny smiling as he forced his car forward crashing again into them. He laid on the horn.

"He's saying something to us," said Jackie looking back. She was hysterical, breathing heavily as she gripped the dashboard in front of her.

Conner turned to see. "I think he wants us to pull over." He flipped the middle finger.

The car pulled closer quickly.

"Step on it," he yelled. And they took off.

Skinny swerved in the wet road.

They rounded a corner, and for a few seconds it looked as though they lost him. But he reappeared, roaring toward the helpless trio, and without regard for oncoming traffic he pulled next to them as the road straightened out.

"Here he comes," said Conner. Then he pushed Jackie's head down and braced for impact. The huge car headed straight for them.

There was nothing she could do but drive as fast as she could, but Skinny's car came on and made contact with their car. Their bumpers had conjoined, and now the two cars moved as one.

Sara screamed, unable to steer her own car.

Conner was about to yell a warning when he looked back at Skinny and saw the angry pimp smiling and laughing as he drove them to the edge of the road.

Jackie was turning white with fright.

Sara tried desperately to regain control of the car, applying the brakes and turning the wheel wildly, but there was nothing she could do to control it anymore.

The cars approached a sharp turn in the road, and Skinny slammed on his breaks separating the two cars and sending the Pinto—with Conner, Sara, and Jackie in it—over the precipice. It slid and hurdled down the steep embankment crashing through tall grass and small saplings, bouncing off one young tree and finally hitting a ditch, which sent the car end over end, and at last coming to rest in the midst of a grove of aspen.

He is Coming

Had the wolves moved on? It was only three hours since he had last heard their bone chilling wails. The wind still talked to the house, despite having no snow to deliver. Its chilling fingers that blew constantly from the tops of the world seemed to play the log structure like an accordion. The fire danced to the tunes. The wolves came back

CJ's temper had soured, and she complained about anything Harry did. She stared at him from across the room; where she sat near the fireplace, not so much for warmth, but to keep an eye on the bag of gems that she stole from Skinny's lair. She looked almost comical, slouched in the leather chair, and barely able to keep her eyes from receding into slits— red and puffy.

"Make them stop Harry," she said, barely moving her mouth. Her chin was resting on her chest so deeply it looked like she was staring at her feet. She had since dressed into something more than a bathrobe, having given up on the lovemaking for the time being.

Harry did not respond.

The wolves howled altogether. Very close. Some were on the porch.

Suddenly they began to scuffle. A fight had broken out on the porch right in front of the door. He had read Jack London's *Call of the Wild* as a child, and remembered how they fought with one another to establish the Alpha. Those were team dogs, barely more domestic than this bunch, but still they answered to their master. These would eat him alive in a second if he had gone out to stop them or chase them away.

From the fireplace, it sounded to Harry like the wind had ripped a hole in the wall and blew in a violent whistling gust, but it was CJ. She screamed and pranced around the room, stomping her feet. She looked like a mother goose chasing off a predator, puffing herself up, and spreading her wings to appear more formidable. She headed for the shotgun that was leaning up against the front door.

Harry jumped out of his chair and headed her off. They struggled a bit with it, but Harry managed to take the weapon form her half-hearted hands.

"Goddamn-it all to hell," she said, walking over to the bar, as far away from the noise as possible. She leaned against it, breathing heavily. Her face was red, and her eyes stuck out of their sockets, veins bulging. He let her get it out of her system. "Why the fuck don't they go away?"

Harry let the rotting flesh angle go, no point in giving her any more ideas to stoke her imagination. He was just as batty as she was, but this outburst gave some relief to his moribund feeling of uselessness.

"They'll go soon. They can't open the doors, after all."

"Shoot the bastards." She pushed him away not wanting the contact. "Shoot them and that'll get rid of them."

Harry looked over at the shotgun leaning against the front door. He went over to the window at the far side of the front porch, slid it open, and stuck the barrel outside.

They sounded close.

He could smell their wet hair and hear their teeth clamping shut. Then he pulled the one chamber.

The fighting stopped, and they all scuffled away whining.

He shot again for good measure. He reloaded the gun throwing the empty shells into the fire and placed it back where it has sat the whole time there. He walked to the bar and found a new bottle of whiskey and poured himself another drink, but left it sitting on the bar, and went to sit down on his favorite chair next to his old pal the wolf.

CJ ran over to Harry, and threw her arms around his chest. They stood like that for a while until Harry felt overcome with fatigue.

"You look like shit Harry," she said, pouting, looking coy, a look that usually aroused in him a feeling of comfort, like a puppy would. He smiled back. He actually felt better, so he began to think of what they should do next. They were in danger as long as they remained at the cabin. There was no way they could return the way they came, and the road would be too dangerous as that would most likely be how Skinny would approach the cabin. He felt almost certain that Conner would not be the first to arrive. He realized they had to do something besides just sit there. Their situation wouldn't improve on its own. He shouted.

"We're sitting ducks here," he said it so suddenly that CJ jumped, spilling her drink. "We should pack and get ready to move." When CJ did not stir, he began gathering things he thought they would need. The first of which was the rifle and the 9mm Glock.

"How long do you think it will take Skinny to get here, figuring he already knows we're here?"

"Well, after the snow stops, if the roads are clear, it should take him about a couple-a... four, or five hours."

"That is if the roads are clear, and I'm thinking they aren't a priority around here so we should be okay for a couple of days." Harry relaxed a bit, but still wanted to pack though perhaps with less intensity.

He took a hot shower and changed while CJ packed the bags, which was something she did better than he did. In one of the bedrooms, he found ample clothing his size and picked the newest and warmest he could find.

While rifling through the closet he found several sets of snowshoes resting against the back wall. Thinking they might come in handy, he placed them by the window, which looked out of the back of the cabin. He opened the window and leaned out to look around. Finally, he closed the window, but didn't lock it.

From the door to the bedroom, he could look out into the main room and just see the wolf sitting between the two leather chairs. He assumed Skinny would approach the cabin from the front, and that CJ and he would make their escape out the back. The house, although well built, had no back door, so he slid the window open and lowered the snowshoes. He leaned them against the back of the building. Then he went out into the main room to see after CJ.

"There's gotta be about four feet of snow on the ground out there," said CJ as she glanced out the window.

She looked worried and Harry noticed. He looked over at the mantle, and saw that she moved the otter, but he said nothing.

"You should shower now CJ," he suggested. But when she looked at him wringing her hands together, he said that he could be trusted if anyone could. "I won't touch them I promise."

"Come with me," she said.

Harry had just showered, and couldn't see the point of tiring himself out, and declined the invitation.

Harry woke to see her standing over him with the shillelagh in her hand. He went to say something, but his mouth had crusted shut. He was thirsty, and rubbed the back of his hand across his mouth to dislodge the glue and free his jaw. He licked his lips and took a drink of water from the glass next to him.

He suddenly didn't feel too well. The thought of dealing with Skinny, and whoever came with him, upset him even more and caused him to relapse just a bit.

"Are you planning on hitting me with that? No? Then how 'bout another glass of water?"

"I heard something outside," she said softly. She was in her blue-velvet robe and slippers.

"What, more wolves?"

"I heard an engine of some sort down the way. They're coming."

Skinny Finds a Way

Skinny sat in the big house pleased at least that he did not have to do anymore killing – for now. Shithead told him about what had happened.

"I thought it was her in that car." He walked around the room touching the cedar walls and smelling his hand afterward. "That bitch must have known something, but why her? Who is she anyway?"

Shithead thought he was asking him a question and said, "Um, I don't know."

"That was a rhetorical question, asshole."

"Are we gonna get them? The snow stopped and it should be clear, at least the roads will be before long."

"Yeah, we're going to get them."

Shithead looked at his boss pacing the floor from wall to wall. "Where are they?"

"They're at the cabin, I'm sure of it. She loves that place and it isn't too far from where they killed Mouse."

That's a fair hike through those hills. Does she even know how to get there?"

Skinny pounded on the cedar wall and swore, "Bitch." Then he turned to look at Shithead as if he suddenly realized he was there with him. "Yeah, she knows. Leastways she should. She's spent enough time with them."

"Are we gonna hike it, too?"

Skinny rubbed his hand across his face feeling his beard growing in, he twirled his mustache away from his lip. "I gotta shave."

He walked towards the exit to the room and told Shithead to get ready and warm up the truck. "Bring the Winchester and a shotgun. Oh, and load up the snowmobile in the back. We're taking the road up and it might be blocked from the highway."

He left Shithead standing alone.

Waiting

"Then I think my 30/06 would do better than that stick." Harry sat up. His leg was numb, but sore to the touch. He got out of bed, and they both dressed. He wanted to be sure they dressed well, thinking they would be outside for quite a while. But he really did not want to run – not again. He would kill the bastard if things got to it, although his first experience at killing did not please him too much.

"Shit," he said, and said it about four more times. "Why the hell does it have to come down to this?"

Harry ran to the front door and looked out. It was late night, almost ready for a new day. He smelled ozone in the air, and sensed more snow on the way. He heard nothing, and ran back to the bedroom.

CJ was closing up the backpacks complete with bags, and tent.

"Are you sure you heard motors?"

"Yes,"

"Were they close?"

"How am I supposed to know," she said, and thought a little, and said, "They did seem muffled. You know, like they were off a bit."

"Ah, it's just the snow. They probably want to sneak up and surprise us. I don't think he knows he hit me with that scattergun. But I'm all right now. I feel good. We should sneak out the back window with the shoes, and make for the ridge over east. We can keep an eye on the house. He'll think we are still here if there aren't any footprints out front. And then we can pick them off. I'm tired of running

He opened the window, and looked out. It was darkening.

"Nothing." He tossed the bags out one at a time.

222

"What about the wolves?" she said.

"The sound of the engine will scare them off, don't worry."

"You know how to use them things?"

"What, the snowshoes? A little bit."

Harry had worked in cold climates before and even had to hike across the Alps. Snowshoes came in handy during heavy snow. He went out first, walked to both corners of the house to look for movement, and then came back to get her.

CJ slipped out, and jumped to the ground.

"I haven't had to do that in a while," she said.

Harry helped her fit the shoes to her feet, and then he put his on.

He and CJ ran toward the east and the deep ravine hidden from the house. They would wait there and watch, unnoticed, from the safety of the ridge.

They rushed along trying to get to a point where they could see the front door of the cottage, and as it came into view, he thought he could see movement. Harry stopped and threw himself and CJ to the ground.

She fell face first into the snow, and came up sputtering.

"Look, did you see that?"

"No," she said a bit annoyed. "I couldn't see anything cause of the snow in my face."

"I think I saw someone go into the cabin. I think it was Skinny and someone else."

"Shithead," said CJ. "His other bodyguard."

What he saw were two men in winter clothing, one in a ski suit with a Russian sable hat followed by a shorter man with a down suit, and ski cap. Both appeared to have rifles strapped to their backs.

It began snowing. The large heavy flakes came down very thick making it difficult to see too far.

Harry took his pack and rifle off his back and set the pack aside. He checked his rifle and made sure that the safety was off and that it had ammunition. He cocked it and a shell appeared. It only held five bullets, so he checked his pack for more, but couldn't find any. He didn't expect an all-out gunfight, but it would be nice to know he had more.

He kept his eyes on the house, waiting. It seemed like a lifetime.

He noticed the chimney was spewing heavier smoke, the lights were on and the windows were steamy.

All of a sudden, the front door opened. He half expected the fat mother in an apron to come out as he had seen before, but it was Shithead. He came out and looked around with a rifle in his hand. He stood for a good five minutes without moving an inch. He was waiting, listening for something. Then he walked around the building.

He must have seen the tracks, because he came running from around the back and into the house. The door closed; he was inside.

"They've found us out," he said to CJ as he turned for the first time to see her, but she was gone. Her pack was still there, but she was not.

CJ sat next to Harry nervously looking towards the house. She was not sure how things would turn out. She knew that Skinny always came out on top, and her confidence in Harry waned.

What was I thinking, she thought. *I owe Skinny a lot.* And she looked over at Harry who kept his eyes on the cabin. He was checking his rifle, cocking it to bring a bullet into the chamber.

Harry had been good to her and treated her as if she mattered. Assuming that they could get away from Skinny, what then? What chance did they have of making a clean get away? Skinny would eventually catch up to them, not for her but for the gems. Greedy bastard. And if they killed him and Shithead, would Harry turn in the gems? Would he turn her in?

She couldn't take prison. Jail was bad enough. Those fat lesbians in Reno's jail were too much. It seemed to her that for her whole life she had been the object of someone's sexual desire. After a while, it wasn't rape. She felt like a punching bag. And Harry was the only one who could take her away from that. But she was sure he would dump her after it was over. Without the gems, her life would be shit once again.

CJ needed to put an end to the tyranny she had lived under for all these years. She did not want Harry to get hurt. Her resentment for Skinny grew, and she no longer felt drawn to that abusive relationship. She wanted to see his balls in the palm of her hand, and him holding on to his crotch pleading with her to stop. She wanted to hear him beg for mercy, for forgiveness, and then she'd put out his lights for the last time. Let them put her in prison. At least she'd be free of him; she'd be free. Then she could bury her past and start anew. Maybe Harry would wait for her, and they could spend the rest of their lives together traveling to exotic places, and dig up bones together.

Slowly, she dug the gems out of her bag and put them inside his. Then, while he was looking at the cabin, she sneaked back. She was going to kill the sonofabitch.

As she headed back to the rear window, she heard them yelling to one another.

"I know you're out there," CJ, she heard him say. And she jumped up to the windowsill and pulled herself inside.

Harry ran back after her footprints and saw her heading for the back of the house. She crouched by the escape window and waited.

He could now just barely see the front of the house.

She was taking off her snowshoes. She looked back at him, waved, and motioned that she was going to go back inside.

Harry motioned wildly with his arms that she should come back.

"That's a really bad idea."

He was going to go back and somehow make a diversion for her sake to distract Skinny.

But that was not necessary. Skinny had come out on the front of the porch, and yelled.

Harry hurried back to his original position, and waited. He aimed the 30/06 at his target.

"I know you're out there," Skinny said. "CJ, honey, why don't you two come on back in and we can talk. Huh? I don't want to hurt no one." He checked his gun and cocked it. He had a long-range scope.

Harry yelled back, "You took a shot at me. That doesn't make me very confident in you."

Before Skinny could reply, he turned his attention inside the cabin.

Harry could hear CJ screaming from inside and shortly she appeared with Skinny behind her holding onto her arm.

"I can't believe you went through all this trouble for one of your girls," said Harry. He paused for a response. Skinny was not playing it Harry's way.

"You've got her now, what more do you want?" He knew what it was Skinny wanted, but he wanted to hear it from him.

Skinny put the tip of the barrel in CJ's face. "I don't like playing games, asshole. Why don't you just come on in and give me the stones."

"What makes you think I have them? Let her go, and we'll talk."

He had her, so he must have the jewels too. Harry couldn't figure it out. Then he saw Shithead crossing the back of the cabin trying to sneak up on him. Harry fired a shot at Shithead and nearly hit him.

Shithead stopped, and sat behind a tree.

"You just stay right there Shithead."

He searched his bag, thinking that he might find the gems, just in case. There, on the top of the bag was the bag of goods. They jingled like before. He put them and some rope in his pocket.

"I'm a pretty good shot with this thing," said Harry. He got up and moved about thirty feet toward

Shithead. He knew that Skinny was probably very good, too, and crazy enough to kill CJ.

Skinny and Shithead were skilled hunters and killers, but Harry was well prepared to hide in the snow for any length of time, and he still had the snowshoes. He continued moving toward the bodyguard, who was moving again to where he thought Harry was.

Harry waited hiding behind a laurel bush until Shithead stepped in front of him. "Don't move pal or this time I won't miss."

Shithead stopped in his tracks and dropped his pistol.

He pressed the barrel of his rifle into Shithead's cheek. Harry took the rope, handed it to the bodyguard, and instructed him to tie one end tightly to his wrist. Then he pushed him to the ground face down, kneeled on Shithead, and pulled his hands behind his back and tied them together.

Get the Girl

Harry turned the bodyguard around and got a good look at him.

Shithead stared blankly back.

"You gonna be in big trouble som-a-bitch," he said.

"You?" Harry was shocked. This is the same man who robbed Nancy and him at gunpoint in Iquique. The pain in Harry's head returned. He felt like returning the deed, but that could wait.

"Small world gringo," Shithead smiled. He had two gleaming gold incisors, the same unmistakable hook-nose, and ponytail.

"You know, I was actually relieved you took the jewels off of my hands. I thought you were some random thief that somehow found out about our hoard. At the time, I never thought we'd make it out of Chile alive."

And now he had the goods and the thief back in his own hands. Why wasn't Skinny there? Was Skinny even involved? It occurred to him he was a dupe, and he got no more out of Shithead, who refused to say anymore.

Was CJ on to this whole thing, or did she simply steal the valuables in hopes of getting back at Skinny? Or maybe she was hoping to take them and get away for good. But now Harry had them, and she did not.

They were on the blind side of the cabin, and hidden from Skinny. Harry rested the gun barrel on the shoulder of his captive, and fired into the far window. Shithead jolted, and winced from the blast.

"Skinny," he yelled. "Let the girl go and I'll give you what's left of your man."

Harry had to let him know that he did not scare too easily, although he knew Skinny could care less.

Skinny came out onto the front porch with CJ in front of him. The gun was pointed at her chest.. "You want her in one piece, you might want to come up with a better idea."

Skinny knew CJ meant something to Harry, although it never occurred to him that anyone could actually love one of his girls. They were just property to him.

CJ tried to break Skinny's hold on her arm, and screamed, "Harry, go away. Don't listen to him."

Harry held the rifle to Shitheads head, and together they walked toward the cabin. She was visibly terrified and Harry could not stand it. He wanted to kill them both on the spot, but his marksmanship was not that good. His blood was hot and he knew it would only ruin everything if he allowed his anger to boil over.

Skinny was smiling with his gold teeth easily visible.

Harry whispered to Shithead, "You tell him to drop the gun or I might get mad." Before he knew it, Shithead took off running not toward the cabin, but toward the road.

Unable to shoot an unarmed man, Harry hesitated.

Skinny did not, and fired at Harry, hitting him in the arm. It hit more of the clothing, but was enough to throw Harry around and off balance.

Harry ran back behind the trees.

Shithead lumbered through the deep snow, falling as he went.

Harry aimed and fired, and Shithead fell. But did he hit him? It would have to do for now. Skinny had retreated into the house with CJ. Taking off his coat, Harry laid it by a tree so that it might look like it could be his unconscious body. He leaned the rifle against the tree, then took the handgun from his pack, and ran for the back of the house.

But why did she leave the gems with him and go inside with Skinny? Had she hoped to plead innocent, or was she letting Harry make off with the goods? He circled around the building, retracing his first steps. There was blood on the ground by the tree where Shithead stopped after Harry fired at him.

It re-affirmed his ability to shoot well.

He wondered if Shithead was dead or merely playing dead. Was he inside with Skinny watching him approach the cabin? There was no turning back now. He had to go on.

The escape window would not budge it must have been locked, and he would have to find another way in. Harry continued around to the other side of the house by the kitchen chimney. There was a small window there, but a bit too high for him to see through. The wall had natural stone sticking out of the white stucco and he could hold onto the stones and climb it. He peered in.

In the living room by Harry's favorite chair next to the stuffed wolf, Skinny and CJ appeared to be arguing. He pushed her to the floor. She got up, and soothed him stroking his arms.

Skinny looked fat and comical in his snowsuit, like an engorged tic. He took off his hat and threw it at the chair, and then his coat came off. Underneath he wore a green chamois shirt over a turtleneck sweater. He looked like Skinny again. He was sweating, and his thin black hair had gone lank. Harry looked around for Shithead, but saw no signs of him.

He noticed a loose stone next to the window. He wiggled it until it pulled out and realized he could stick the bag of gems inside it. When the gems seemed secure, he put the stone back concealing everything. Then he jumped down and continued to the front of the house.

In the dim light of the early morning, he rounded the corner of the porch and saw Shithead's body face down in the snow. He walked over to it, and saw blood soaking the snow around what used to be his head. Harry turned around to look at the house, its windows still steamed up, hoping Skinny could not see him standing there. He bent down and patted the dead man's pockets. He found two pistols, and a watch.

I'd better not let Skinny catch me here, he thought. Then he slowly moved toward the house. When he reached the porch, he heard something in the bushes by the road and turned with his gun pointing toward the sound.

The dry laurels shook vigorously.

He saw only shadows until he drew near. He nearly shouted when he saw that his friend still lived. Harry walked through the deep snow over to Conner. When he got there, he stared in surprise. He hadn't expected Sara to be squatting next to him.

She motioned for him to duck down and come closer. And that is when he saw another girl, who smiled apologetically.

He said little more than, "Good to see you," since he was feeling a bit confused and disoriented by the situation. He looked back and forth between the three waiting for some explanation.

"She's good," Conner said. "She's on our side." Then he quickly told Harry about his experience and how Sara rescued them. "You were shot again," Conner said. He reached for Harry's arm, but Harry stopped him.

"It's okay, only a flesh wound."

They all looked at the cabin now, and no one spoke. That is when Harry noticed there was one more person with them: a ranger.

"Is this all you brought, one guy?"

"The others were out on patrol and are on the way," said the ranger. "Officer Renaldo," he said, extending a hand.

Harry shook it.

Renaldo was about six foot, had broad shoulders and a square jaw. He looked frightened almost to the state of being petrified, but he tried to conceal his anxiety. His normal daily routine did not include stand offs with criminals. Bears and timber wolves were dangerous enough, but they could not shoot back.

Harry understood that. He never thought himself the type who could stare down the barrel of a .45 and not piss himself, but he had no choice in the matter now. Renaldo could turn and leave, and no one could blame him, but himself.

Harry wondered if they saw him on the ledge stuffing the jewels into the wall. But it was shadowed in the early morning light and maybe they saw nothing.

"We're going in. Is he in there?" said Sara.

"Yes, but that won't do. He's got CJ, and I can't jeopardize her life. Listen," he said after a second of thought, "I have an idea."

Skinny's Part

Harry was impressed with Conner's new friend, and was even more impressed that Sara was a cop. They stayed behind, all four people waiting outside the cabin. Harry understood Jackie's interest in Skinny. She had to promise not to interfere with the police, though Conner had to vouch for her character before Sara finally acquiesced and allowed her to come along.

"I want to see what happens to that scumbag," Jackie said.

Harry had no plan really, but hoped they would buy it. He was going to go in, confront Skinny, and somehow goad him into going outside for the gems, which he would say are in Shitheads pockets, and hope that was enough. Conner and Sara asked him as much, and he reassured them he could do it. He started toward the cabin now, and paused to look back at Conner and the others, wondering if he would ever see them again.

Harry was never one to fear the inevitable. He could never imagine going through life afraid to die. His father would laugh. He had seen his father stare death down many times. Even when it finally overtook him on top of the waterfall in Venezuela, it was at his own hands. Harry could not see his end, which made it easier to walk in its shadows. He thought of his father again about to jump off the cliff, and then took the first step toward his own fate.

He walked up to the cabin and approached the porch. "I'm coming in, Skinny, don't shoot."

He stood alone in front of the door waiting, his gun still in his back belt. Sara and the ranger had the front door covered, but Harry could not be sure how good their aim was, and had to trust them not to shoot until he gave the OK. His adrenaline surged in him and he began to tremble. He took a deep breath and turned the doorknob.

Slowly, it opened, letting the quiet glow of the house spread out onto the shadows cast by the low morning sun. Harry stood, silhouetted, looking at only an opened door.

"Come on in, Georgia," he heard a voice call from inside.

As he entered, he saw CJ standing in the middle of the room looking calm and defiant. Skinny stood close to her, then her arm slipped under his and she snuggled close to him. All the while, Skinny pointed the rifle at Harry.

"Well, it don't look like I hit you square enough. CJ here told me all about your little adventure. But I think she left out some juicy details, like I'll bet you owe me for a whole lot of screwin'."

CJ looked up at him, as if they were discussing her next customer. Cool and unaffected, she walked over to the kitchen bar—seductively swaying—poured a whiskey and sipped it while looking over the rim at Harry with cold unresponsive eyes.

Asshole. Harry looked down at his foot. "I can manage," he said, rubbing his arm. "That's twice I owe you for."

"Close the door, take off your coat, and stay a spell."

"No, thanks. I just came to get what belongs to me and leave."

"Ain't nothin' that belongs to you here. Especially them jewels you got of mine."

Harry threw up his arms. "I don't have them. You can look for yourself."

"I didn't think you'd be stupid enough to come in here with them on you." He pointed the gun again at CJ and said, "But you are goin' to tell me where they are."

"I'll make you a deal," said Harry.

But Skinny blew up, and cut him short. "Too later for deals partner. I ain't leavin' here without them. You and your stupid friend got in my way and I'm pissed."

"What'd you do with Conner? I have to know if he's alright."

"You don't have to know nothin' asshole."

Skinny walked over to CJ and stroked her hair. He reached his hand down and cupped her breast. She jerked back.

"Aw, what's the matter Honey pie? Ain't you got no more for ol' Skinny?" Then he grabbed onto her hair, and pulled it hard enough to knock her off the stool.

She fell to her knees. She held onto her hair, trying to free it from his grasp. The rifle was pointing at her head now, and Skinny looked as if he enjoyed it.

"Harry, don't give him the bag."

Skinny backhanded her face, and she fell to on the floor, wiping the blood from her lip. "Shut the fuck up."

Skinny dug a cigarette out of his pocket and lit it. He drew in long and slow on it, and held it a while before letting the smoke out. "Oh man, I needed that."

Harry walked over to the kitchen bar and poured himself coffee whiskey. He looked at Skinny as he did, and poured another for him. He handed the cup to his host and said, "Prost."

"Oh very good, 'Prost,' to our little Russian connection," Skinny said, "Put it on the bar." He would not take it from Harry's hand. Their eyes never left on another's gaze.

Skinny lifted the glass, and they both drank together.

"I started putting everything together just after our little lesson in economics in your room. I thought I recognized you although it's been two years."

"I had a beard and long hair then. I cleaned up a bit since."

Harry still was not sure how much Skinny was involved in all of this. He helped himself to a cigarette.

It felt good going into his lungs and calmed him down a bit.

"I work with a lot of shitheads, not just the one you knocked off out there. You caused me a bit of grief. But it was worth it. I liked the way your little wife moaned. Gotta love the moaners, huh Harry?" He imitated Nancy moaning during sex, the pet name she called Harry, "My little Viscacha," and poured another drink for the both of them.

CJ sat still on the floor next to the fireplace.

"What the hell are you talking about?"

"After Shithead stole my property back from you, I realized he had only gotten half of them. So I followed you on board, and paid off the crew to keep dumb. I hadn't been to Lima in a while."

Skinny was rubbing the salt into the wound. Harry made an easy target for someone like Skinny. He wanted to make him squirm before he killed him – like pulling the wings off flies.

Harry had a puzzled look on his face, "How? Where? What?"

"Who," Skinny finished mockingly.

It was coming to Harry a bit slowly. He had never expected to meet up with the mastermind of his failed trip to Chile. He felt nauseous. His head swam. He thought of Nancy.

"It's a big boat, and you two spent a lot of time in the cabin I gotta say." He gave a wink and nudge with his elbow. "I bet you could teach little CJ here a thing or two couldn't ya? Besides, I didn't have anything against your little bride, what's her name? Nancy was it, it's just I really wanted the other half of the goods you took from me."

"You took from me, you mean."

"Oh no Buck, they belonged to me, they always did. Dago owed it to me. We were partners, not the fucking Russian. Anyway, I wanted to keep it clean. No mess, you dig. She didn't even scream when she went overboard. What a good little girl."

Harry lunged at Skinny. "You bastard," he said.

He heard CJ yell his name, "Harry don't!"

The butt of the rifle struck his head and he went down.

When he woke up, CJ had his head in her lap cradling his face in her breast. His arms were splayed out on the floor. Skinny was standing above them both dangling Harry's pistol in the air. Harry could not believe what he had just heard. He thought Nancy had fallen off the boat during the storm. That is what the mate told him.

"Tsk, tsk, tsk, where'd ya get this little thing?" Skinny held the 9mm in his hand. "Think you was gonna use it, Harry? Okay now, you've wasted enough of my time with all of this memory lane bullshit. Where is the stuff?" He flipped the gun around his finger like a gunslinger and pointed close to Harry's nose.

Harry could smell the gun oil.

"Leave'im alone will ya Skinny. He don't know where it is. I had the bag and I hid it outside by the woodshed. I'll go and get it."

"Man, you two play me for some kind of fool?"

Harry hoped that this would work his little plan. The last thing he wanted was to die at the hands of a sociopath. At best, he wanted to protect CJ from harm. Now she was screwing it up. He tried to sit up, but Skinny held his arm down with his foot, and fired the pistol into Harry's hand hitting it dead in the middle.

"There, now I know I hit you."

The shock prevented the pain from registering too quickly. He knew if he had seen it happen it would have hurt even more. He felt it and pulled his hand to his chest, sitting up completely free of CJ's embrace. The pain soared through his whole body. He wanted to say something, to hit him back, to kill him, but reality had set in. Hc had to produce or else. CJ muttered under her breath, and went to get something to wrap around his hand.

"Your wife kept walking around the deck disrupting the crew. I stoppcd hcr once. Pretty little thing. You shouldn't have let her walk around without no bra or stockings, gives the men some ideas. I guess she thought I was a crewmember, because she never paid me no mind. Well, she got to know who I was before the end. Yeah, she even liked it, I think. Maybe you weren't man enough for her." He walked over to the fireplace next to CJ and continued. "I still got her panties; pretty little pink things. Not typical jungle-ware." And he pointed the gun at Harry and cocked it.

But Skinny was a congenital liar. Harry tried not to let such talk bother him. And he could not remember if she was wearing panties or not, so he cooled himself down and counted to ten.

"But you two were never together long enough for me to check the cabin except once, and I couldn't find them anywhere. So I waited for the perfect opportunity. The captain never knew who I was, or what I wanted. I told him nothing, but paid him well, and I stayed out of the way. It wasn't easy but I managed to pull it off. I waited for you to sleep. I was going to break into your room and kill you both but then I saw her walking on the deck, I grabbed her and took her back to my cabin and made her hand the shit over. Brave little girl—at first. But she finally gave it up. I'm afraid I broke her nose."

CJ fussed over Harry's hand. She and Harry were both on the floor.

Skinny wanted to hit him below the belt. "You know Harry, she screamed for me too, even gave me a little scratch."

Harry felt sick. Could Skinny be telling the truth? He wanted to die, but not before killing Skinny. He got to his feet.

Skinny pointed the rifle at his face.

Harry had to think of now. That was past and he would have enough time to think about that later, at least he hoped he would, so he laid out his plan.

"It's outside in Shithead's pocket. He took them from me and ran, that's why I shot him." He paused to check Skinny's reaction. "He didn't look to be heading toward the cabin when I shot him either. I wonder where he was going. Maybe he wanted them for himself and meant to leave you behind. I suppose if he thought it out, he'd have tried to kill you first, but what can you expect from someone called Shithead?"

Skinny's eyes lit up. Harry could almost see the light bulb go on over his head—and he headed for the front door. He hoped Skinny would make it out the door before the gears cranked on and the dust cleared.

Suddenly, he stopped.

"Oh no you don't." He turned quickly and pointed the rifle at Harry. "Do you take me for some kind of fool, Georgia?"

Harry had not really thought out his plan too well. He thought he could wing it and hoped for the best, somehow catch him off guard, if that were possible. But Skinny scared Harry, not physically, but psychologically, Skinny was a real loose cannon. If the others outside got involved, the wrong person would get hurt.

He left the cabin without a coat and headed towards Shithead's body.

Skinny watched from the window, the barrel of the rifle aimed at Harry and following him as he walked in the snow like the eyes of a tiger waiting to pounce.

Harry didn't know what would happen when he returned to the cabin without the gems. . If he thought he was alone, he could just kill them both and wait for the spring thaw to melt the snow and simply pick up the jewels. But that was unlikely. Skinny wanted it now.

And what would he do when he realized that the bag was not on the body at all? He hoped that the ranger was inside the back window by now, and ready to take Skinny out.

Harry approached the body lying in the red snow. Its arms and legs were bent in unnatural angles. He thought back to what seemed years ago, to the beginning of his journey into the cold and treacherous mountains, when he stood over another body whose life he had also taken. That was only a week before, but seemed to Harry like some story in a book, or a cheap "B" movie he remembered from his past. This is the second life he had taken is less than two weeks. Maybe for someone like Skinny or the two fools he killed this would be a typical week, but for Harry it was cosmic. He never wanted to kill Shithead.

It seemed like only seconds passed before he heard struggling and yelling inside. He turned, and ran back. He threw the door open, and saw Skinny and CJ struggling. She kicked and screamed, but Skinny swung his hand, cracked her head with the butt of the pistol, and shot her as she lay on the floor.

Harry rushed at Skinny, throwing his weight at him, and they both fell against the bar, knocking over the stools. The gun came down, and Harry knocked it away. It slid across the floor towards the door. Skinny's eyes spotted the shotgun by the fireplace, and he lurched for it. But Harry dove, reached it first. As he slid across the floor, he took the gun, turned, and shot Skinny as he fell on him.

Conner stood at the cabin door, staring. Sara, right behind, pushed past him and ran over to Harry, as he kicked Skinny's body off to the side. She bent down to render aid, and asked if he was all right. Blood was everywhere.

He pushed past her and ran to CJ's side.

She was still alive.

Harry knelt on the floor next to her, and cradled her in his arms. She looked up at him unable to move. Her eyes were bloodshot and wet. She tried to talk, but nothing came out. She tried again, and said with a fragile whisper, "Oh Harry," as blood oozed from her stomach. Her hands reached up and cradled his face, wiping away the blood that dripped from it.

Ranger Renaldo was already inside and knelt next to Harry and CJ. He tore open her shirt to inspect the wound, and placed Harry's hand over the hole in her abdomen. He told Harry to apply pressure while he went outside to get more supplies. The blood seemed endless and his hand kept slipping, but he managed to slow the bleeding.

Harry looked over at Skinny, who laid flat and lifeless with a hole the size of a melon in the middle of his neck. Sara stooped over him, checking that he was indeed dead.

The fire in CJ's eyes dwindled, washed out by the tears that flowed down her cheeks. Her lips, crusted over with blood and saliva could barely move. Harry kissed her and encouraged her to hold on. The ranger returned, and forced his way between them. From a case marked, "First Aid," he quickly assessed the wound and produced a large bundle of cotton. He asked that Harry hold it firmly against the gaping wound while he checked her pulse and eyes.

"What the hell happened here?" said Conner. He seemed in shock and walked back and forth trying to help where he could.

CJ sputtered blood and heaved, her back arching high almost jerking out of Harry's embrace. She gripped his shoulder and looked into his eyes. And as she expelled her final breath, he would swear to his dying days that she smiled as her eyes dimmed and saw no more.

Harry cried. He was exhausted and could do nothing but give himself up to the loss of his friend, his companion, his short-lived lover.

Sara Reveals All

It seemed that a throng of people, mostly police and rangers, had invaded the cabin. Jackie's father even made an appearance, and talked extensively with Conner. When he told him about the car exploding in the dingle, Conner explained that they had enough time to jump out of the car before it started to burn, and that he was worried for Jackie because gasoline was dripping on her as she passed through the door. She had cut her leg on the twisted frame, which had a jagged piece sticking out. They managed to hide long enough for Skinny to leave. Then, they caught a passing car and went straight to the station.

Harry ignored the questions and looked only at CJ.

The sun rose and crept into the cabin through the opened front door. Outside under a blue morning sky, the snow already began to melt. Help seemed to come all at once: medics, more rangers, and state police. Shithead's body lay alone, unattended for a while, on a bloody island in the middle of the front lawn trampled by swarming people.

Harry stared at CJ, ignoring even the pain of his wounds until the rangers lifted her body away. Now the Harry and Conner were reunited, and with them were Jackie and Sara.

The helicopter waited in the open field that lay at the end of the drive. Harry refused to leave just yet. He wanted to hear more from Conner and Sara. The medics were prodding him with needles, testing his blood pressure, taking samples of blood, and injecting him with antibiotics. He sat on his chair holding CJ's blue velvet robe. His leg had received a clean bandage, and so had the wound he got when Skinny shot him the second time. He would say often in years later that he was still picking feathers from his arm. He walked over to the door and looked out as they took Shithead's body away.

His hand hurt like hell. "How do you figure that Skinny and I would finally meet and neither of us knows what we had in common?"

"Oh, he knew," said Sara. "At least he thought he recognized you, but never made the connection. Like you Harry, who would have thought it'd be such a small world. You never met him so couldn't know who he was. And after CJ took the contraband, he threw it together."

"But I never knew until we got here that she had it. And I still wasn't sure they were mine until I saw the Inca pieces."

"I'm glad you said that Harry because I thought for sure you knew about it from day one."

"I sure misread Skinny. I thought he was just a pimp."

Sara got up and walked over to where Harry stood and said, "Skinny, just a pimp? We've been on his tail for ten years. He smuggled eastern European girls in here promising to marry them off to rich Americans when they arrived. He had entire dossiers on these alleged husbands – all fabricated. He made thousands. He could have retired, but he would never do that. He worked for some old friends of his he met while serving in the army in Germany during the war. They were tough characters. Dagon was one of them. There are still two out there. But Skinny skipped out on them—and us—and disappeared for about three years and resurfaced in Reno."

"Reno?"

"Yes. That's where he met CJ." Harry said. "She told me about that. But that was before Chili."

"He'd been in Reno for quite some time. He met her after his trip to South America. In fact, he had been doing that almost immediately after he left the organization in Germany."

"Doing what, pimping?"

"No, smuggling diamonds, and anything of value out of Argentina, Chile, Bolivia, wherever."

Harry thought about the time in Chile and the two men that came asking for Dago. "The two guys that came to our camp in the Andes, The Russian. Where did he come in to all of this?"

"We had one of our own working with Skinny's friends in Europe undercover, and found out about his operations over here."

"You mean Shithead worked for the FBI?"

"No. Shithead worked for Skinny. The Russian worked for us. We had caught up with him with enough incriminating evidence to put him away forever, but convinced him to work with us so we could stop Skinny. But the Russian still operated with them all the while."

"But how did he know about our expedition in the top of the mountain?"

"Are you ready for this? It seemed that Dagon Benicia was double dipping. He worked with Skinny, and also worked with an outfit out of the Soviet Union, a private company called The Russia House. The Russian worked for them from the beginning. They have been smuggling goods out of Europe, and funneling money into a company called Trireme, and other businesses for years since the war. They sent the Russian to South America to check things out. They suspected Skinny was cheating them for some time, but couldn't prove it. And he was too valuable to do away with without good provocation. They let him work his little operation because he produced good results just the same. The Russian knew Dagon was cheating Skinny. He and Skinny had been smuggling contraband out of historic sites in South America. Skinny would sell it here in the US, and share the profits with Dagon and the Russia House."

Harry was flabbergasted. He took a few minutes to take it all in.

"But how about Don? He wasn't in on it was he?"

"Wait, the Russian found out about it in Chile when you were there, and was prepared to take Dagon out of the picture, but he died before we could do that. As for Don, he and your wife were innocent bystanders, dupes like you were. Sorry Harry."

"What ever happened to him, to Don?"

"Skinny caught up with him in Bolivia and found out about you and the gems from him. Sorry Harry, I'm afraid it wasn't pleasant for him when he died."

"So," Harry filled in the blanks, "When Dago died, Skinny's supplier in the south was gone, so he came home to Reno."

"Well, yes and no. We think that Skinny killed Dago by poisoning him somehow. But that wasn't our concern. We wanted Skinny, the stolen property, and the whole operation. We were willing to go back and get Dagon later. He was easy. The Russian sent us a telegram from La Paz warning us that Don was dead, and no longer suspect."

Conner interjected with a question of his own. "What ever happened to the Russian? Is he here?"

"He suspected Dago and Skinny of cheating him and skimming off the top. But he had to trust them, because they were selling the goods on the black market for years, and the Russian was one of the original war buddies."

Sara continued when she saw the puzzled look on everyone's face. "Skinny was taking good merchandise and giving them less and less for it. I don't think he was ever on to our operation. But by that time, he had a whole web of markets, so he did away with the Russian in Lima after your boat reached shore with the gems. That is where Skinny came on board the boat.

"Skinny was using legitimate businesses to move his goods. He had a bank in Chicago, a curator in DC, and shipping lanes from Philadelphia to San Francisco. We had him red-handed on that, but we needed to stop his whole smuggling operation. We're rounding them up now, as we speak. It might all fall apart now that he's dead. All we need is the bag."

The police were wrapping up. The captain of the state police called Sara over by the kitchen. He notified the owners of the cabin about what had transpired. There was no way they could come out, and as far as the police were concerned, nothing they could do here anyway. The officer Renaldo knew the owners well, and promised them to have the place cleaned up before the end of spring. He would stay long after the others left to secure the building. Now they wanted Sara to finish up with her end and move the others into the helicopter so they could get Harry to a hospital.

She returned to Harry and said, "So Harry, where are the gems?"

Harry turned around with a surprised look. He smiled and walked over to the kitchen to get a drink of water. "Funny thing is, I never did have them. CJ never gave them to me, and she didn't get the chance to tell me where she hid them."

The thought of putting them in the pockets of Shithead did come to him out there. Whether or not he should turn them over to Sara didn't occur to him either, until he realized how much trouble he had gone through to get them and until after listening to her story of the parallel universe surrounding it.

He toiled with that notion, weighing right from wrong, and most importantly, could he get away with it? What did he owe, and to whom? He played his part, and she gave him the jewels. He knew in the end that he would have to return them to the Chilean government, not to his. Sara wanted them as evidence, but they were actually his problem. Skinny merely provided a means of getting them into the states. For now, no one had them and he wanted to keep it that way.

"I remember my father," Harry told them, "on our last adventure together he said, 'Son, in this world we each have to follow our own vision.' Then he explained,

'You don't have to watch this if it makes you so goddamned worried. Just keep the camera rolling.' And then he jumped off the top of Alfred Falls with only a winged body suit. He wanted to be the first human to fly like a bird."

"Come on Harry, are you kidding?"

"Way to go Harry," said Conner. "The case of the missing family jewels."

"This isn't for the sake of one of your plays Conner. I don't have them. Really."

"So what were you going to do when you got back in the cabin without the stuff?"

Harry thought about that, and after some lengthy silence said, "My father once asked me if life wasn't worth a little risk once in a while. He told me that in order to get what you want out of life you had to take a little risk; anything worth having is worth losing." He sat down on the bar stool and said, "I have no idea what-so-ever what he meant by that."

Harry doubted that Sara was going to let it go that easily, but she would have to wait, at least until spring thaw. He had a feeling that she'd be keeping a close eye on him.

When they stepped onto the porch of the cabin, Harry looked around at the distant mountains that he had not really seen until now, and he took a deep breath of the icy air. He thought he caught a faint whiff of pine. Then, he thought about the wolves. They were gone, chased away by the noise, and people. *They'll be back,* he thought.

In fact, the wolves were close by, watching from a safe distance, smelling them, tasting the air. Harry and the others walked off the porch, and headed down the road.

He didn't look back.

The Ride Home

On the helicopter ride back to civilization, Harry sat with Conner and Jackie who sobbed into her hands. On occasion, she would pause and look out at the passing scenery, but what she thought about she kept to herself.

The helicopter churned its loud engines and the rotors quickly began to spin. It lifted suddenly. Harry's family used to make airplane parts for the military and then for the public, so he had ridden in these machines many times before. It was nothing new to him, but Conner held on to the seat and wouldn't let go until they were down again.

It rose slowly and made a sweep over the cabin, rising in a circular pattern until it was above the trees, and Harry had the chance to see it as if it were a map showing all of the key places of the story that played out that week. He thought of CJ and how she impacted his life so heavily in so short a time. He could see it all like life passing before his eyes, all too quickly, and he thought to himself; *anything worth having is worth losing.*

He looked over at Conner who was sallow and appeared as though he was going to throw up. Then he looked back down at the valley and the high pass and stared long at it disappearing beneath them. He thought he saw blood on the snow in front of the cabin and it hit him that he had just killed not one, but three people that week. He didn't care what happened to him because of it, because it was something that had to happen, as naturally as having to sleep. He had to survive, but it meant nothing to him now because CJ was dead.

Why had she done it? That she used them to get away from Skinny and take the gems with her was obvious. But why did she go back inside with Skinny? Had she met the end of her determination, and lost her resolve to free herself? Or, was she trying to save Harry?

The helicopter took its last swing around the cabin and headed for Jackson Hole. Harry looked around at the motley crew assembled there. Jackie was still crying. Conner and Sara were still staring out their respective windows. Then pilot radioed ahead to an ambulance that was waiting to carry Harry to a hospital. He began to feel the pain; his hand and shoulder started hurting more than his leg ever had, though there would be no infection this time.

Harry looked at Conner who had been looking at him. Harry tried to smile, and said to him, "I didn't even get the girl."

Conner looked at his friend, put his hand on Harry's shoulder, and said, "Yes you did, Harry. You did."

Silence returned to the mountaintop, the last of the noisy humans gone. The alpha male cautiously approached the front of the cabin, while the others remained hidden to all but themselves. Slowly he stepped out, nervous and shy, ready at a second to retreat into the forest. He could smell them, still very much there. His sense of smell was like another sense altogether; a sixth sense, in which odors left behind by anything organic created a vivid dimensional image, a shadowy representation of what had been there moments earlier.

He had hoped to find something good to eat. They usually left something behind; like the guts of a deer, elk, or even one of their own. The others crept slowly into the clearing behind him. He stood over the bloody snow, digging and sniffing. He looked up and turned his head both ways, looking at the others as they came into the clearing.

He looked towards the distant peaks of the Teton Range, perhaps even to the Heavens beyond, and howled as though saying, "Oh Great Wolf, the Humans are gone." The others gathered there also joined in, and soon they began shoving and growling and biting for the food the humans had left behind.